What Happened to Michael

N. F. Paupe

Copyright © 2018 N. F. Paupe

All rights reserved.

ISBN:1987700007
ISBN-13: 978-1987700008

DEDICATION

For my daughters, Eva and Alice, without whom I would never know the love a mother feels for her children, and so would not have been able to write this book.

CONTENTS

	Acknowledgments	i
1	Prologue	Pg 1
2	What Happened to Michael	Pg 5
3	Epilogue	Pg 346
4	About the Author	Pg 351
5	Questions for Discussion	Pg 352

ACKNOWLEDGMENTS

A huge thank you to my brilliant editors: Ann, who possibly spent as much time editing the book as I did writing it, and who not only dedicated endless hours of her time and asked important questions, but also pushed me to achieve my full potential; and Aleks, whose thoroughness and meticulous proof-reading deserved a medal, as it helped me immensely in ironing out the story and making it as close to perfection as humanly possible.

Many thanks also to my photographers, Zoran and Amanda, for their help with the cover, and of course, the model, my Michael: Teddy.

Much gratitude to all my friends for reading drafts, comparing covers and giving me constant support and crucial feedback, and to all the people along the way, from primary school to the present day who told me I should, 'be a writer', who encouraged and inspired me, and without whom the book probably would not have been written. You all know who you are.

Finally, to my ever supportive parents for letting me choose the path I have chosen, who have always been my biggest cheerleaders, and to my love, my husband, Ju, who has always believed in me, for looking after our daughters while I was locked away, typing furiously at my desk. I hope you love the book as much as you love me.

Prologue

'Now we are going to roll the sugar fondant out, into a big circle; that's it, add a little bit of icing sugar if it sticks to the rolling pin.'

'Like this, mummy?'

'Yes, darling, just like that.' I fed my flour-covered fingers through my son's silky, chestnut-coloured hair.

'Is it big enough yet?'

'Nearly, but it needs to be really, really big to cover the cake.'

He nodded, and rubbed his nose with his hand.

'Aw, look at you, you've got flour all over your face,' I laughed, and wiped it off with a tea towel. He looked up at me with his big brown eyes.

'This is so long, are we nearly done yet?'

'Yes, sweetie, we are. We just need to put the icing onto the cake; here we go, one, two, three, oops!'

The sugar fondant had ripped in two. Michael looked at me, guilt written all over his face.

'I'm sorry, mummy.'

I picked him up, and sat him on the kitchen top.

'Don't ever apologise for trying to be helpful. It doesn't matter, we can just roll it out again. OK?'

'OK, and eat some?' he asked cheekily.

'Well, it wouldn't be much fun it we didn't, would it?' I giggled, and ripped off another corner of the icing. He stuffed it into his mouth.

'Mummy?'

'Yes, my love?'

'Why do I need to know how to make a cake?'

'Well, why do you think you need to know how to make a cake?'

'I'm not sure, 'cos I've got you to do that.' He smiled a big gappy grin.

'Well, one day, you might get married, and make cakes

with someone else.' I tried to explain slowly, choosing my words very carefully. 'Then you won't need mummy any more. So I need to teach you how to the make the best cakes in the whole wide world, so that you can make them for someone special, someone that you love.'

'But I love you, mummy.'

'And I love you my gorgeous boy.'

'But I don't want to make cakes for anyone else.' He looked sad.

'Come here baby.' I scooped him up into a big hug. 'Listen to me, OK? I promise that however old you get, and however far you go, I will always be here to make cakes for you.'

'So I don't have to get married?'

I smiled, 'Not if you don't want to.'

'I can live with you?'

'For as long as you want, my sweetest boy.'

'Forever?'

I held him tightly, the smell of icing sugar in his hair, his hands sticky from the bright blue fondant.

'For ever!' I whispered.

Now

It was a road that I knew by heart. Blind, I could find my way. The twists and corners seemed natural, etched in my memory. My hand knew when to turn the wheel, which gear to use, my foot, when to brake. My heart achingly remembered the way. Over the past year and a half I had driven maybe twenty times, fifty, a hundred, I had lost count, along the expanse of grey concrete. I never found solace coming here; it became more of a ritual, a rite, a date in my diary that must always be kept. As if returning to the place where Michael died would bring him back somehow; would fill some part of the gaping hole in my embittered heart; replace pain and loss with some form of memory and love. And each time I sat in my car, making the seventeen-minute drive to the end of my world, the answer seemed cruelly so much further away. Seventeen minutes, seventeen lonely minutes between truth and lies, seventeen minutes of asking myself what I could have done to prevent it, how much my baby suffered, for what cause, and at whose hand. Until tonight. Tonight I'm going to find out everything. If it breaks me, if it kills me, I will know what happened to my son, and this will be the last time I make this drive.

Missing

I was sitting at the dining table at my parents'. It was winter, but these days I seemed to be immune to the cold. I took tiny sips from the tea my mother had made me, wishing it was something stronger, something to take the pain away. My parents sat opposite me, my mother crying silently into a handkerchief, my father's stony gaze focused on nothing in particular. Nobody spoke. All I could hear was the ticking of the clock, and the sound of an occasional car driving to the end of the street, turning around in the cul-de-sac, then leaving the same way. Is this what my life was going to be like from now on? A silent concerto, playing on repeat, never interrupted by the sounds of children's laughter, never broken by the noise of a cup being dropped, the splash of bathwater, the cries of a boy who couldn't get back to sleep.

The doorbell rang, and my mother got up automatically to answer it, returning a moment later,

'Ann, there is someone to see you.'

Without needing to be asked, my father got silently to his feet and slipped out of the room, and I was vaguely aware of somebody else entering it.

'Hello, Mrs. Peters, I'm so sorry to drop by like this, unannounced; my name is Inspector Paul Stone.'

'Yes,' I said, blandly, not really listening; barely existing.

'I just have some routine questions for you; I can see that you are obviously distressed and not ready for visitors, but we really do need to talk. The sooner we can piece together what happened to your son, the sooner I can find him.' I didn't reply.

'Very well, I'll give you time to compose yourself; your mother has offered me a coffee; you take a few moments, and I'll come back in here in ten minutes or so.' He turned to leave.

'Michael.' I murmured.
He turned back, 'I'm sorry?'

'His name is Michael,' I whispered.
He approached the table, warily, 'I'm perfectly happy to come back in a few minutes.'

'It doesn't make any difference. I'm not going to be in any better frame of mind in a few minutes. I don't know why you're here; I already spoke to someone down at the station, when we reported him missing: Sergeant Miller, I think it was. I already gave him my statement; it hasn't changed.'

'Of course. It's just, well, this is more official, and sometimes, when we are in shock, we forget details, get times mixed up; we don't see everything as clearly as we might, after giving the event a few days distance, if that makes sense.'

'I honestly don't know how I can help you; I didn't see anything, or hear anything, and I certainly haven't remembered any other details since giving my original statement.'

'That's fine, and of course, I completely understand, and I know this may be a bit tedious for you, but Sergeant Miller is no longer assigned to this case, so...'

I stood up and smoothed down the wrinkles in my dirty shirt. 'How come?'

'Several reasons; I don't want to bore you.'

'Bore me.'

'Well, as I said, for several reasons really, but the most pertinent one being that this is now not just a missing person case.'

'I don't understand.'

'Well, Mrs. Peters, in these kinds of circumstances, especially with a little boy of his age, and a good, close-knit family like yours, we tend to rule out the possibility of the child just running away. It doesn't really fit the profile.'

'Michael, his name is Michael!'

'I'm sorry, the possibility of Michael running away for no reason is very slim. To be on the safe side, and to cover all bases, we are treating this as a kidnapping, and therefore, I have been assigned to the case.' He waffled on for several more minutes: explaining himself, outlining his role in the investigation, and what the next steps were to be. I felt a sense of dread that Michael wasn't just down the road hiding with his friends, or in the woods, trying helplessly to find his way home, but in actual danger, at the hands of a predator who might do him some real harm. But I also felt hope, and a strange belief that here was someone who would help find my son and bring him back to me. There was something honest and disarmingly open about this man I barely knew, and yet in him I sensed a determination to do his job, and keep his word.

'Can you just tell me a few things about Michael, Mrs. Peters?'

'He is the sweetest boy you'll ever meet: so polite and friendly, but, at the same time, outgoing and funny. He always pulls the silliest faces, and comes out with the funniest expressions. He knows how to ride a bike. He can swim underwater,' I took a breath, 'he loves to run, and play with his friends, his favourite food is pasta, he's scared of the dark,' my voice cracked, 'he likes animals, and watching cartoons, he plays with Lego and Play-Doh and his trains.' I looked down at the broken wooden pieces: the parts of my son's train set that he had received for Christmas the year before, a circuit that could no longer be connected. 'He's smart, he's so full of energy and love; and he loves me, oh, god, he loves me so much! What is he going to do without me?' For the first time in two days, I grabbed my son's favourite teddy, a dishevelled blue thing, a gift from my sister, Alice, when he was born: Bear Bear. I held it to me, my tears soaking the soft fabric, the salty taste on my lips. Inspector Stone approached me and gently removed the teddy. He patted my back a little awkwardly and brushed my hair out of my face. He looked fuzzy through my tears, and I couldn't make out the expression on his face.

'That's a great start; thank you, Mrs. Peters; I already feel like I'm starting to get to know him,' he smiled, 'now, I'll go and have that coffee, and then we'll continue.'

2 Weeks Missing

Relationships are complex: they need foundations, insulation, walls and maintenance. Doctor Blunt's words hummed relentlessly in the back of my brain, challenging me to face the realities of my own marriage. But what did that mean exactly? That I should stay with Dave right until the very end, until he lost all his hair or developed some kind of incurable disease. We did take that vow, for better or for worse, although I admit, the vows were more for my parents than for my love of God and respect for the institution of marriage. What if the foundations were being undermined? What if the insulation wasn't keeping the house warm any more? And what if the little cracks in the plaster on the walls were becoming holes that could cause the roof to cave in at any moment? What if they were real cracks: real open sores, wounds from the fighting, and the resentment, and the cheating and every other sign that perhaps we were doomed to fail? What if we were simply not meant to be together?

Back when I was working as a waitress, Dave had been my favourite customer. He would come in every Friday evening, alone, and request a table in my section. He would always order the same dish, *risotto gamberi*, and a bottle of Riesling. He seemed charming, and funny, and a complete gentleman, and being only 21, I think I deliberately chose to ignore the wedding ring on his third finger, and the time it took him to polish off an entire bottle of white without seeming even the slightest bit tipsy. He appeared articulate, worldly and intelligent. At the time, I was a drama student, working in an Italian restaurant to pay my university fees, and he was certainly appealing. After a few months of this routine, he eventually asked me out to dinner. I said yes. He was a big, strong man, almost intimidatingly big, but I think that excited me and drew me to him even more. Eighteen years older than me, he knew so much about everything, and I would sit listening intently as he described his travels, his passions, and his plans for the future, all of which included me, he would add, reassuringly. We would stay up all night, drinking wine and talking to each other. We would have sex, order a Chinese take-away, drink more wine, and fuck some more. Yes, the fucking; Dave certainly knew how to do that. He hands would travel over my inexperienced body as if being guided. He knew where to touch me, how to kiss me, and how to get me off in ways that I never even knew existed.

And after a year of the drinking and the fucking and the talking, Dave divorced his wife, and asked me to replace her in their suburban house. It's surprising to me now, how, as a young woman, I was so incredibly selfish; as if his wife was a piece of broken crockery, to be thrown out for something shiny and new, something more beautiful; as if their years of marriage meant nothing, and her feelings were of no consequence. She was a loser, as far as I was concerned: some trophy wife, who had not given her husband the things he needed to be happy; she had pushed him away, out of her house and into my bed. She was ungrateful for the life they had, unappreciative of the man he was, and blind to the inevitable fact that if she didn't take care of her marriage as she should, then he would just walk away. Just like that. I was convinced that I was the one who could change him; to me he would always be faithful, after all he left his wife for me. He loved me.

And yet, here I was, ten years later, in the same position as his ex-wife. Only now I was the loser, the trophy wife who hadn't taken care of her husband's needs, who had pushed him into three affairs, who didn't really even care any more if the marriage worked or not. Our son, Michael, had been missing for two weeks. This should have been a time to grieve together, to make everything bad go away, to mourn and to unite. Instead, I couldn't even look at Dave. Everything about him disappointed and disgusted me. I finally saw who he was, and it wasn't the big, strong lover who could take me in his arms and protect me, nor was it the intelligent, well-read man I had believed him to be, who knew his wines, and knew how to treat a lady. He was an abusive, unfaithful drunk, constantly unhappy and easily bored with women.

'Dave?' I shoved his foot to try and wake him. He continued to snore, loudly. What man sleeps when his son is missing, when his wife is sick with grief? 'Dave?' I spat into his ear. 'Wake up!'

He opened an eye, groaned and rolled onto his back. His breath smelled of morning, of dry saliva, and bourbon. He was hideous to me.

'I'm awake.'

'Good. How's Helen?'

'Not this again; listen, Ann, I'm tired; I have a lot of work to do; it's going to be a busy day.'

'It's about to get even busier!'

He sat up, and cocked his head to one side. His hair was receding now, and the lines in his face made me realise just how much older than me he really was; old and ugly.

'What did you say?'

'Call Helen. Tell her you'll be staying with her tonight.' He was fully awake now, and he reached into his bottom drawer and pulled out a pack of Marlboro cigarettes.

'I'll be staying where, with whom?' He lit the cigarette and took a drag. Smoke filled the air as he exhaled, catching the sunlight that peeped in through a gap in the curtains. 'Aren't you going to bitch about my smoking?'

'Speaking of bitches, call Helen. You don't have much time; your taxi will be here in a few minutes.'

'I'm not going anywhere!' His voice changed so suddenly; it was almost a growl. His eyes, bloodshot and thirsty bored into mine. 'Oh, there you are, nice to meet you.' He laughed, and scratched his crotch.

'I want you out of this house and gone.'

'Well, sweetheart, that's not going to happen anytime soon.'

'You really are repulsive, you know.'

He leaned in, 'That's not what you used to say.'

'How can you be so cruel, so…'

'So what, Ann?'

'Michael is missing.'

His face hardened, and he got out of bed.

'How many times have I told you not to mention his name!'

I began to back away.

'I want a divorce, Dave, I don't want anything else, I just want a divorce; you can keep everything; I just want our son, that's all I want.' My lip was trembling. He continued to move towards me, his fist raised, I felt an excruciating pain in the side of my face, and then nothing.

When I came to, I was lying face down on the bed. I could feel someone stroking my hair.

'Shh! It's OK, Ann, it's OK, everything's going to be OK.'

For a second, I felt relief sweep over me; I was safe, I had imagined all of it: Michael, my marriage, Dave.

'I forgive you, Ann.' I opened my eyes groggily, and twisted my head round; my husband's grim face slowly swam into focus.

'No!' I tried to move, but realised my arms were bound to the bed above my head.

'It's OK, Ann, I'm here; everything's going to be OK.' He kissed the back of my neck, and moved his hands down my naked back. Fear and dread engulfed me, and I tried to protest, to move, but he had tied my hands so tightly that I couldn't.

'We all know this is how you like it, bound, beaten and completely helpless,' he rasped.

'Please don't!' I sobbed, snot and spit smearing across my flushed face.

'Shh! It will all be over soon.' and then he was inside me, moving back and forth, grunting like an animal. I screamed into the pillow, frantically trying to free myself somehow, but he was quickening his pace. He let out a muffled cry as he came, and fell onto me to rest for a minute.

He unbound my hands and started to dress. I lay there, not daring to move, watching his reflection in the mirror, the look of pure satisfaction written all over his vile face.

'You can have your divorce. I'll have my lawyer see to the paperwork.'

Then he was gone.

*

'What is it that you want me to do, Mrs. Peters?'

I was at the police station, with Inspector Stone; he seemed a nice man, a good man. But can you really trust any of them? After Dave's assault I had waited until I heard his car pulling away, before gingerly getting up from the bed. I had dressed, cleaned myself up, turned off the video camera that I had built into my jewellery box four months previously, and driven directly to the station.

Inspector Stone had looked shocked, watching back through the repeated scenes of violence and rape. I had planned to use this to help with my divorce, before Michael went missing. Everything had been set up and prepared: Michael and I would stay with my parents until I could find somewhere to live permanently, and hopefully, with the help of the incriminating footage, Dave would be rotting in prison. But I had been overtaken by events. Everything that had seemed so hopeful, so positive, was now destroyed. Months of self-sacrifice, of letting Dave attack me, were now worthless. I had always been able to cope, because no matter how painful his attacks, inside I was laughing, watching the tiny red light of the video camera, and knowing that the future was just going to be Michael and me, and never being scared again. But now, it felt as if all of it had been for nothing; all that pain and sacrifice, for nothing! But something worse had occurred to me since Michael's disappearance: was a man of such violence capable of hurting a child? It was a question that I had, unfortunately, had to ask myself, and so I kept going back for more, to see to what lengths he would go; for my son, my boy.

'We can arrest Mr. Peters on a rape and battery charge.'

'I don't know, Inspector, I just don't know what is the best way to proceed. If you arrest him now, and he has

Michael, what if he kills him, what if Michael…?' I couldn't find the words.

'Mrs. Peters, sit down; have a glass of water.'

I obeyed silently, interlocking my fingers, pressing them together until my knuckles became white.

'I want you to listen to me very carefully; Mr. Peters has an alibi for the day Michael went missing. It's a pretty watertight alibi, too.'

'But how can you… you saw the tape?'

'There is no denying that Mr. Peters is a sadist and an extremely unpleasant person, but that doesn't make him a murderer, or a kidnapper, or the person who took Michael; you do understand that, don't you?'

I nodded, my hatred for Dave bubbling over.

'We can charge him with aggravated rape and battery; he will spend a long time in prison.'

'Not nearly as long as he deserves,' I mumbled.

'What would you have me do, Mrs. Peters? I don't know what it is you are asking of me?'

'What if there's a chance his alibi is fake? What if that woman is lying for him?' I said, urgently. 'I don't want him to know about these videos yet. I want to use them as my last resort. After all, I'm in them too,' I added, quietly.

The inspector came round to my side of the table and held my shoulders:

'No woman should ever be treated like you have been. No man should ever do that to a woman. What you have suffered and gone through I can't even begin to understand.'

'I did it for Michael.' I started to cry. 'I did it all for him, and now he's gone!' He lifted my face and held it there with his smooth hands, wiping away my tears.

'We can arrest Mr. Peters. We can bring him in for questioning, and if we are sure that he had no part in Michael's disappearance, then you can decide what to do with the videos. OK?'

I left the police station, Inspector Stone's words still fresh in my mind, but still unsure about how to proceed with Dave. He was a hateful man, and yet I couldn't help but pity him. I had never had that feminist angst, that fire of freedom and fair play. I found myself sympathising with the unsympathetic and always finding excuses for the way that they behaved, however callous and dark. And even now, with Michael gone, no matter how unforgivable his actions were, I always seemed to forgive him.

The police station was on the corner of the main street. There was a car park on the left, followed by a row of mostly abandoned shops, with a post office, a pharmacy and an off-licence. Opposite was a Korean takeaway, run by a friendly couple, Sandy and Suntae. They made the best kimchi I had ever tasted, and always insisted on thrusting extra fortune cookies into my bag as I was leaving, with mottoes like:

'Success lies in the hands of those who want it.' and 'To avoid criticism, do nothing, say nothing, be nothing.'

'Fucking Kinks!' Dave would growl under his breath as we stepped out of the warm kitchen into the cool night air, and: 'Bye Suntae, see you next time, thanks again!', his arm wrapped tightly around me, and then: 'Don't even know their own fucking culture!' And he would empty all the fortune cookies into the bin, laughing in a mean-spirited way. 'Do... They...Think...They...Are...Chinese?' he would say.

'Oh come on, Dave, a lot of Asian restaurants mix up the customs and cuisine; it's commonplace. Hell, Karen said she'd had the best sushi ever at a Vietnamese restaurant.'

'Sacrilege!' He raised his eyebrows, 'Let it go, will you?'

Sandy had loved Michael; they had a little girl, only a year behind him in school, and she would often make pretty paper lanterns and good luck charms for him. Sometimes, when I unpacked Michael's school bag, I would find broken prawn crackers at the bottom. I never scolded him for it, it only made me smile.

I continued to look down the street: just an ordinary street, in a very nondescript town, and yet there was something out of the ordinary about all of this, something all wrong and bent out of shape. I took off in the direction of Michael's school. My therapist, Jane, had brought up the idea that Michael might have left of his own accord, that perhaps something had been troubling him. I had never got that feeling from him, but I felt like all the loose ends should be tied up, and all the bases covered. The school was about a mile from the police station, and I decided to walk. The wind felt good against my bruised skin. A few heads turned as I walked. I could hear whispers; a hum of sympathy following me down the street. I quickened my pace until I'd left them behind. The school itself was quite an impressive building, or at least it must have been once: wrought iron gates and beautiful stonework. The playground was big, with netball posts and a set of swings. I remembered Michael playing on those swings. I remember calling from the gates for him to come, and his obstinate refusals.

'Just one more go, mummy!' he would scream to an empty playground.

He was always the last one to leave. I made my way through the gates and into the entrance hall. My heart ached a little as I saw the coat pegs, each with a child's name and picture above it. Amy, an apple, Katie, a balloon, Jake's horse, and for Michael a blue clock. I reached out and stroked the little laminated card, which was peeling slightly at its right-hand corner. I gripped my pendant, a gift from Michael on Mother's Day, a gift I later found out had been my sister, Alice's idea, of course, not my husband's. Our faces lined the two halves of it, connecting us for ever. I knelt down, holding onto the peg, leaned forward and whispered:

'Where are you my baby?' My heart felt like it had broken into a million pieces. I was imagining him hanging his little duffel coat on his peg, tucking his shoes neatly under the bench, then later, at break time, running off to play with his friends. I missed him so terribly. How could I have failed him so badly? How could I have let him down like that?

'Ann?'

I turned quickly and got to my feet; the head teacher, Mrs. Cliff, was smiling kindly, her hands clasped together. She was a lovely woman. Long blonde hair braided into a French plait, bright blue eyes, and a wonderful smile, and whereas I was rather awkward around other people's children, a maternal light seemed to radiate from her. The children loved her, and she seemed always to have enough time for each of them.

'Kristin, Hi!'

She came forward and embraced me. I'm not a huggy person, but her hair smelt like lavender, and her wool-blend jumper like warm biscuits. I let her hold me for a few minutes, feeling like one of her schoolchildren, savouring every moment of the wonderful way she made me feel.

'Come on, I'll make some tea.'

She directed me into her classroom. Kristin was far too humble for offices and desks; she was the kind of teacher who preferred cushions on the floor, music playing in the background, and finger painting. There seemed little organisation in her classroom; how childhood should be, I thought. 'How have you been?' she asked kindly.

'Like hell,' I responded, not looking up.

'Of course, what an insensitive question! I'm sorry; it always seems to be the appropriate thing to say, but how can anything be appropriate in these circumstances?' She sighed, 'If only we could do something, if I only could do more to help.'

'You can help me Kristin.'

'Oh, tell me, anything you need.'

'I was wondering how Michael had been, in the weeks before... you know...'

She nodded, and poured us both a cup of tea: green, of course, no sugar.

'I have rarely met a child like Michael,' she began, clasping her mug in her hands. 'You have children who are bright, and children who sometimes need a little encouragement.' Classy Kristin; she never put her students down, would never even think to use the words 'behind' or 'slow'.

'But Michael was neither, and he was both,' she mused. 'That is to say, he was incredibly good at music, at sports, and during story-telling time, and then maybe he needed some persuasion to do the more curriculum-based activities.' She smiled to herself. 'I have been saying for years that this school, and all schools, should be encouraging the arts, and making them just as important as mainstream subjects, but you know how governors are: school politics and all that.'

'Hmm.'

'And they never have approved of my way of teaching and what I do here. Education should be about colour and life, laughter and music; but what do I know?'

I took a sip of my tea; even Kristin Cliff's green tea was perfect.

'Michael was such a fast runner. The way he used to run during breaktime, up and down, and up and down, and then he would be at the window, panting, 'Miss Cliff, Miss Cliff, please can I have a glass of water, Miss Cliff, I'm so thirsty, I'm PARCHED!'

We both laughed. Michael would learn new words and then use them repeatedly, until everyone got sick of hearing them: 'parched' had been a particular favourite; 'devastated' another. 'I miss your son very much, Ann.' Her face suddenly looked very sad, too; as if she was mirroring mine.

'The week before he went missing, or in the days before, was he different? Did he seem angry or afraid, or sad?'

She considered for a moment:

'Not afraid, or particularly sad really, but there was the incident with Billy Stevens.'

Therapy with Doctor Blunt

'Ann?'

'Mm?'

'You don't seem to have very much to say today.'

'What do you want to know?'

'Whatever it is that you need to tell me.'

'We have been trying for a baby, Dave and I.'

'But that's wonderful news, congratulations!'

'Is it?' I looked up at her, and into her grey eyes. It was a genuine question.

'Why do you think it wouldn't be?'

I turned to look out of the window. It had started to rain, and I was suddenly aware of how dull and sombre the colours outside were.

'Dave has promised me that he will remain faithful this time. I don't know; I want to believe him.'

'That's good,' she nodded encouragingly, 'as your partner and husband, you should trust him implicitly. But then again, trust has to be earned. How is your relationship currently?'

'You mean the sex?'

She smiled.

'Not just the sex, Ann. Marriages and relationships are complex things. They need foundations, walls, insulation, care and maintenance. Do you have a solid friendship?'

I shrugged,

'I used to think we did. I was convinced I knew Dave's soul and he, mine. But you don't hurt your soul mate, do you?'

She considered this for a moment, and wrote something down in her notepad,

'This isn't about my opinion, Ann. I'm here to listen, and to help you understand yourself and your own relationships better, but only you know how you feel and how you can answer questions about your marriage.' She paused: 'Let me re-phrase the question. Do you love Dave?'

'Yes.'

'Then that's a great start, Ann. Not everyone is lucky enough to have married, and stayed married, and even fewer to have fallen in love. Love is a wonderful medicine, and a great starting block to build the trust back up again, and to be together.'

'Jane, I...' my voice wavered slightly. 'I want to be really honest with you.'

'Honesty is good.'

'But I'm afraid of hearing myself say this out loud.'

She leaned forward, and held my hand between hers.

'You have nothing to be afraid of. Anything you say here stays with me and my notes. I want you to feel comfortable, safe. Don't be scared to be naked here. That's what therapy is, after all: getting naked, and being unashamed of the stripped truth, no matter how unpleasant it is to look at.'

I smiled; she really was good at this. I took a deep breath,

'I'm worried that I want a baby, more than I want my marriage to work.' I didn't look at her.

'Go on'

'I'm thirty-one years old; I don't want to have to start all over again with someone new, and wait another five years to have a baby. I know Dave, we have ten years of history together; it's comfortable, and familiar. What if looking the other way is just the price I'm going to have to pay for having the baby that I know I want?'

Doctor Jane Blunt glanced at her watch.

'Excellent progress today, Ann, we will pick up from here next week.'

3 Weeks Missing

I stood at the school gates, watching the children greeting their parents and leaving on foot or in cars. Toddlers and babies screamed, and laughter and shouts filled the air. I clutched the iron railing as if to steady myself, feeling as though my legs could give way at any moment. My breath made clouds in the cold air, and my eyes watered in the wind. I waited until I could make out Billy Stevens and his mother clearly, about to get into their car, and I approached.

'Mrs. Stevens?' She turned and stared at me.

'Yes?' She pretended not to recognise me.

'Hi, I'm Ann Peters, Michael's mum.' Her face was unreadable. 'Michael Peters, the boy who was kidnapped...' She cut me off:

'Yes, I know who Michael Peters is. What do you want?' Her abrasiveness stung. She finished buckling Billy into his car seat and slammed the door. 'What do you want?' she repeated.

'Just to talk to you, about Billy and Michael, if that's OK.'

'I have nothing to say to you about Billy and Michael. And in any case, I'm surprised you want to talk about it now, when you were so uninterested before.' She rummaged in her handbag, searching for something.

'I don't understand; I've never spoken to you before. It's just that I spoke with Mrs. Cliff a few days ago, and she mentioned that something had happened between them, just before Michael went missing, and I'm trying to piece this thing together.'

'That's an unusual choice of words. Something happened all right, and you are lucky that we didn't take it any further than we did.'

I was completely at a loss as to what she talking about.

'May I ask what you remember of this incident?'

'No, you may not! I promised that I would drop it and I have. I don't want to discuss it and I don't want you to contact me ever again, Mrs. Peters.'

I was so taken aback. I had no idea what she thought I knew, or what she believed me to have done.

'Maybe you're getting this situation confused. I wasn't aware of this incident, until a few days ago. I'm trying to find out what happened to my son.'

'Then let me suggest you focus on that, and leave my Billy out of it. He had nothing to do with your son disappearing.'

'I'm not suggesting he did, I just want to know…'

'That's enough!' She was face to face with me now, her expression hard and menacing. She pointed a finger at my chest,

'It was made clear that we should drop it. I have dropped it. I don't want to discuss it any more. Is that understood?'

'Yes, OK. I'm so sorry I bothered you.' My head began to throb, as I watched her get into her car, her eyes still fixed on me. 'Wait!' I ran to the window.

'What?' she snapped,

'Please, who made it clear to you that you should drop it?'

She laughed, in complete and utter disbelief.

'Your husband, of course, who do you think?'

I drove straight to Karen's house after the confrontation with Billy Stevens' mother. I felt the strongest urge to drive to Dave's hotel, but I didn't have the energy. Karen lived at the other end of town, on what you might call the 'rough side'. A divorcée, she could no longer afford the beautiful house she had previously shared with her banker husband and their three children, and now had to make do, living in a two-bedroomed flat that overlooked the river. Karen was my best friend, my soulmate, my partner in crime. She was everything a friend should be: she never judged, always brought alcohol, and never let me down. When I started sleeping with Dave, while he was still married, she advised from a distance, recommended lingerie stores and sex positions. When Dave first began assaulting me, she tended to my injuries, gave me support group contact numbers, and a place to stay until Dave was sober. When I found out I was having a boy, she bought baby blue blankets and baby grows, bibs, and a breast pump; and when my baby went missing, she came with flowers, with gin, with kisses and never-ending hugs. She was my safety net, my airbag, my flash-light in the dark.

I pulled up in the car park. It had started to rain. Her block of flats was old; the once cream paintwork was now a dark urine colour. Battered cars filled the car park, and kids hung around smoking and riding their skateboards. Despite the depressing façade, I felt incredibly happy to be here; much happier than in my perfect suburban house, which was now only filled with emptiness and loss.

Karen greeted me in her usual fashion: with warmth and wine. It was only 4pm, but these days there was never not a good time to drink. She poured a glass for each of us and we sat in the kitchen, eating cashew nuts.

'It's certainly very strange,' she pondered, 'I mean, if something serious happened, then why didn't Dave say anything to you?'

'But the implication was that I knew what she was talking about.'

'And you have no idea?'

'Absolutely none; it was only when I spoke to Kristin that I had any idea that anything unusual had happened.'

'And what did she say exactly?'

'Well that's the weird thing, she didn't actually seem to know what had happened. Billy's mum, who is an absolute bitch, by the way, filed a complaint to the school board about Michael, the week before he went missing.' Here, Karen nodded knowingly, and refilled my glass. 'It's all confidential and private, when it's done officially like that, and Mrs. Cliff has no idea what it was about, apparently, only that Mrs. Stevens withdrew Billy from school for a few days.'

'That's a little extreme,' frowned Karen.

'I'm telling you, she is a bitch; so then, you know what Kristin's like: anything to keep the peace and make everybody get along; she persuaded bitch woman to drop the complaint and speak directly to me or Dave.'

'Which is reasonable enough.' Karen lit a cigarette and offered me one. 'Don't worry, the kids are with their dad, and it's not like you have places to be.'

I took one, and ploughed on: 'Yes, it's reasonable enough. So she dropped the complaint, and next thing, Billy was back at school, and then Michael… well, you know…'

She clasped my hand,

'So, something happened between Dave and Billy's mum?'

'Yeah, but I get the impression it was something very nasty; I mean she said, and she repeated it again at the end of our conversation, that she had been made to "drop it", so what does that mean?'

'I have no idea,' she shrugged, 'Nothing good, knowing Dave!'

'Knowing Dave!' I repeated, and held my head in my hands. 'So what did he do, threaten her? Get lawyers involved? Pay her off? Or what if it's something far worse than that, Karen?'

She looked at me a little alarmed for a second.

'What are you getting at Ann?'

'I don't know but he's been acting so strange.'

'Dave is strange, he's a loser, I've always told you that.'

'No, I mean, different strange. He never wanted a baby in the first place; he hardly even communicated with Michael, apart from to punish him when he was naughty, or to criticise my parenting style.' Karen measured out another refill; I was starting to feel the buzz, and yet everything seemed clearer than it ever had. 'What if the answer to the problem was getting rid of our son? I can't bear even to think that, let alone utter it out loud, but this is all so weird, and it keeps getting stranger and stranger.'

'Oh, Ann!' And she was hugging me, as she always knew how: holding me tightly, kissing away my tears and stroking my hair. 'You mustn't think like that, you mustn't! I'm sure there's a reasonable explanation for all of this.

You're obviously tired and stressed and sad all the time, and I know it makes it easier to believe that Dave did something, because then all the hate you feel for him would be justified. But being an arsehole doesn't make you a murdering arsehole...' she stopped herself, her eyes wide, 'I didn't mean... I shouldn't have said... that was the wrong choice of words.'

'I should go,' I said miserably.

'Go where?'

'I don't know, but I can't stop until this thing is finished. I can't sit here drinking with you, as if nothing has happened, pretending everything is how it was before. I can't be drunk. I need to find my son, and I guess I'll have to start with Dave.' I sighed heavily. She poured herself the last of the bottle, and gave me a quick hug.

'OK, go. If you need anything...'

'I know, thank you.'

Therapy with Doctor Blunt

'So, Ann, what have you decided?'

'About the baby?'

'Yes.'

'We are going to keep it.' Saying the words out loud gave me butterflies. 'I mean, I don't trust Dave; I probably never will. In fact, I'm not even sure that I love him any more, but that's OK.' I paused, waiting for her to interject, but she just continued to listen, and scribble away at her notes as I spoke my thoughts. 'If Dave fucks up, then it's over; he knows that, and I have more than enough love to give this baby: baby Michael.'

'It's a boy?' She sounded genuinely pleased.

'I can feel it. I won't know till my 16 week scan, but I can feel it.'

She smiled warmly.

'You seem to have made peace with your demons,

Ann.'

'I have.'

'And the drinking; do you have that under control?'

'I haven't touched a drop since I found out, and I feel something else. I'm less paranoid, anxious, sad.'

'Yes, sobriety is good like that!' We both laughed. 'You have made such progress.'

'Thank you, Jane, I feel a lot lighter.'

'Ann, you have been blessed with a wonderful gift. Whatever the future holds for you, there will be a baby, and babies always bring happiness.' She searched my face for a moment. 'Do you have any concerns?'

'Several!'

5 Weeks Missing

It was a Sunday. I'd not slept well. My dreams were dark. Eight hours of broken sleep, of nightmarish thoughts and memories. I dreamt of the woods, of the sounds of breaking branches beneath my bare feet; of Dave, raising a whip and bringing it down on my naked back again and again, whilst singing the theme tune to a butter commercial I could no longer even remember the name of. And all the while, Mrs. Stevens kept weaving in and out, shaking her head and pointing a long fingernail at my chest, chanting:

'You know what he did, you know what he did!' on a loop.

I was drenched in sweat and did not smell good. I had spent the night at my parents' house, a haven of sorts, where I found peace and familiarity; a place where I could sit and cry, and not be reminded of Michael's voice, or

Dave's blows, just my mother's warmth, and my old bedroom, which had remained untouched since the day I left for university. This was a house of only good memories, of unconditional love, and of hope. I would sit in this room and have so many dreams for the future: the person I would become, the career I would pursue, and the children I would raise.

Hope can be such an incredibly positive influence on a young teenage life, and yet such a burden to me now, as a woman, holding on to every last thread of it. I'd lost my virginity here: James Wood; tipsy on Lambrini, and high on a nicotine rush from a cigarette I hadn't had the first clue how to smoke. He'd been inside me before I knew it, tearing through, without the faintest idea what he was doing, and I'd squirmed in pain: uncomfortable and unhappy. A few thrusts, a drop of blood, and we were done. I had become a woman, at the age of fifteen. It had been hope that had got me through: I was hopeful that the next time would be less painful, hopeful that the next guy wouldn't smell like his dad's aftershave and cats, hopeful that life had so much more to give me than that moment; but it didn't, and here I was, pining to be back there, even if for only a few seconds.

I pulled on my jeans and an old top, and went downstairs. My parents were both sitting at the dining table, my father pretending to read a paper, my mother absent-mindedly stirring a cup of coffee that had neither milk nor sugar.

'How did you sleep, my lovely?'

'OK, I guess.'

She put a hand to my forehead.

'Terribly then, in other words.'

'No, I'm fine. Who needs sleep anyway?'

She boiled the kettle.

'Cold forehead. You're still tired, you should probably get some more rest while you can.'

I ignored her and made myself a cup of tea. My father folded his newspaper in half with purpose, and took off his reading glasses.

'We wanted to talk to you, Ann.'

I drank some of my tea, allowing it to burn and sting my throat. I didn't care. It felt good to feel something. He ploughed on;

'Your mother and I are worried about you. Obviously, this is an extremely testing time for all of us.' They exchanged glances, and I didn't respond. 'Is there anything you want to tell us, anything at all?'

'About what?' I felt light headed, and suddenly in desperate need of a drink.

'There's no easy way to say this, Ann but...'

'How could you let this happen?'

My father's eyes widened, and we both turned in my mother's direction. She was staring at me, with a look of... contempt? Disappointment? I couldn't tell. My eyes felt heavy;

'I beg your pardon,' I cleared my throat, 'let it happen?'

'I'm sick of us all walking on eggshells in this house, and nobody being honest about anything!' Her voice was mounting. '36 years I have been a mother, 36 years, and I have never let anything like this happen, in my own home!'

'What do you mean, let this happen? I left him for a second!'

'I'm not talking about that!' There were real tears in her eyes, now, and she was practically shouting. 'I'm talking about all of it! Marrying someone like Dave, I mean. What possessed you to even be with someone like that, somebody who was married? We didn't raise you like that! Allowing yourself to have a child that he didn't really even want, and that you were both too busy to see had problems, and then carrying on in the way that you and Dave always did, with poor Michael in that house. It was wrong! I don't understand how you could have done this to our family!' She burst into tears and buried her head in my father's shoulder. He held her for a few moments, and fixed me with a look that Inspector Stone usually reserved for me: pity. I felt betrayed.

'This isn't about you and dad; it never was, and it isn't even about me, although it's nice to know how you really feel. It's about Michael; we just have to find him, and all of this, everything, will go away, and it will just be like it was before.'

My mother continued to sob uncontrollably on my father's shoulder, and I felt sick in the pit of my empty stomach.

The three of us stood there, awkwardly, for what seemed an eternity, in my mother's kitchen, my safe haven, a place where I never thought I would feel so outnumbered and abandoned.

The phone rang and broke the silence.

'Hello!' my father answered. 'Yes, speaking. She's here. Where? Probably not. Of course. I understand. Goodbye.' My mother had stopped crying and was staring at him, her eyes rimmed with red. I put down the cup I was holding and stared at my father's back.

'What is it, John?' She knew something was wrong. Eventually he turned round to look at us. I had never seen my father's face so etched with misery, with complete and utter devastation. He put the phone back on the hook and turned to me directly.

'They have found Michael.'

*

I abandoned my car at the bottom of the hill, and began scrambling up the embankment, in the direction my father had indicated. The ground was wet, and my shoes kept sinking into the mud and slime, nettles stinging my ankles. I could see police cars, an ambulance, and hear voices in front of me. I couldn't stop, I had to make it to the top and see for myself; I had to save him; I had to get to him.

I had left my parents' house in my own car. My father had tried to stop me, my mother's screams echoing in my ears, but I couldn't stay; all I saw was Michael's face, and the knowledge that whatever I might find, I could touch and know was real.

'You're in no fit state to drive Ann, please wait here. Inspector Stone said to wait here, and someone would come and collect you.'

But I was gone.

I slowed down as I reached the top of the slope. The gushing of the river was deafening after heavy rain. Everything looked blurred and out of focus. I could hear murmurings and whispers all around, but none of them had a face or a purpose. I went a few steps further and saw a white tent down by the widest part of the river. I looked down; I could see Inspector Stone talking with some of the other officers. He glanced up and caught sight of me amidst the brambles lining the embankment.

'What is she doing here? I told them not to let her come.'

I started to move towards him, and he shook his head.

'Mrs. Peters, you need to go, you shouldn't be here.'

'I need to...'

'No! Will someone get her out of here!' He was shouting now, and I felt hands on my arms, voices begging, pleading with me to go back up to the top of the hill.

'No, please! Don't do this! I need to see...'

He was motioning to other officers now, to remove me from the scene, and I fell to my knees:

'I need to see my son? Please!'

It was as if the grief was being injected slowly into my veins. It started slowly and uncomfortably, and became stronger, as the full realisation of what was down there became clear.

'Where is my baby?' I was screaming now, an animal noise that came from somewhere I never knew existed, 'Let me see my baby, let me see Michael!'

The woods suddenly fell very quiet, and I was aware, for a moment or two, of just how unbearable that silence was, of how everything would be silent from now on. It only took a second or so for me to grasp that life would never be how it used to be, ever again. There would be no more kisses with my son, no more late nights eating cheese on toast and watching cartoons, no more outgrowing pyjamas. I would never be able to hold my baby again, to breathe in his golden brown hair, to wipe jam and breadcrumbs from the side of his mouth, and tell him how cute he looked. I would never be able to bathe him in the tub, listening to our favourite songs, and splashing the tiles with water, even though we knew how angry it made Dave. There would be no more picking him up from school, or taking him to get ice cream; Christmases when we would choose the tree, and buy one new special bauble every year; kisses goodnight, and stories, until he fell asleep in my arms. And then there were all the things that he would never get to do: fall in love, graduate, travel, get married, have children of his own one day; all the things that we could have done together, the journey that we were supposed to take together, we could never take, because life had been cruelly snatched from him, so early, so unnecessarily. In that moment, I realised something else, before I passed out, one final thought, which struck like a knife to my chest: it wasn't only that I now didn't have a son, it was that I was also no longer a mother.

Therapy with Doctor Blunt

'You seem a little out of sorts today, Ann.'

'Is that a question?'

'More like an observation. Do you want to talk about it?'

'That's a question.'

'That's why we are here: to ask questions about ourselves. To be honest with ourselves, if only in here, for one hour a week.'

I sighed. I had been sitting sulkily for ten minutes, saying nothing. Truth be told, I really didn't feel like it today. I was tired, sick from the pregnancy and irritated by the smallest things. I stirred my finger round the water in my glass. I had been seeing Jane for three months now. Aside from the huge expense, and the twenty-five minute drive to Greensworth, I did feel strangely liberated when I was here. A friend of Karen's had recommended Doctor Blunt, and although at first I was somewhat reluctant, it felt good to be held up to a mirror, to be forced to examine myself with a microscope. Picking over all the flaws, all the mistakes, and being told by a total stranger that having these flaws made me somehow more human, and therefore imperfectly perfect in my own little way, felt reassuring. It was good just to talk, and to have someone listen, someone without judgement, without hostility or persecution, just an ear, and a voice. It made me feel safe.

'Therapy?' my mother had said, with one of her perfectly plucked eyebrows raised. 'I was under the impression your father and I had done rather well, both with you and your sister.' That was my mother all over: kind and loyal to a fault with her own children and those closest to her, but absolutely no time for bullshit. She called a spade a spade and never had time for fancy names for illnesses she considered imaginary.

'Oh come on, mum, it's 2017; everyone has a therapist. It's nice to talk to someone about things, you know.'

'Can't you do that with me, over cocktails, or with your girlfriends?'

I shook my head;

'There are some things that I wouldn't want even you to know!'

She looked surprised, and then hurt.

'I'm intrigued, and also a little insulted. I thought we told each other everything.'

I hadn't pursued the conversation, and my mother was too much of a class act to berate me into a confession.

'Ann, are you with me at all, today?' Doctor Blunt was tapping her foot insistently on the parquet floor.

'I'm sorry, I'm not feeling great.'

'I can see.'

'It's just hormones, and the sickness is pretty grim. I haven't been able to keep anything down. I thought this was supposed to have stopped by week fourteen.'

She scribbled something down; I wish I knew what she wrote about me.

'Some women can experience morning sickness right up until the birth.' She faltered when she caught my horrified expression. 'Oh don't worry, Ann, I'm sure you'll be fine; I felt great after sixteen weeks.'

I looked up. 'Oh? I had no idea you had children.' It was true, there were no photos in the doctor's office. She looked down for a moment and her expression was pained. This was one of the few times I had seen true emotion on her beautifully made up face.

'Three miscarriages,' she said, simply. I flinched at the word.

'I'm so sorry, Jane, I mean, Doctor Blunt, I had no idea. I obviously wouldn't have said anything...'

'It's quite all right. And now you know something dark about me. I have let you in to something very personal and private; maybe now you can let me in a little bit more.'

Gone

Trying to figure out why Michael was missing had filled my days with a sense of impending doom. I spent hours watching the clock, waiting for the phone to ring. I would jump at the sound of a car pulling up outside, and peel back the curtains when I heard voices nearby. I had been afraid of waking up every single morning to an unknown future, to another day without my son, not knowing where he was, who had him, or what they were doing to him. I couldn't sleep, because my dreams were filled with Michael's face, his voice, his energy. I couldn't eat because everything in my house tasted of nothingness. It's strange how everything feels so different now: it's almost a relief. Knowing that my son is no longer in pain is somehow more comforting than living off the hope that he might return. It is exhausting to spend the days waiting and praying and hoping, and never getting any answers.

Now, I don't have to check my phone, wait by the door, or stay at home with the lights on, just in case, because he's never coming back, and he never was. Life has taken on a new meaning and mission: to find out exactly what happened, and who was responsible; nothing else matters.

I set off on foot from my house to retrieve my car. I hadn't been back for it in over two weeks, but then I hadn't needed it. Our town is fairly small, and I could walk pretty much anywhere for essentials. I passed several parents from Michael's school, noticed their heads turning, the tuts and the sighs, and then the heads pushed together again to whisper. It felt good to be outside. I hadn't gone anywhere since Michael's body had been discovered.

A jogger had found him that morning: barefoot, lying on the riverbank. How the police had missed him on their numerous searches I'll never know; they had already found his trainers some way downstream, so I suppose they must have assumed that he would have been found a lot nearer to where he lost them. The shoes; I still didn't understand why he wasn't wearing them, why he had taken them off, and whether it was of any significance. He had been drowned. Marks around his neck indicated that he had been held under the water for several minutes. How could anyone physically hold a child under water until the life left them? He was still recognisable, despite the length of time he had been in the water, so that I could still tell it was him, with his round face and smiling eyes. He was still my baby. I held him, as I had held him when he was born. I remember thinking how precious and how entirely perfect he was. When he grabbed my finger for the first time, my heart doubled in size. He had been the most beautiful baby, and even in death he was perfect, so still and peaceful.

Nothing prepares you for losing a child, for seeing the body, or for burying your child; it is an experience no parent should ever have to undergo. Nobody can possibly understand the loss, and the never-ending ache that you feel, imagining all the things that might have been done to him: how he might have suffered, how he must have called out for me, how he must have asked just to go home, and hold his Bear Bear again. After identifying my five-year old son's body, and making a promise to myself to find whoever was responsible, I had walked home in the rain, climbed into Michael's bed, held his Bear Bear that still smelt of him, and cried into the pillow for days.

I turned the corner onto the street where my parents lived. It was raining again, and although the walk only took ten minutes, I was soon drenched. My legs felt stiff, reminding me that I hadn't moved in days. My eyes hurt from squinting in the daylight. I was out of breath. I made my way up the street until I reached number 19, my parents' house, with its bright red door; I saw my sister's car parked outside, next to mine. That lifted my heart a little, and I went inside.

'Oh, thank goodness, she's here.' I heard my father say. I stood in the hallway, soaking wet, my hair stuck to my forehead like some goth rocker, and I was shivering. My mother ran down the stairs; she had been crying by the look of it, and drinking too, by the smell of it. She clasped my cheeks in her hands:

'Ann!' she looked at me desperately. 'Oh, Ann!'

I looked back at her, seeing my mother, my best friend, realising how much I needed her now, more than I ever had, and everything just became too hard to bear.

'I miss him so much,' I wailed.

She pulled me to her, and we sat like that on the stairs, she stroking my wet back, and peeling aside the strands of hair from my face, kissing my cheeks, my forehead, my nose. We must have stayed that way for a quarter of an hour, just silent and holding each other. I had forgotten, since becoming a mother myself, just how much I loved mine, and how good it felt, even though everything was so desperate, just to be kissed by her. I almost felt like she could make it all go away.

'Alice is here,' she said after a while.

'Yes, I saw her car outside,' I replied. 'How is she?'

'Oh, you know, same old, but I think she's happy to be out of hospital and in a comfortable bed.'

I tried to laugh;

'I'll go and see her.'

'She'd like that; you can change in your room; there are still some clothes and a dressing gown in your wardrobe.'

My mother kissed my forehead and watched me, with a pained look on her face, as I climbed the stairs to see my little sister.

'Annie?' I heard her call down the landing.

My parents' house was a typical three-bedroomed semi. The long upstairs landing had doors leading off to bedrooms, and a large bathroom at the end. My sister's room was the last door on the right, and her voice was like music to me. I put my face around the door and looked in. She was propped up on the bed, typing furiously on her laptop, glasses resting on her nose, her hair scraped back. She looked pretty. She was pretty. She looked up at me, her big doe eyes shining.

'Annie,' she breathed, and slowly rose to hug me.

My sister, Alice, had been diagnosed with MS several years ago. She was still a firecracker, and nothing seemed to keep her back, despite repeated hospital visits and episodes of reduced mobility. She was one of the most extraordinary people that I had ever known: loving, kind, and gentle, yet feisty with it. She was never sad or down, and she certainly never appeared to be resentful about the life that she was forced to lead, the cards that she had been dealt. I envied that lust for life; she made the most of every minute, appreciated every new day she got to spend, and spent it always smiling and laughing. She had the most irrepressible spirit. I often found myself wondering why I had not been more like her: carefree and indifferent to the restraints and regulations of this world. But then, perhaps I would not have married Dave, had Michael, been here. I sometimes tried to calculate: was it better to have lived my life, and had five wonderful years with Michael, or never to have had a child and never known the pain. But feeling this pain stems from knowing a love like that, and I suppose I would rather have experienced that feeling, no matter how much it hurt now.

'I miss you, Annie!' She held my hand across the bed.

'You know,' I sighed, as I sat down next to her, 'you are the only person in the world who calls me that.'

She smiled. 'You are too special to be just plain Ann.'

'So how are you feeling, anyway?'

She closed her laptop, and leaned back on the bed.

'I feel OK, I'm less than pleased with the doctors over at Barts, but it's fine, it's fine. There are much more important things.'

'Alice, there is nothing more important than your health.'

'Yes, there is: finding out who took Mikey from us.' she interrupted. She barely missed a beat, and her expression was bold and unabashed.

'Alice, sweetie, it's my burden, it's my fault...'

'Stop blaming yourself; you are the best mother anyone could wish to have!'

'I was the best mother, past tense.'

She looked at me sadly, and rubbed my knuckles with her thumb.

'You will always be the best mother to him, Annie. Don't let whoever did this take that away from you too; they already took your son.'

'You know you are the only person who called him that.'

'What?'

'Michael, Mikey,' I laughed. 'I'm pretty sure he hated it.' We both laughed. 'He loved you, though, so much.' My words stuck in the back of my throat, and my saliva made strings between my lips. Alice was such a positive person:

she always managed to see the good in this incredibly bad world. 'When do you go back up to London?'

She opened up her laptop again.

'As soon as I can, really,' she sighed. 'I have got so much work to do, and my stay in Barts hasn't helped.' She began feverishly typing away again, her eyes wide, darting across the screen, her face lit by the white word document.

'What are you working on?'

She didn't look up, 'Just research for a few articles I've got to get out by the end of the month; nothing headline-worthy, yet, unfortunately!' she added, somewhat bitterly.

I got up from the bed and moved a bit nearer to her. She glanced up from her laptop and caught my eye.

'I love you Alice!' I kissed her forehead. 'You're tired... your forehead's...'

'Cold! Yes, thank you, mother!' she laughed. 'I'll get some rest while I'm here; please don't worry about me.'

I hugged her and started to leave.

'Annie?'

'Yes?'

'Come and see me when you're up in London. I can help you with this. I can do some research and digging of my own, I've got several contacts there.'

'Maybe I will.' I blew her one last kiss and stepped back into the hallway. I saw my mother standing at the top of the stairs, holding on to the banister as if to steady herself.

'You staying, Ann?' she asked, as I reached her. 'I'll make something nice if you are.'

'I said I'd meet Karen for a drink. Maybe next time.'

I left my parents' house, and after stopping for petrol on the main street, I drove to The White Horse, an old favourite, where Karen and I had spent many a late evening, eating cheese platters and downing glasses of *Pinot Grigio* and house red. It was somewhat posh: there were no unemployed wasters at the bar, or underage girls in push-up bras. In fact, there wasn't even your usual middle-class family with its train of screaming kids, playing on their tablets and whining for yet another diet Pepsi. It was mainly couples, young and old, obviously still crazy about each other, or humouring each other's need for romance and fine dining, and friends like me and Karen: divorcées, women with baggage, who didn't really need an excuse to meet up and spend an afternoon drinking and confiding all their deepest and darkest secrets. Karen was already there when I arrived, and already on her second glass of wine, judging by the half-empty bottle on the table. She was perusing the menu while sucking on her e-cig; she looked up and waved when she saw me. The pub was empty, apart from one other couple, and a man drinking a pint at the solid oak bar. He nodded politely as I ordered a drink: a large glass of Merlot.

The pub was divided into two spacious rooms. Both were full of dark wooden tables and chairs. The floor was made up of old paving stones, and above, fairy lights hung from wooden beams. There were photographs, some old and some new, of past pub landlords, of village carnivals and cricket matches. It was cosy and comfortable. I made my way over to Karen, who threw her arms around me in her typical over-dramatic, tactile way:

'What took you so long? I had to order myself a drink, sorry.'
I nodded.
'I can see!'
She stuck out her tongue, and took another sip of wine.
'The kids with Tom?'
'Mm.' She opened her menu again. 'I'm thinking I want something light today, like a Caesar salad, but then I'm drinking red, so maybe steak, or half a roast chicken.' She continued to stare intently at the menu, and then passed it to me. 'What do you fancy?'
'I'm not hungry, Karen.' I took a sip of my Merlot.

'You have got to have something, you need to keep your strength up.'

'Then you order for me. I don't care.' I looked out of the stained-glass window by our table. It was still raining, and cars drove past splashing passers-by with murky water.

'Fine.' She got up, and went over to the bar, asked for something, paid, and returned to our table. 'So?'

'Please don't ask me how I've been. If one more person does that...' my voice trailed off.

'I wouldn't dream of it, but we do need to talk about things.'

'I suppose.'

'So, have you seen Dave?'

'Only at the police station, and the funeral; not to talk to.'

This was a lie. I had, in fact, seen Dave a few times at the house, but I didn't really feel like admitting this to Karen; she would only scold me. He had come round to talk twice. Talking had turned into sex. Ours was a complicated relationship that I couldn't expect anyone to understand.

'Do you still suspect he has something to do with this?' She took a slug of wine.

'You know Dave.'

'That's right, I do know Dave.'

'He's a passionate person.'

'Passionate? He's abusive and violent, and dangerous, Ann!'

'Yes, I know; it's complicated.'

'Well what the hell does that mean?'

She continued to rant about Dave, and I continued, lamely, to defend him, until our food arrived. Karen had chosen steak and kidney pie, soaking in thick brown gravy. The smell of kidney turned my stomach. For me she had ordered a small portion of chips. I smiled at her, remembering times past. She knew me so well. As if reading my thoughts, she took a chip from my plate and popped it into her mouth.

'Well, Ann, how is it complicated?'

'I need to find out what he knows about Michael and Billy's incident at school, because Mrs. Stevens definitely isn't going to tell me, and Kristin has no idea.'

'So ask him?'

'If I just come out and ask him, he'll shut down, or he'll play mind games and never tell me the truth. I need to either get him drunk or...'

'Well, that shouldn't be a problem, the guy's a textbook alcoholic.'

'Granted! Alternatively, I could try to convince him that I still love him and want us to stay together, and wait for him to tell me himself.'

She snorted, 'I somehow doubt very much that that is going to happen.'

I shrugged, 'I don't know yet; I had another idea, though, but...'

'But... what?'

'But you'll think I'm insane, and I don't need you to tell me what I already know.'

'I would never do that.' She took a large swig of wine, her lips and teeth were now stained slightly, and her glass left a red ring on the wooden table. 'You're my girl, I'm in this with you, whatever happens, you must know that!'

Karen was tipsy. You could tell that, as soon as she started using phrases like: 'you're my girl', and 'ride or die'. She won't remember this conversation tomorrow, I thought.

'Well, I was thinking of visiting Helen Anderly.'

She put down her fork and looked at me:

'The mistress?'

'Whatever she is: girlfriend, bit on the side, pussy, as Dave calls them, but yes.'

'But why?'

'Well, I think he might have told her something, unintentionally. She may not think it's important, but it could be.'

'But she'll never go for it; she'll never talk to you in a million years. She thinks you're out and she's in, and that the divorce is going ahead!'

I dipped my finger into my Merlot and sucked it slowly, considering this.

'It depends from what angle I play it. I'll tell her that Dave's abusive, beats me. I'll show her the marks on my ankles and wrists, hell, I can even show her a video if I need to. I'll show her the kind of person he is, and get her to tell me everything she knows. Two birds with one stone, so to speak. If she believes me, which she will, if presented with hard facts and video evidence, she may leave him, which means that I can keep Dave close to me.'

'For how long?'

'Until I figure this thing out, until I know who's responsible, and if it's Dave, then I have to know, I have to!'

'But isn't it dangerous? I mean, Dave is dangerous. What if you do all that, and she leaves Dave, and he moves back in with you, and it turns out he did kill Michael? You could be in serious danger in that house!'

I sat in silence for a few minutes, thinking this over, 'I don't think Dave would ever try to kill me; not if I could manipulate him into thinking that we were happy and still in love.'

'I think you're crazy.' Karen had finished another glass of wine, and got up. 'Nature calls!' She announced, walking across the pub in the direction of the toilets. I sat thinking about this plan, and what I needed to find out from Helen Anderly. Had I left the door unlocked the night before? What had Michael done to Billy at school that was worth silencing his mother over, and where was my husband when Michael was kidnapped? If I could just get to the bottom of those questions, it would be a start. The door to the pub opened, and Inspector Stone and another man walked in. He approached the man standing at the bar, who muttered something in his ear. He turned in my direction.

'Mrs. Peters!' He strode over.

'Inspector Stone,' I nodded.

His eyes took in the empty bottle of red, and my glass.

'I'm with someone; don't worry, I haven't had a bottle all to myself!' I tried to smile.

'I wouldn't judge you if you had. How have you been?'

'OK,' I replied, numbly.

'Listen, I meant to call you last week. We have a few leads, and I wanted to fill you in on a few things and see if you can answer some questions, help me out with a few things, if you don't mind.'

'Yes, of course; anything I can do to help.'

'Has your husband been to the house?' He was frowning.

'No, no, he hasn't been back.'

He sat down next to me.

'Mrs. Peters, Ann, I'm on your side here. I'm trying to do everything I possibly can to help you and to find whoever did this.'

'I know, and I believe you will.' I was suddenly very aware that I was being backed into a corner. Paul Stone was inches away from my face now. He smelled of whisky, but not in the stale, repulsive way that Dave did. It was more of an attractive smell; it suddenly made me want to drink some too, and to be alone with him.

'It's not a good idea to lie to me then, is it?'

'About?'

'We have been watching the house, Ann.'

'Why?'

'Well, partly for your safety; I mean, you came to me with those videos. I have seen the kind of man that Dave Peters is; but also to see if anyone else is watching you, or stopping by when you aren't there.'

'He just came round to drop off his key,' I mumbled, staring at the ground.

'The curtains were closed.'

'The curtains are always closed. I can't bear to see outside, to look at the garden, to see Michael's bike.'

'Unfortunately, I don't have anyone else to confirm that, do I?'

'Karen Williams, I don't believe we have met.' Karen had appeared from nowhere. She had an odd expression on her face and her eyes were slightly glazed. The Inspector got to his feet and moved around to the other side of the table.

'Paul Stone.' He shook her hand. 'Come down to the station, later this afternoon, Ann, and we'll talk some more.'

I nodded, and he rejoined his friends at the bar. Karen rounded on me.

'I don't mind you lying to him, Ann, that I can understand, but if you want my help, then you have got to start being honest with me, about Dave, about Michael, about everything!' She looked hurt and annoyed. Her make-up was smudged slightly, and she had red wine on her blouse.

'OK.' I leant forward onto the table with my head in my hands. 'But I don't know how to say it, and I know how it sounds, and it's not good.' My hands were trembling. Karen noticed too, and she clasped them together in hers.

'Whatever it is, I'll understand, ride or die!' she whispered.

'OK.' I took a sip of my wine, and looked directly into her eyes. 'I don't remember where I was when Michael was taken.'

*

I hadn't wanted to expand on what I had told Karen over drinks. An empty pub is perhaps worse than a busy, rowdy one. It only takes one person to overhear a conversation, and seeing as one of the few other people in the pub was the policeman in charge of the case, I decided I did not want him to be that person. Instead, Karen had diverted me with stories from work: who had slept with whom, who was getting a rise, or getting fired: general office gossip, and I pretended to be interested and laugh along at the pointless scenarios, and soap-opera coincidences. But, surprisingly enough, it felt good to hear somebody else's drama, another woman's heartache, another bastard's betrayal. It lifted my spirits a little, and helped to lighten the load.

We had said our goodbyes around six-o'clock, after a couple of bottles of bad wine, and the decidedly average food. I decided to walk to the police station to see Inspector Stone, giving me time to think a little more about the day that Michael went missing. Not remembering where I was. It was an admission I had never made to anyone, and I often pretended even to myself that it wasn't the truth.

It had been an ordinary Monday. The night before, Dave had been out for drinks with the other lecturers at the University. Actually, he had been screwing one of his students, a young woman named Helen Anderly, the latest of many affairs and indiscretions. I had read Michael a bedtime story: 'We're Going on a Bear Hunt', his favourite, a book that I had read to him ever since he was baby. His chubby fingers had turned the pages for me. I had tucked him up in his little pirate bed, and he had fallen asleep cradling Bear Bear and smiling, his night light projecting stars and moons onto the cracked ceiling above. I had gone to bed not long after.

The next morning I had taken Michael to school. There had been nothing unusual about any of it so far: no matter how many times I kept thinking back, trying to remember the smallest detail, the slightest thing, nothing came to mind. I had gone into the main street after dropping him off and bought some things from the supermarket: apples, cheese, rice cakes for Michael, wine, milk, toilet roll, and then gone home to do some housework. Since Michael's birth, I had been a stay-at-home mother, revelling in the delights of home baking and finger painting, breastfeeding and Play-Doh. I had never gone back to my job, as Dave's salary was more than enough for our needs, and I was toying with the idea of putting it off some more and having another baby. I had been a Drama teacher at the local high school, and though once it had been a passion of mine, I found little pleasure in trying to encourage the kids to open their horizons to Stanislavsky and Brecht, when the only things they seemed to care about were their iPhones and reality TV. At least at home, Michael appreciated me, loved me. It was nice to feel necessary, to feel needed.

After I had finished the housework, I had showered and gone to collect Michael from school. As always, he had rushed out of the school's blue door first, with his green school bag that was far too big for him hitting his legs at each stride. First out, last to leave, that was Michael. No matter how quickly he emerged, he would make straight for the swings in the playground, swinging higher and higher, until all the other children had disappeared, and he was alone, with me waiting patiently on the other side of the gates. I never rushed Michael, and I never forced him to leave. That is one of the things that I am happy about now. I used to watch him on those swings for ages until he was ready to come home. I'm glad that I took the time to enjoy those moments, instead of pining over them now he was gone.

We had walked home, Michael kicking the leaves and running a little ahead of me, telling me about the painting they were doing at school, using sponges and plastic knives. He had drawn a huge sun with yellow and orange spots of colour, and during break time, he had shared his snack with his best friend, Tony. I loved to listen to him ramble on, as there was so much enthusiasm and excitement in his voice. It was as if he was ready to take on anything that life would bring, and he would always see the positive and the good. It was an endearing naivety that I thought was one of Michael's many strengths.

We had stopped at the Korean takeaway as we passed through the main street. I'd chatted with Sandy about school, the kids, this and that, all and nothing, and she had given us some free prawn crackers. By the time we got home, it was already 4 o'clock. Michael had insisted that he play outside for a bit and, as usual, I was unable to refuse him, his head bobbing up and down like a dog's, panting for acceptance and encouragement.

He had put on his new trainers and run out into the garden. I remember it being very windy. I had watched him from the lounge window as he played in the dirt, making gravel stew and mud pies, pulling up flowers from the flower bed that had been largely untended anyway. I had poured myself a small glass of vodka in one of the crystal tumblers engraved with the names: 'Ann' and 'David', a wedding present from my parents. I had stood at the window, continuing to watch my son happily playing in the mud without a care in the world.

And the next memory I have of that day is waking up on the floor of the lounge. The lights were off, and it was dark outside. I hadn't a clue what had happened, or even really what time it was, but I knew that something was horribly, horribly wrong. I could hear an unbearable squeaking noise, like the sound of a door opening and shutting very slowly, its hinges in need of oil. I had rushed out onto the porch and seen Michael's bike, abandoned and on its side, the wheels turning in the wind.

'Michael?' I had called out, aware how husky and unfamiliar my voice sounded. 'MICHAEL, sweetie?' I had run to the edge of the garden, down the steps and onto the pavement. There was nobody on the street, not a soul, and it only took a second or two for me to realise that he was gone. Everything felt incredibly cold, and I knew instinctively that something very bad had happened, and that I could not explain any of it.

This was a chilling memory that I kept to myself, that I only thought about when I was alone, as if I was afraid that someone would jump into my head and examine my thoughts. Occasionally, when Inspector Stone looked at me, I felt as if he was doing that, and I was always careful never to think about the real memory. But something certainly haunted me about that day, other than the obvious. Somebody else must have known that I wasn't with my son, or they knew that I would leave him for a few minutes; even worse, they knew that I was a drinker, and they knew which drink I would choose, or had all my bottles been spiked? That scared me more than anything else, that whoever had done this to my child knew me in an intimate way, and I couldn't shake the feeling that perhaps I knew them too.

Therapy with Doctor Blunt

'Tell me about your childhood, Ann.'
I was back in the white office with the red curtains and the overbearing smell of roses,
   'What do you want to know?'
   'Whatever you want to tell me.'
   'Can you be more specific?'
Doctor Blunt smiled and shook her head good-naturedly,
   'Ann, I want you to confide in me. I can't force you to share with me anything that you don't want to, but it is important you give me something.'
I returned the smile and caressed my belly.
   'Why don't we start with your parents? What was your relationship like with them?'
   'Good, fine.'
She raised her eye brows, 'Fine?'
   'Yes, well, I suppose you could say with my mother it's fine. We've always been very close, in a kind of sister or

best friend way. We drive each other crazy, but she's always been very supportive of me and my decisions. She loves me a lot, and I guess I feel in awe of the sacrifices she's made for her children.'

'Interesting, How so?'

'She's from a different time, a different world, where marriage was for life, and divorce was for the weak.'
She frowned, 'I see.'

'Not that I think she actually believes that, but it's her general philosophy on life. For example, she stayed with my father, even though she wasn't always happy with him. She could have thrown in the towel years ago, but she stayed for her children. I think that's pretty amazing. And she always cared more about us, and how happy we were, than about herself.'

'We?'

'My sister Alice and me.'

'Go on.'

'She's a very brave woman; but not in the outwardly confident sort of way, but in her own brilliant way, she's probably one of the strongest women I know.'

'And you are afraid of disappointing her?'

'I'm always afraid of disappointing anyone, but especially my parents.' I looked down at my hands, feeling a little uncomfortable.

'What exactly are you afraid of doing or not doing that might disappoint them?'

'Divorcing Dave; or even just admitting out loud that I don't want to be with him any more.'

She nodded thoughtfully, and wrote some more in her notebook:

'But you said she had always been supportive of all your choices. Perhaps you aren't giving her enough credit.'

'You're right; I'm sure she'd say it was fine. It's probably not the best idea to have a baby with someone I don't love, but I'm sure she'd support me through it anyway.'

'So, the disappointment that you're feeling, where is that coming from?' She leaned forward listening intently.

'I guess, myself.'

'Go on.'

'I suppose deep down I know that I would not be, am not, capable of staying in this marriage, even for this child.' I looked down at my swollen stomach. 'He's not even here yet, and I'm already talking of abandoning my marriage, not even willing to give it one last go, or to try one more time for his sake. What kind of a mother does that make me? I see my mother, who put everything on hold, and sacrificed her entire life, and perhaps her happiness, to raise me and my sister in this happy family home, and I can't even keep it together for the birth. I don't feel ready to sacrifice anything. I guess I'm incredibly disappointed with myself.'

9 Weeks Gone

My answerphone was flashing; I had two new messages. I threw my keys onto the sofa and pressed the menu button, grabbed a beer from the fridge, and replayed the messages.

'Hello, sweetie; it's mum, just checking in. Your father and I are going up to see Alice next week, and I wondered whether you fancied a change of scenery. Anyway, I'll probably see you tomorrow or at the weekend, and you can let me know. Love you.'

I blew into my scarf, allowing my breath to billow back onto my chin and cheeks. I'd forgotten to put the boiler on, or light a fire, and my fingers were pink and swollen from the cold.

'You have one new message, today at 7.15am'

'Ann, it's Paul Stone here. I've tried calling your mobile but you're not answering. You really need to come down to the station as soon as you can. There's been a... development.'

His voice clicked off and I sat up. I could feel the blood pounding in my ears. Everything seemed heightened; it always did, when I believed I was getting closer to the truth. I chugged down the rest of my beer and popped a breath mint to mask the smell. It was 9.30, and even I knew that it was a little early for beer. I jumped into my car and drove to the police station.

As I pulled into the car park, I was aware of several things: firstly, the absence of police cars. I could make out Paul Stone's battered mushroom-coloured Vauxhall, its yellow magic tree dangling from the rear-view mirror, and maybe one police car, and that was it; secondly, on the steps to the station there were several people, and as I got closer, I realised they were reporters. My phone vibrated again in my pocket and I picked it up.

'So you do know how to answer your phone now!' He sounded irritable and extremely tired.

'Why are there reporters here?'

'Come round to the back entrance, Sally will open it for you.' He hung up. I turned right, instead of continuing towards the steps that led up to the main entrance, and ducked down a narrow side alley that led to another door at the back of the building. The receptionist opened the door in her usual discreet fashion, nodded, with a hint of a smile to welcome me, and closed and locked the door quickly behind me, before pocketing the key.

'Inspector Stone's in his office.' She motioned to his door; all the blinds were down. I thanked her and knocked softly on the glass window.

'Come in.'

As I entered the room, the first thing I noticed was the overpowering smell of Scotch, and thought to myself that I clearly hadn't needed to bother with the breath mint this morning. His desk was awash with papers, his phone lay off the hook, and a cigarette was burning down to its filter. He looked beaten: defeated and done. It was not a look I was used to seeing in him; he was always so determined and thorough, no matter how desperate things seemed to be getting, but it seemed as if he was really at the end of his rope, almost as if he just didn't want to do this any more.

'I came as soon as I could; what on earth's the matter?'

'Yes, thanks, Mrs. Peters, Ann. I had to get you to come down here, tell you in person.'

'Tell me in person what?' I felt alarmed, and then excited at the same time, thinking that perhaps, by some miracle, they had made an arrest.

'You'd better sit down.'

'I'm fine standing.'

He sighed.

'Spit it out, please!'

He looked up at me, the dark circles under his eyes highlighted by the desk lamp, giving him an almost ghoul-like appearance.

'Another child's gone missing!' He spoke every word clearly. I sat down slowly on the plastic chair.

'When did this happen?'

'Well, her mother reported her missing yesterday, but it had only been seventeen hours.'

I was shaking my head; this could not be happening.

'I don't understand.'

'She didn't report it here; she must have gone to Wreathwood to file the report, as that's where her daughter's father lives; they're separated...'

'It's a girl?' my throat felt incredibly hoarse.

'Yes, and obviously they didn't make the connection between her and Michael, and they told her to go home and wait, and that it hadn't been long enough. Plus, there have been incidents apparently where she'd run away from her dad's house before, and the police had been called out for no reason.' He was shaking his head from side to side, as if he knew that saying all of this out loud only confirmed just how ridiculous it all sounded, and just how crucial this could have been if he had known about it yesterday. 'I spoke to the police down there and I asked them why we hadn't been called. They didn't seem to make the connection, or see that there were any similarities between the two cases, and it had only been seventeen hours.'

I was nodding, but I couldn't really focus on anything that he was saying.

'So in other words, you could have been out looking for her yesterday; whoever took her has had almost a two day start.'

He poured himself a coffee and added a splash of bourbon to it.

'I somehow doubt that's going to help!' I snapped.

He rubbed his forehead and loosened his tie.

'Have you even been to sleep?'

'I was called out at 3 this morning.'

'You look like shit!'

'Uh-uh.'

'So what happened? Where was her father? When did she go missing?'

He rifled through the papers on his desk, 'Well, according to her mother, she was dropped off at her father's on Friday evening, after school. The dad says they went to McDonald's for tea, came home, watched some soaps and went to bed. The next morning, she had dance class at the town hall, and then came home for lunch. She was outside playing, and...'

'Yes, I know how the rest goes.' I held my head in my hands. 'But he didn't report it?'

Inspector Stone let out a long drawn-out sigh; I could feel his despair.

'Apparently, she runs away quite frequently. They don't have a good relationship, and this isn't the first time she's just run away. They found her once at her friend's house; once, she'd gone to her grandparents', so the father just carried on as usual, and waited for someone to call. Then, when his ex-wife called to speak to her daughter, and he explained that she wasn't there, she reported it to Wreathwood, and they said to wait until Sunday, and I know what you're going to say, that this is on me, and that I should have done more, but I'm doing everything I possibly can. I've got cars out looking for her, and we even have a description of the kidnapper.'

I stood up, knocking over my chair. I was trembling;

'Somebody saw?' I couldn't believe it; this was the first break we had had since Michael went missing. Inspector Stone looked down, and pulled out another sheet of paper from the pile.

'Yes, a neighbour, Mr. George Young.'

I snatched the piece of paper from his hand.

'Well, we have to go and see him right away.'

'WE do not have to do anything. I only invited you down here out of courtesy. You are not police, and officially, you shouldn't even be here.'

'Then why am I?' I spat.

'Because I respect you, and I didn't want you hearing about it from the little press broadcast that they will be filming shortly outside. I thought you would rather have heard about it from me.'

'Oh come on, this isn't about respect! It never was. You wanted to tell me yourself, yet again, how you have all failed me, and this girl's family too. You thought maybe seeing how down you looked would make me feel some sympathy for you, that you have it hard and that I understand. Well, guess what, I don't understand, and I don't feel sorry for you. I feel sorry for myself, and this girl's mother and the children.'

'Ann, sit down, and keep your voice down.'

'I'm sick of being treated like something breakable. Nothing can destroy me any more than I already am. You saw Michael's body; you of all people should know that.'

He looked at me in silence, for a moment,

'I thought you would appreciate being kept in the loop. If you would rather I didn't inform you when we get updates, make progress, or have other leads to follow, then I won't.'

'Then don't!' I shouted. 'Let's not pretend that that's really why you bring me down here: staring at my chest while you tell me there's been another kidnapping, stroking my arm while you watch videos of me being assaulted. Why don't you try being honest: that my being here in an "unofficial capacity" has nothing to do with this case at all.'

'Ann, that's so far from the truth'

'Bullshit! I have seen the way you look at me.'

'Ann, you inspire me; you help me to see this thing clearly.'

'I'm not your muse! I was Michael's mother! If you can't inform me about what's going on, or allow me to be a part of this, then I will go about it in my own way. I have my own contacts.' I thought back to what Alice had said. Perhaps it wasn't such a bad idea after all.

'That would be a very unwise decision,' he said, guardedly.

'But it's mine to make.' I reached for my bag and opened the door. I was very aware of Sally putting her head down as if she hadn't really been listening to our entire conversation. She suddenly became very interested in her screen-saver. 'I'll see you, Inspector Stone!'

And I left the police station, through the front door, braving the baying pack outside.

Therapy with Doctor Blunt

'How many weeks are you now, Ann?'

'Twenty-six.'

'Lovely. And everything is OK? Is the baby fine?'

I patted my bump. 'Yes, he's doing just fine.'

'And how are you feeling about everything now?'

'A lot better I think. I'm adjusting to the idea of being a mother.'

'Adjusting?'

'Well, making compromises, I suppose.'

'Such as?'

'I'm not drinking or smoking. I'm learning to make decisions based around the baby, rather than thinking only about myself.'

'That's great progress Ann, really. And how is Dave preparing for the baby's arrival, mentally, physically?'

'We don't really talk that much about it.' It was true; I remember when Karen had her babies, the amount of planning and brainstorming she and Tom did: suggesting names, painting the nursery, buying the cot. The truth was, Dave seemed even less interested in me than before I became pregnant, and I found myself being even more repulsed by him as the pregnancy progressed. I wasn't sure what I expected, but something made me question whether this was a healthy way to prepare for a baby with your husband. 'Do you think that's weird?' I found myself asking abruptly.

'I choose not to use that word if I can help it, Ann.'

'OK, well what word would you use to describe it then? Different? Unhealthy? Narcissistic?'

She sighed and wrote a few notes down.

'Labels, Ann, all labels. I choose to look at the situation carefully, and to understand the thought processes of the people involved. I'm really not here to judge anyone, just to hold up the mirror, and let them examine the reflections.'

'OK, well, can I ask you what you think about it? I mean, before you, I'm sorry, before you lost your babies, did you and your husband talk about them; their names, for instance?'

She looked a little stunned, and I thought I had pushed the question too far, but she recovered quickly, giving me a weak smile.

'I think all expectant parents deal with pregnancies in their own ways, and it's completely normal to talk about the baby constantly, even talking to the baby, and gushing to everyone who will listen about how it's kicking, when it hiccoughs and what names you have picked out for him or her, just as it is OK to wait until the baby arrives before allowing yourself to get fully excited about it.'

I nodded, unsure that I really believed this.

'I don't think Dave really wants this baby.'

She stared at me for a moment.

'But you do, don't you?'

'Of course I do, he's all I have thought about for the past five years, but I can't help worrying about what's going to happen if he arrives, and only one parent loves him.'

'Is Dave capable of that?' She looked puzzled.

'Is he capable of having a baby, and not loving it?' I repeated her question out loud, pondering it in my head. 'He's capable of many things. I believe he thinks he needs the baby to keep me, and I need the marriage to get the baby, so I guess we're both happy, or...'

'Or both miserable,' she finished for me.

I looked up, 'Yes, exactly.'

10 Weeks Gone

My meeting with Inspector Stone had left me confused and disconcerted. My feelings were bubbling in my stomach like a bad cocktail, sour, about to come back up again. I felt incredibly angry still, an anger that I wasn't used to experiencing on this level. Part of me believed that he had been sincere when he talked about wanting to share details of the case with me. I thought he had been on my side, my team, that we were in this together, to find Michael's killer, whatever the cost, but then a part of me also thought that maybe he had been using me, either to get information about me or about my husband. I didn't like the fact he had been watching my house, or that he seemed not to trust me in some way. I called bullshit on his refusal to share important details of the case with me. Perhaps I couldn't accompany him to interview a witness, but I sure as hell wasn't going to be happy about it! I felt used and betrayed, which were both feelings that I was beginning to think I had left behind. I thought perhaps I had been naïve and vulnerable with a person who had made me feel something. Maybe I had made bad choices regarding what to tell him about myself, about Michael and our life, but the biggest regret was allowing myself to imagine that my own stupid romantic notions might be returned. Paul Stone, and the kind of man he seemed to be, threw up several kinds of red flag. Nevertheless, I still couldn't stay away, even amidst all of this mayhem. I was used to having control over most aspects of my life, and when I lost that control, there was only ever one way to get it back. I picked up the phone.

*

Dave burst through the door like a cowboy in a saloon bar. He always had that animalistic way about him that either made women despise him or turned them on. Judging by the number of women that Dave had had in his life, I guessed that the majority of them, against their better judgement, and despite what they might tell you, felt the latter. In the early years of our marriage, I had been incredibly attracted to that side of him. The way he could scoop me up in his strong arms, throw me down onto a bed and treat me like a thing he desired, and simply had to devour, was wonderfully exciting. Over the years, of course, as soon as I realised that there were so many other women being devoured across town, while his wedding ring was stuffed in a sock drawer, and condoms were bought with cash, it all became less appealing. He was a dinosaur; again, a characteristic that intrigued and excited me at first, but that simply disgusted me now.

'Why are you sitting with the lights off?' He came into the lounge and took off his shoes. I was sitting in the armchair furthest away from the window, sipping gin on ice and rolling my toes into the carpet repeatedly. He made as if to open the curtains, but I stuck my foot out to stop him getting past.

'Keep them closed,' I muttered.

He took a seat opposite me. 'So?'

'There's been another kidnapping, Dave.' I didn't look at him; I didn't want to be disappointed by a fake expression or lies. 'A girl, Michael's age.'

'I already know.'

It was my turn to be surprised, 'How?'

'Your Inspector Stone invited me down to the station, yesterday.'

'My Inspector?'

'Don't start with me!'

'I'm not starting anything, and he's certainly not *my* anything.' Steering the conversation back on course, I continued: 'So what did he want you there for?'

'To ask me where I was last Saturday; if I had been to Wreathwood lately; if I was a stone-cold murderer, in a nut shell.'

I looked up at him, 'And what did you tell him?'

'What do you mean, what did I tell him? The truth, obviously: I was nowhere near Wreathwood last Saturday, and I didn't really appreciate being called in like that. He's such a prick, that guy.'

I got up, 'Well, you know what they say, Dave, takes one…'

'Really? They say that, do they? It's funny because there's something else that the Inspector you have a crush on said.'

'Will you stop insinuating whatever it is you're insinuating.'

'So you don't have a crush on him?'

'No, I don't.'

'So do you just want to fuck him, or have you done that already?'

'You're disgusting.'

'No, what would be disgusting is fucking the policeman who is trying to find out who murdered your son, when you're still married to his father.'

'I don't have to explain anything that I do to you, Dave.'

'No, I suppose you don't; that's the joy of being separated. And I get to sleep with whoever I choose, without using a condom.'

'I'm confused; didn't you do that when we were together?'

He shook his head, 'No, I didn't. I always wore a condom.'

I slapped him hard across the face. I was suddenly very aware that inviting Dave over was an incredibly bad idea. He grabbed my wrist so hard, I could feel the blood at the end of my fingers tingling.

'But you know what else your Inspector said, and I found it really strange?' He was leaning into me, and I could smell stale smoke on his breath. 'He said he was happy I was only a wife beater, and not a child killer.'

I felt cold all over.

'Now why on earth would this policeman, who you are in no way, shape, or form sweet on, you say, think that I'm a wife beater?'

'Let go of me, Dave; I have no idea what you are talking about.'

'Shame, because I think you know exactly what I'm talking about; there are only two people who could possibly talk about that, and they are both standing here in this room. And I don't see anything in it for me, to go down to the police station and confess to beating my wife, do you?'

I started to cry.

'Oh, don't be so pathetic!' He snapped, and pushed me back down onto the arm chair. 'I wonder how your policeman would react, if I told him the truth, hmm? Shall we do that, shall we pick up the phone and tell him what really happens in this house, and the kind of woman that you are, hmm?' He began to unbuckle his belt, slowly.

'Please, Dave, you should leave.'

'Really? That's funny, because I seem to recall that it was YOU, who called ME, not the other way around.'

'I made a mistake,' my voice was tiny now.

'On... Your... Knees!' I slowly got down onto the wooden floor, my knees skimming across the rough surface.

'Please, Dave,' I whimpered, 'please!'

'I think Inspector Stone needs to know who you really are, and maybe then he would think twice about flirting with you, hmm? Take off your skirt.' My hands trembled, as I slowly unzipped my skirt. 'And those!' He circled my crotch with the belt buckle; I removed my knickers, and knelt there, naked from the waist down. 'Now turn around!' I obeyed, silent, sniffling and wiping away tears. 'Because you know what I think, Ann? I think once he knows that this is how you like it, I don't think he'll be coming back for more any time soon. Now ask me!' I shook my head. 'Ask me, or I will walk away!'

'Please, Dave, please hit me!'

And he did.

That was how our relationship had always been. I had never met anyone like Dave, who could put me back together, make me feel whole again. When life got out of control, his beatings were the only thing that could make it right again. They helped me to regain control of my life, to help calm me when everything seemed so confusing. It was not something that I was open about, or proud of, but I had always been this way. I had just never found anyone cruel enough to give me the pain that I required to function, to survive. The more pain he inflicted, the more free and focused I became. In our own twisted way, it was perhaps a form of love, and something that had certainly not stopped, even when Michael was born. And although I had never questioned Dave's cruelty, I had never believed him capable of anything worse. I truly thought that I had seen into his soul, and understood the ugliness that lay within. But in recent weeks, I have only had one thought, and that terrifies me more than his blows or his words ever did: the idea that he could have channelled that anger into hurting our son, and however crazy it sounded, I somehow found myself believing that he could.

3 Months Gone

The room smelled, unsurprisingly, of coffee and, unusually, of coconut. Phones buzzed, the steady hum of conversation hung in the warm air.

'Mrs. Peters?'

I looked up.

'Can I get you a coffee or some water while you wait? Inspector Stone will be with you shortly.'

'No, but thank you.'

The police station was a dilapidated building, the ceiling lined with polystyrene squares, some cracked and yellow-stained from years of cigarette smoke. There were three or four police officers, all talking manically into phones, scribbling notes, throwing files across desks, writing reports. I felt dizzy. I shuffled my feet in my brown loafers, aware of how scruffy and unattractive I must have looked. The thought didn't bother me, though; attractiveness was a thing of the past, a characteristic that belonged to the world of desire, happiness, love; it wasn't a word I was familiar with now. Nothing in my life was attractive. Everything was black and ugly. Inspector Stone emerged from his office, the blinds slapping loudly on the glass as he opened and closed the door. He looked harassed, irritable; I wondered if he remembered how we had parted on my last visit.

'Ann.'

'Hi.'

'Come in, come in; sorry to keep you waiting; we are up to our ears in all sorts this morning.'

'Really?' my eyes widened.

'No, no, nothing serious, Ann; come in and sit down.'

I followed him into the room and took a seat. Up close, he appeared even more exhausted. Deep lines etched his otherwise handsome face. His eyes were red and sore; he looked like a bad hangover.

'The secretary called me Mrs. again,' I said numbly.

'I'm sorry about that, Ann, I'm sure she wouldn't have done it on purpose.'

'I told her last time I was here. I took great pains in explaining to her. It's Miss, or Ann, but...' my voice trailed off. I sensed Paul Stone was humouring me. 'Never mind.'

'It won't happen again, Ann. I'm sorry.'

He seemed a kind man. Or at least maybe I would have found him kind, back in a time when I cared for people and their niceties. He looked like the sort of man who would open the door for you, pull out a chair, rub your back after a long day, and cook you dinner if you didn't have the energy. He looked as though he would have made a wonderful husband. He had that homely, fatherly air about him, and apart from the drink, I couldn't think of any other reason why he had never settled down and had a family of his own.

'So what can I help you with today, Ann?' He sounded a little exasperated.

'Oh, just the usual. But I also remembered something else about that morning, and it might be nothing of course, but you say, and my therapist says, that every little detail is important, and whatever we can salvage from that day is of the greatest importance.'

He smiled:

'That's wonderful, and of course she is right! Memory is the key here, and details of that day, or anything at all during that week, are very important. As for the case, I can't...'

I cut through him:

'Tell me anything official, I know; you tell me every week. But since the Haddison girl went missing, I thought maybe you had more evidence, or you might have found something.'

He leaned back in his chair, rubbing his thumbs together and considering me for a moment. He always looked at me with such pity. Not even sadness any more, just pity. What a tragedy I was. He always pretended that he didn't, and I pretended not to notice. He sighed:

'We found her shoes.' Four words. The same four words he had said to me, seven weeks ago, four weeks after Michael went missing. Four weeks after Michael had disappeared from the front garden, his little blue and white trainers had been recovered in the woods, near the river, not far from the main road; they were flecked with mud.

'I don't want to upset you, Ann; you know it's the last thing that anyone here wants to do.'

I nodded, helplessly, feeling the walls closing in around me, trying to keep it together, to keep my feet firmly on the ground, to hold back the tears that pooled in my eyes.

'This really is completely confidential, and I wouldn't be telling you, but I know how involved you are with the case, and I know you like to get all the information and...' he stopped, as if uncertain as to how to continue.

'What, Paul? Inspector Stone.'

'Paul is fine.'

'Paul, what?'

'I think it is important that you know we are treating this as serial. Jennifer Haddison was the same age as Michael. She was also alone in her garden playing...'

'Michael wasn't alone!' I found myself shouting. Conversations stopped, and faces turned towards the office. I was on my feet before I knew it. I couldn't reign it in. I couldn't stop it.

'I know that, Ann.'

'I would never... I never left my son to play alone. I was with him the whole time!' And off I went, on the same rant that I nearly always recited, as if the more I said it, the more they would believe it; believe me. 'I only went into the house to get a drink...' my voice broke, as the pain of the memory came surging through, like a knife ripping at my insides '...for Michael.' I finished, in the tiniest voice, looking down at my hands that were wet from the tears now falling onto them.

And he was holding me, as if instinctively. He stroked my tears away, and rubbed my back awkwardly. What a scene, what a state, what a pity.

Inspector Stone led me into an interview room. The paint was peeling like sunburnt skin, patchy and discoloured. There was no air-con in here, but a fan circulated the smell of summer and sweat round and round in the air. This was not my first time in an interview room, and I found the hard metal chair almost comforting. Within these four walls, I had been told about my son for the first time; I had talked and cried, been questioned, been accused, accused my husband, and cried some more. It was a place in which I felt almost safe to talk about Michael, as if I trusted these old peeling walls to keep my secrets and share my pain. Inspector Stone perhaps shared my feelings; maybe he felt we had more intimacy in this room than in his glass office, with prying eyes and bottles of Scotch hidden in his drawer. Here there was no judgement. Just the two of us, and my sadness.

'So.' He licked his top lip. Not in a seductive way though, God, that's if I even knew what seduction was any more. 'This thing you remembered, Ann. Do you want to tell me about it?'

'Yes, yes I do!' I placed my hands on the desk. I felt calm and back in control. 'That morning…' I have stopped saying 'the day Michael went missing,' or 'the day Michael died,' or 'the day my beautiful son was ripped cruelly from my life.' I almost feel like people are bored with hearing it. Now I stick to the simple: 'that morning.' They know which morning I'm talking about. It was the last day of my life. Every single day since has had no structure, no schedule, no ambition. It's not a life. I'm alive, but it's not a life. Paul had fixed me with an intrigued stare, my calmness perhaps encouraging him. I had maybe remembered a car parked somewhere it shouldn't have been, or seen something that was out of place, something important, something crucial, something that would lead us to the answer and possibly save another child's life. I cleared my throat. 'That morning, when I came down stairs, the back door was unlocked, with the key inside. I'm a very organised and efficient person. Was. I was a very organised and efficient person.' I paused. 'I locked the door before going to bed. Dave came in around 2.30am; he would have used the front door. Only the front door. And they were my keys in the lock.' I waited for a reaction: for Inspector Stone to pick up the phone and call someone, to call Lee Haddison, and ask if his door had been unlocked, as mine had, a gasp, or a look of relief, as if we finally might have the missing clue. Nothing. 'Why aren't you writing this down? Isn't this important? What if this is a way to...'

'Ann.'

'Inspector?'

'Paul, please.'

'Paul?'

'Ann, do you remember your husband's statement?'

'Yes, of course I do. Dave has always been very honest and open with me about his whereabouts that night.' Perhaps a little too open, I thought, bitterly, in my head.

'And do you remember Miss Anderly's statement?'
I tasted bile in my mouth and stared at him for a few moments.

'I vaguely remember something about her confirming my husband's whereabouts and activity that night, yes.'
He looked at me, unsure for a few moments:

'Ann, what are you trying to tell me? That your husband kidnapped your son, and his mistress had something to do with it?'
I didn't respond.

'Think back to Dave's story. He had left the back door open himself. He didn't know what time he would be back, and he didn't want to wake you by opening the front door.'

I laughed in spite of myself. He frowned.

'I'm sorry, Inspector. So let me get this straight: lying, and fucking somebody else is fine, but heaven forbid he wakes me up by opening the front door!'

'Listen, Ann, I know you are confused about the events leading up to what happened. Those memories will come back, your therapist said, and I don't have any cause to think she is lying. But let's not go round in circles with facts we are already sure of, and scenarios we have discarded.'

I got to my feet.

'So in other words, I'm a confused, crazy lady who is wasting your time.'

'No, Ann.'

'Mrs. Peters!'

'OK. Mrs. Peters.'

'Listen to me, Inspector; I'm crazy yes, I'm crazy angry because my son was snatched from my arms and murdered, by somebody in this town; by somebody he knew.'

'I disagree; there is plenty of evidence to suggest it was a stranger.'

'Michael would never leave my side, or his house, with a stranger. He would never go off on his own. Hell, even in the supermarket he would hold my hand the whole time. At school he would hang on the gates until I was gone, waving through the bars the entire time. So yes, I'm crazy angry that someone has taken the most important thing from me. I'm confused as to why you haven't found who did this or why, and the only time being wasted is Jennifer Haddison's, who is about to killed, if she isn't already dead.'

I stood there, defiantly; my whole body trembled and ached. I could feel all my pain rising to the surface.

'I don't care what Dave thinks he did, or what he remembers. I don't trust Dave Peters, or Helen Anderly, or you. The only person I trust is myself. I remember locking the back door, and checking it twice before I went to bed that evening. In the morning it was unlocked with the key inside. You can either take me seriously, and call Jennifer Haddison's father and ask him if he remembers a similar thing. Or you can ignore me, and have it on your conscience when this happens again.'

I picked up my purse and turned to leave, fixing Paul Stone with one last look. This time, there was no pity in his eyes. And I noticed.

4 Months Gone.

I took it upon myself to take the train up to Wreathwood. Of course I could have driven, or asked Paul to give me a lift, or even gone with Karen, but I was drinking more frequently again. I didn't feel safe, didn't trust myself to make the 40-minute drive without stopping to buy booze, or have a glass of wine somewhere. I would have made the idea of buying a drink rational, reasonable even, and turned any situation to my advantage in order to get it. So I removed the threat. This way, I could have a drink and not feel guilty or worried about getting into my car. I could drink without judgement, and the only punishment would be a hangover. Paul Stone had left numerous messages on my answer phone, apologising for our exchange at the police station, although it really wasn't necessary.

'I was the one being a bitch.' I had told him. But I also felt that somehow it was better to stay away for a while; I felt as if every time I put my foot in his office I was being watched, read, almost. I had the uneasy feeling that perhaps they hadn't ruled me out as a suspect, and I really didn't have the energy to defend myself against that. Besides, I thought I'd make a few house calls in Wreathwood and then hop on the train and carry on up to London, see my sister, and perhaps take her up on her inviting offer of help. I needed a change of scenery, to visit places that were not tainted by memories of my son.

The memories seemed to be everywhere: his laughter in the house, his singing in the bath; at the supermarket, he was sitting in the seat of the trolley, trying to grab snacks and chocolate that he always wanted, and that I always tried not to give in and buy for him; at the petrol station he was blowing air onto the windows, his warm breath steaming up the glass, on which he would draw a heart or a smiley face; in the park he was running wildly after a football, swinging as high as he could on the swings, and asking a million questions about the flowers, the trees and the birds; at the school gates, he was playing hopscotch in an empty playground, watched over by Mrs. Cliff, who would ruffle his hair and tell him for the last time that break was over and it was time to go back inside. My baby boy was everywhere; there was no escaping his infectious smile or his soft voice, but he had never been to Wreathwood with me, and I felt that going there would give me some insight into what had happened to the little girl that had been taken: Jennifer Haddison.

Wreathwood was a much bigger town than ours. It had a secondary school opposite the train station, and a football pitch. There were several pubs and restaurants along the main street, and it even had a clothes store, a book shop and a library. It was split into two parts: Upper Wreathwood and Lower Wreathwood, and as with most country towns, they were set apart by wealth and class. Upper Wreathwood had a rugby club, a high-end cocktail bar and several banks, Lower Wreathwood had the rest, but the houses were all owned by the council. I clutched my bag, and looked down at the piece of paper that had been screwed up into a ball in my pocket.

Lee Haddison

36 Parkwood Avenue

Lower Wreathwood

I turned right, upon leaving the station, and made my way along the main road before crossing over. Parkwood Avenue was like any other street. There was nothing special about it; it had a little less glamour about it than mine, I suppose. Some of the gardens were unkempt, the cars a bit more dated than those parked on mine, but it was not the hole I had expected. From what I had heard about Jennifer's father, I imagined him in some grotty drug den, with mattresses piled outside the house, and old bikes with missing wheels in the drive. Number 36 was the last house on the street, and there was nothing significant about it; it also bore no resemblance to mine. A red Volvo was parked out front, and a gnome that was missing half of his hat stood alone and sad on the front step. I knocked once and waited. A light flickered inside, and a shadow appeared behind the door. Someone opened the letter box. I could see a pair of eyes behind glasses looking through.

'Whatever you're selling, I'm not interested!' He slammed the letterbox shut and started to move away.

'Mr. Haddison, my name's Peters, Ann Peters.'

His shadow stopped abruptly in the hallway, and he turned around. There was a pause of a few seconds, and I could imagine him debating whether or not opening the door was a good idea, but he came back, and I heard the jingle of keys and the clicking of the lock. The door swung open.

'Come in,' he said.

Lee Haddison was not very tall; his hair was turning grey in patches, and it was receding slightly. He had a sort of lopsided mouth, and a droopy moustache; he was absolutely nothing like I imagined.

The house was very clean. It took a while for this to register, for two reasons: one was that I had been living in such squalor since Michael went missing. I couldn't remember the last time I had taken out the bins; my kitchen reflected my misery, and was disorganised and desolate. Secondly, it was so different from what I had expected that it left me speechless. Mr Haddison's house was - there was no other word to describe it - immaculate. I don't really know what I was expecting to find, but on hearing that Jennifer's parents were divorced, and that Jennifer didn't get on with her dad, and had run away previously, I had pictured some depressing slum, with beer cans lining the hall and cigarette butts in shallow shot-glasses, but it was not the case. The house was not nicely decorated, or pretty, but it was clear that Mr Haddison ran a tight ship and took the expression "house proud" to the next level. The hall was empty, except for an umbrella stand with one navy blue umbrella inside, neatly furled. There were no pictures, or mirrors, just some drawing pins, where something must have once hung: a calendar or a postcard, perhaps; taken down in disgust, or removed due to heartache.

'I'm sorry for your loss.' His voice broke through my thoughts.

'I'm sorry?'

'For your loss. I heard about Michael; what a shame! Your handsome, blue-eyed, innocent little boy; it breaks my heart.'

I nodded. 'Thank you.'

'I guess I'm holding on to the hope that Jenny's OK, and that this is just all one big mistake. Would you like a cup of tea?'

'Do you have anything stronger?'

He shook his head.

'I'm sorry, I don't drink.' That surprised me; I had been under the impression that he was a bit of a boozer, or maybe Inspector Stone had just told me that in passing; I couldn't remember. In any case, he didn't smell of alcohol, and the house was so clean that I had no reason to suspect that he could be lying to me.

'Tea's fine, unless you have coffee, no, forget it, tea is fine.'

'Why don't you go into the lounge and I'll bring it through.' He opened the door to the right and pointed with his finger, before going to the end of the hall, and into a kitchen. I caught a glimpse of stainless steel before he closed the door behind him.

The lounge itself was not very large, and painted beige. An ironing board was open and an iron steamed on the rest, next to a basket of incredibly neatly-folded shirts and jeans. There was a television in the corner of the room, a computer against the left-hand wall and a small, green two-seater sofa. Other than that, there was nothing personal: no photographs, no pictures, no pets, nothing. It was odd, eerily so, but then, I thought, people live differently. We all have different personalities that are reflected in how we live, our artwork and our choice of furniture. Perhaps Lee was a simple man, or lonely, or just weird. I couldn't decide yet, but I was certainly glad to have come. I felt sure that I could get some information out of him that Paul hadn't been able to.

'Are you here officially?'

I jumped. Mr Haddison was standing in the doorway, holding a tray with a cream teapot and two cups on it.

'Officially?' I frowned.

He set the tray down on the coffee table, and poured me a cup.

'Yes, I heard that you were working with the police, after what happened.'

'No, no, nothing like that. I often go down to the station to see if there are any developments, or if they have any suspects, you know. I'm sure you must know how I feel. It's frustrating. I can't sleep, I can't clean, I can't eat. So I try to search for answers.'

He was nodding.

'And do they?'

'Do they what?'

'Have any suspects?' he asked quietly.

'I'm not sure, and it's something I wouldn't be privy to, anyway.'

He smiled. I was definitely leaning towards weird. He was what my father would have called an 'oddball'.

'I just wanted to share my grief, I suppose, and ask you about Jennifer. I mean, I believe she was in Michael's class, but I don't have any memories of her.'

'Jenny,' he sighed. 'Jenny was... nice' He seemed to pause as if he were searching for the appropriate word.

'Nice?' What about her passions, her personality, her likes and dislikes, her spirit and her heart? I thought.

'Yes,' he smiled. 'Nice.'

What a strange way to describe your child.

'She got into her fair share of trouble, mind. She was always running off, doing her own thing, always coming

back only when she was ready to. She could be a handful.'
I couldn't shake the feeling that he was referring to his daughter in the past tense, as if he was certain that she wasn't ever coming back this time.

'So what happened, when she went missing? Did she just take off?'

'Yes, it's unfortunate, really.'

I frowned, 'Unfortunate? How so?'

'Well, I'd only gone inside to wash my hands. You can never trust McDonald's or supermarket trolleys. I usually carry hand sanitiser around, everywhere I go, but I'd run out, and we were late for Jenny's dance class. So I had to make sure I washed them when we got back home.'

'I see.' Weird, he is definitely weird, I thought. 'So she was playing outside and you were inside washing your hands. For how long, a couple of minutes?'

He laughed, a sort of high pitched giggle.

'Goodness! It takes a lot longer than that to wash your hands properly.'

I smiled politely, realising that I hadn't taken a shower in three days, and he would probably be disinfecting my seat once I had left.

'I was maybe inside for a total of five or six minutes, and then I came back outside and she wasn't there.'

'And you didn't report it, you didn't find it unusual?'

He took a sip of tea, almost delicately:

'As I said, and as I told the police, Jenny was always running off. I wasn't alarmed at all, until Sue called me,' he added, with a hint of bitterness.

'And she realised something was wrong?'

'My ex-wife has been waiting for something serious to go wrong ever since we started weekend custody. She did not really want me to see Jenny - ever.'

That gives you a motive, I thought.

'She wasn't genuinely concerned about our daughter, more excited about using this against me in court in a couple of weeks' time; they're building a case against me.'

'They?'

'Mm. Sue, and her lawyer, who also happens to be her new boyfriend, or so I have heard. In fact, for the first day I thought they had deliberately told Jenny to run away, or to wait at the end of the road and go back with them, just to create more drama, so they would have something else to use against me. But then I realised that's too low, even for Sue.' He remained quite composed, despite the bitterness in his voice. 'But they never really won.' He seemed to be talking to himself now, rather than me. 'And they certainly never will now.'

I thanked Mr Haddison for the tea and left. I looked down at the piece of paper again. I was feeling more excited about this one.

George Young

13 Fleet Road

Lower Wreathwood.

It took me a good ten-minute walk, at a rather brisk pace, from Mr Haddison's freakishly clean semi to Mr Young's red-brick terrace. This was what one might call the really rough part of town: the ghetto, at least for someone like me, with my upbringing. Fleet Road was one long row of terraced houses, two up, two down, by the looks of them from the outside. All old, with smoke billowing from chimneys, and all with tiny front gardens. At the end of the street was a big brick wall, with a little alley to the right that connected Fleet Road to the next road over. It was certainly depressing: concrete had replaced most of the flowerbeds, and some windows were covered by chipboard panels, victims of stray bricks thrown during drunken brawls, no doubt. There were no children playing outside, although it was 8pm, I reminded myself. The overall atmosphere was one of despair and emptiness. It was certainly not an inviting street, and I had to really push myself to walk down it, knowing that it was the means to an end that I couldn't possibly turn my back on. The door to number 13 swung open before I had even reached it, and a man in his fifties stood in the doorway staring at me. He wore a long-sleeved blue t-shirt that barely hid his beer belly, and which was dappled with orange stains. He was smoking a roll-up cigarette and scratching his bald head. He was certainly in stark contrast to the person and the house that I had just left.

'I've been waiting for you,' he said, which took me by surprise.

'Oh?'

'Lee called,' he shrugged, 'said you might pop by with some questions.'

I smiled. 'I had no idea that you were close.'

'Me and Lee? Oh, we go back a fair bit. I was the first friend he made when he moved here, six years ago.'

I nodded. 'Time passes.'

'It sure does! Anyway, come in and have a drink.'

I hesitated, looking uncertainly at the house and Mr Young's unkempt appearance. He seemed pleasant enough, and I had come this far, I reasoned with myself. I stepped inside.

'Coffee? Beer?'

'Beer, please.' Relief flooded over me; finally, a drink!

'It's *Stella*, I'm afraid, and I've not had time to put it in the fridge.'

I waved a hand.

'It's fine.'

I waited for him to get up and go to the kitchen to retrieve the warm beer, but instead, he just slid a hand down one side of his grey sofa and unhooked another can from an eight-pack. He chucked it over to me. I nodded politely and opened it slowly. Taking a gulp, I looked around the seedy room.

As opposed to Mr Haddison's impeccable minimalistic interior, this was full to bursting with things. It looked as if an impromptu car boot sale had erupted. The walls were covered with paintings and plates, medals and rosettes.

There was an old grandfather clock in the corner, broken, by the look of it, a rocking horse, a basket holding children's dolls and stuffed animals. There were several, large, coloured rugs placed on top of the beige carpet, and there must have been thirty photo frames on the window sill, all of children: some on horses, some with other children, laughing. A fire burned in the grate, and *Eastenders* was playing in the background on an old-fashioned TV. All kinds of paraphernalia littered the fireplace: matchboxes, paperweights, snow globes, more photographs, an ashtray, lidless pens, packets of chewing gum; on the table, there were candles, a teapot, newly dried clothes waiting to be folded, light bulbs, screws. I had never seen such a random collection of possessions, and wondered, to my amusement, if Mr. Haddison had ever set foot in here, and what he would have thought.

As if reading my thoughts, and following my gaze, Mr Young stood up, and pointed to some of the photographs on the mantelpiece and the window sill.

'My children, my grandchildren, my godchildren; good memories; that's what I'm hanging on to here.'

'Memories?'

'Yeah. Life goes so quickly, and before you know it, you're divorced and made redundant, and your kids grow up and move away, and the only reliable thing you have is the drink, and the memories.' He waved an arm around the room at all the things he had kept over the years. 'I keep everything; it helps remind me of a good life that I did have once.' He looked sad.

'I'm sorry, Mr Young.'

'Oh, never mind; we all have our baggage. Why else would you be here?' He sat back down. 'You're wondering about what I saw when Jenny went missing, I suppose?'

'Yes,' I said, quietly.

'I'm not sure how much good it will do.'

'How's that?'

'I already told the police everything that I know, gave a description, made a statement, but they don't seem to take an old drunk like me very seriously.'

'I'm sure that's not true. I know the inspector in charge of the case; he seemed to think that you were a reliable witness.'

'Then why haven't they made an arrest?'

'I don't know, George; can I call you George? I've been asking myself the same question. I just want to find out what happened to my son, and help in any way that I can to find Jennifer.' He seemed to be warming to me; I felt him relax. He knew I wasn't police, and perhaps I could gain his trust, if I opened up a little.

'You seem like a nice person. I'm sorry about your boy. I wouldn't wish that on my worst enemy. Hanging's too good for the monster that did that; just give me a stool, and a bit of rope!'

We sat in silence for a few minutes.

'She knew him, you know.' He was the first one to break the silence. He finished his can and squeezed it, until it collapsed in his big hands.

'I beg your pardon?'

'Jenny.' He looked directly at me. 'I was checking on my mother. She lives across from Lee's. I often see Jenny playing outside, or riding her bike up and down the road. Sometimes she's with her little friends, sometimes she's running away from Lee; she can be awkward with him sometimes, I think, but he's a good mate, and he's trying his best with her.'

'Go on,' I coaxed.

'I was fixing mother's curtain rail. She'd been moaning about it for weeks, so I'd bought her a new curtain pole from Homebase, and she was happy enough with it, and my girlfriend Andrea, she'd bought her some lovely new curtains, only a few quid from a charity shop, but she'd washed them, and my mother was very pleased.' He was waffling, but I humoured him, sure that it would be well worth the wait. 'Anyway, this car pulled up outside Lee's house. Jenny was on the lawn, playing. I stopped to look, because it's not often you see a nice car like that in our end of town, if you know what I mean. It was a big black Land Rover, shiny and new-looking; and I only saw the back of his head, when he stepped out of the car, but Jenny knew him, 'cos I could see her face, and she smiled and ran over to him. They talked for a bit and then she got into his car, and he drove away.'

I held my breath. 'And that's it?'

'That's it,' he finished, lighting another roll-up and cracking open another beer. I finished mine, and accepted a second.

'So what did he look like from behind? His hair colour? His clothes?'

'Well, I'm not one for details, really, you know; if it had been a young woman such as yourself, I might have paid a bit more attention. He was about my height, thin and had brownish hair, that's probably all I could tell you about him.'

My heart was thumping so fast now, I could hear it getting louder and louder, the beats faster and faster.

'And the car, can you remember anything else about that? Any specific details, other than the colour? Number plate, for example?'

He shook his head. 'Not one for details, I'm afraid. It had tinted windows, and it was black, or navy blue; I'm colour blind, you see, so maybe I got the colour wrong.'

My heart sank a little:

'Was there anything else that surprised you, or that looked wrong or out of place?'

'I'm sorry, love, that's all I remember, and that's all I told the police.'

'And you didn't see Mr. Haddison?'

'Lee? No, well, he came out about five minutes later and was looking around. I saw him walk down the road and then go back in; I just thought he must have known the person too. I didn't say nothing to no-one, until I heard she'd been kidnapped. Poor Jenny!' He sighed. 'Me, I've got seven kids, maybe more that I don't know about,' he chuckled, 'and they are everything to me, but Lee, he only had Jenny, and she was a lovely little girl, always happy and cheerful. I don't know how Lee will get over it if anything happens to her.'

I frowned.

'You adjust,' I muttered.

He slapped his forehead.

'I'm sorry, love, here I am talking about all this, forgetting that your son is...'

'Yes, thank you, it's fine. Listen, I'd heard that Lee was not a great father: that Jenny wasn't happy visiting him and had run off a few times.'

He stood up and moved over to the fire to put more wood on.

'That's what Sue would like everyone to think. Unfortunately for her, I couldn't disagree more. I have known Lee for six years, and he was a great father to Jenny.'

'Thanks, George, you've been really helpful.' I got up to go, when suddenly the phone rang. It made me jump, and Mr Young moved over and picked it up. He stood talking for a few minutes, and then put the phone down, off the hook:

'My mother, she likes to talk before she goes to bed; she feels safe hearing my voice. I hope you don't think I'm being rude.'

I placed my empty beer can next to the first one, and opened the door.

'Of course not, thank you so much for your time; you have been incredibly helpful.'

I ran down the front steps and out onto the street. The cold hit me instantly. My chest felt ready to explode, and my head was pounding. Something that had happened at George's house had made me remember. It was only a tiny feeling, a hint of a memory, but I knew that it was real. I fished out my phone as quickly as possible and dialled Paul's number; it went straight to voice mail.

'Paul, it's Ann. I have just remembered something, and I think it might be important. When Michael went missing, just before he was taken, somebody called me on the house phone. I can't remember why, or who it was, but I remember watching Michael through the window, and I was about to go and give him his drink, when the phone rang; that's why I didn't go back outside. Call me back when you can.'

Therapy with Doctor Blunt

'I wanted to try something new today Ann, if you'll let me.'

'OK.'

'Well, don't agree too quickly; first, listen to what it is: I want to hypnotise you.'

I suppressed a snort, thinking about what my mother would have to say about hypnosis, but tried not to disrespect the Doctor.

'Hypnosis is often used in therapy sessions, and it's a technique that I have used many times with different patients, for various reasons and with varying results. It doesn't always work, and not everyone is receptive to it, but I do think you could benefit from at least trying, if you are open to doing it, that is.' She smiled warmly, and the sceptic in me remained silent.

'OK, that's fine, but, I mean, why do you think it will help me?'

'For several reasons: one is that you already feel safe here; I believe that you trust me, and that you are very relaxed when you come to my sessions. That is a wonderful base to build on with hypnotherapy. Secondly, being hypnotised may or may not allow you to extract, and isolate perhaps, painful or difficult feelings and memories from your past that you may have blocked or tried to hide from your conscious mind.'

'OK, so what? You think I'm perhaps unintentionally hiding something painful from my past that might explain why I have difficulty opening up and trusting people?'

'It's possible; I'd at least like to be given the opportunity to try.'

'Is it safe to do that with me while I'm pregnant?'

'Completely. In fact, a lot of women use hypnotherapy to prepare them for childbirth, or to overcome morning sickness and other pains and complications of pregnancy.'

'OK, go ahead.'

'All right then, if you are sure that you are ready; lie down for me, over here.' She indicted a long white leather couch in the corner of the room. I made myself comfortable, aware that I was suddenly very tired, and hoped that I would not fall asleep during the therapy.

'Try to relax... remove any tension; shrug your shoulders and let them go. That's it, we need to relax the muscles... good. OK. Now take a deep breath... and release, and another, breathe and release. Allow yourself to relax even more... and take one more breath... breathe out and allow yourself to let go... good... become aware of how you are breathing... your breath moving gently in and out... in and out. Relax a little more... with every gentle breath out... you are relaxing deeper and deeper. Now close your eyes and think just how nice it is to close your eyes and fly... wherever you want to go... Try to imagine a quiet, peaceful spot... maybe on a warm, summer afternoon... somewhere nice... somewhere you feel very safe... calm and peaceful... your mind is drifting away... your arms and legs are beginning to feel heavy, now. Just let them go, let everything go, and drift peacefully away... imagine a room, somewhere familiar; there are stairs in the middle of the room. You can go down those stairs; you are perfectly safe here... go down the stairs, and with each step, your body and mind relax more... Good, good; there are ten steps going down... and you can go down those steps now... going deeper and deeper with every gentle breath... 10... 9... more and more relaxed... 8... more comfortable... 7... and 6... deeper and deeper... and as you go down each step, you are feeling more and more safe and at peace... 5... and 4... and 3... and you are drifting off to an endless soft dreamlike place... and now let's focus on your eyes... they are so relaxed, so tired that you just cannot open them, the lids are glued together... you are so relaxed that even if you try, you simply cannot open your eyes, they just don't work. That's good... that's exactly the way it should be... now imagine being in a comfortable chair... just relaxing somewhere... breathing gently...and letting your mind drift away... you don't have to think... you don't have to do anything at all... except enjoy that lovely feeling... nothing bothers you. You are calm and relaxed... that's good... and just allow your mind to relax even more. While you are in this state, your mind is open to many possibilities... you can imagine things clearly... you can recall feelings and memories... you are aware of everything, inside and outside your own body, you are flying, weightless and open to anything. Now, become aware of your hands... think about how they feel: the weight, the texture, the temperature; you become aware that your hands want to move, just a little, allow that to happen, good, now it's time to return to the present; back to reality. I am now going to count from five up to one, and when I get to one... you will be back in the present, in this room with me, OK... five... four... three... two... one!'

5 Months Gone

I had caught the afternoon train back from London. I'd spent three days with Alice, at her London apartment, and on two of those we had both been so inebriated that I couldn't even remember everything that we had talked about. I'd been going up to see my sister every couple of weeks, since she had first suggested the idea, and not only did the visit itself do me good, but so did the journey. On the crowded train I was able to sink into the background and appear to be just another commuter like everyone else. I didn't receive any pity-stares or platitudes. I was a nobody, untouched by tragedy, as far as they were concerned. It felt good to fade into anonymity, and get back some peace of mind and privacy. It was a one-hour journey: ample time to allow me to write down developments, clues, questions, and to put in my earphones and listen to Imogen Heap, holding my pendant with Michael's face and mine, and to disappear to another place, somewhere pain free.

Alice lived in an average apartment building in an average area; her building had a lift, and her flat had a small balcony with a view over the park. There was a 24-hour supermarket right next to it: although she moaned about it, due to the constant hum of people shopping even in the early hours, it gave me a sense of security. Sometimes, it felt nice to be surrounded by noise and traffic, to confirm that the rest of the world carried on living and breathing, food shopping, filling up with petrol, taking kids to school, visiting the doctor, and posting letters. Also, I had to wonder why Alice had come to a city that didn't sleep if she wanted peace.

My sister worked for a local paper, writing short articles on current affairs: nothing fancy, but she loved it. It had been a dream of hers ever since I could remember. She had always had her head in her books, and seemed to practically inhale literature: anything from Roald Dahl's *Going Solo*, to Brett Easton Ellis's *American Psycho*. Crime, mystery, fiction, non-fiction, romance; she read everything, and her love of writing had only grown stronger as she had grown up. She didn't let her condition interfere with her work, and we were all happy for her, knowing that no matter how MS affected our wonderful Alice, it would never take away her love of writing and journalism.

Visiting Alice was my equivalent of writing a diary. As opposed to Karen, who loved to argue with everything I said, and always gave her two penn'orth, Alice listened. This allowed me to clear out my head, to get rid of useless information, and only retain the important things. I could say out loud what I was thinking, pick it to pieces and put it back together, or simply lock it up and throw away the key. It was nice to have Alice to listen to me. She had loved my son, and I knew that she could be depended on when I truly needed something. Besides which, she had friends in high places, and unlike me, she hadn't slept with anyone to make those friends. Alice was fiercely independent, a credit to herself and to all of us, never willing to compromise who she was for anyone, and she would certainly never sell her soul to the devil. But it was definitely useful knowing that for all the little pieces of information Paul could not give me in an 'official capacity', such as tracing phone records, recovering deleted text messages etc., there were others that I could access by other means, using Alice and her contacts. It was a relief to know that I could go about my own investigation, whether Paul chose to include me or not.

It was raining, as usual, the rain hammering against the windows on the train, the grey sky a mirror, as usual, of my heart. I wondered when the sun would shine again, both metaphorically and literally. I longed to feel its touch on my face, the warmth spreading to my finger-tips, my toes, every inch of my body. I was so tired of being constantly in the rain. As we pulled into the station, I immediately noticed Paul Stone standing on the platform. He looked solemn and drawn, but then he rarely looked anything else these days. I made my way through the passengers on the train, savouring for a last few seconds the feeling of complete anonymity, and then stepped out onto the platform, back into the world where everyone knew my name.

'Ann?' He moved towards me. We hadn't really spoken properly in a few weeks, and his greeting seemed somewhat awkward and forced.

'Inspector Stone.'

'I wish you would call me Paul.' He smiled half-heartedly.

'Why are you here, is everything OK?'

'Been to see your sister, have you?'

'How do you know that?'

'Oh, don't worry, I've not had you followed; I just popped round to see your parents yesterday. They mentioned that you've been going up to see her quite a lot.'

We started to walk.

'It's nice to get away from this place. I feel liberated.'

'That's good. Although I don't think that pursuing your own investigation is going to help anyone, least of all Michael.'

I stopped walking.

'You're not the only one snooping around, Ann. I happen to have friends in London, too.'

'I'm not doing anything wrong.'

'Wrong, maybe not, illegal perhaps.'

'Bullshit! Maybe if you had filled me in a little more, and stopped messing me around…'

'Messing you around?'

'Calling me in one minute to tell me about leads, then shutting me out the next. If you didn't want me around, you could have just told me.'

'Ann, I…'

'I'm sick of it; of everyone tiptoeing around me, scared to tell me the truth, worried how I might react. Listen, yes, I've been up to see my sister, although I don't think it's any of your business.' I turned, and he grabbed my arm.

'And what about interviewing fucking witnesses!' he hissed. It was the first time that I had seen Paul actually look angry. I remained silent. 'Jesus, Ann. I could arrest you right now!'

I shrugged him off.

'For what? Tampering with the case? What case? You have nothing. And I'll bet both Jennifer's father and Mr. Young told me more than they gave you.'

'So, you admit to tracking down victims' families and cross-examining valuable witnesses, then?'

'That's strange, because George Young said that you thought he was an unreliable drunk. Valuable witness now, is he?'

'I'm warning you, Ann!'

'What? What? You're warning me of what, exactly? God, Paul, either spit it out, whatever it is you really want to tell me, or leave me the hell alone.'

He stared at me, breathing heavily, as though two voices were fighting in his head, unsure what to say.

'What is it?' I shouted, loudly enough for several people to turn their heads in our direction.

It had started to rain heavily now, and I began to shiver. We stood like that for a few seconds, me, willing him to speak, to say something, and then he leaned forward and kissed me. I pulled back at first, surprised and indignant. He tasted of Scotch, his mouth hot. He kept kissing me, and before I could really stop and think to myself what a horrible idea this was, I was kissing him back, urgently, our mouths on each other's, my fingers grasping at his hair, his around my jaw, a thumb on my throat. And then it stopped, almost as suddenly as it had begun. He was smoothing down his jacket, shielding his already soaking hair from the rain with a newspaper, looking anywhere but directly into my eyes.

'There's a reason that I came to meet you off the train.' he said quietly.

'Oh, was that not the reason?' I teased lightly.

'No.' He looked deadly serious again.

'Well, what is it?'

'We found Jennifer Haddison'

'Alive?' I whispered.

He shook his head, once.

6 Months Gone

Jennifer Haddison's funeral was a simple affair; not that I had expected anything different. When we had said goodbye to Michael, I hadn't had the strength or the inclination to organise anything other than a plot at the graveyard, in the small area set aside for children. There were only two things that I wanted, or that I knew Michael would have wanted: Alice singing *Be Still*, a song that we had both sung together as choristers when we were younger. I had an old tape-recording of her singing it, and when Michael was a baby, it was one of the few things that helped him sleep. As he grew a little bit older, it was a song that I often played to him before bed, or to calm him down when he was over-excited, and when his hamster died and he didn't know how to express his sadness. He said that Alice sounded like an angel. And she did. Children always say it exactly as they see it. He had no ulterior motive; he just loved that song, and her voice. I managed to persuade her to sing it in the church, as people entered, and on their departure. It was beautiful: *a cappella*, her voice wavering with emotion, trying her best to keep it together until the very last note of the song.

And the second thing was birthday cake. I refused all offers of catered food: sausage rolls, finger sandwiches, pizza. I spent two days making five Victoria sponge birthday cakes, oozing with butter cream and raspberry jam, and covered in blue and white fondant icing. This was Michael's favourite cake. It was the only cake that I had taught him how to make, partly because it was my favourite too, and partly because I was hopeless at baking, despite my mother trying endlessly over the years to teach me how to measure out ingredients precisely, and attempting to enforce the rule that 'baking is a science'. Well, I had failed science, and it was certainly reflected in my cakes, but not this time. This time, I had spent all day mixing, sifting, measuring, whisking, rolling, and spreading, until I had five birthday cakes to celebrate each of my son's five years of life. And they were perfect.

I decided, at the last minute, to attend Jennifer's funeral. Part of me thought it might have been inappropriate. I didn't want to risk running into Billy Stevens' mother, either, and I didn't want to appear insensitive, but then another part of me wanted to share my pain with the only other person right now who could possibly identify with it. I longed to hold Mrs Haddison's hand. I wanted to help her by letting her know that she wasn't alone, and as opposed to saying that everything would be OK, that she would feel OK again one day soon, I wanted to be honest with her, and tell her that she wouldn't feel right for a long time, that her daughter's memory would haunt her house and her dreams. Living, when your child has died before you, is utterly terrifying, and the feeling of complete and total despair never goes away. I wished somebody had been there to say that to me; it might have helped to lighten the load a little.

Karen was going anyway as her youngest daughter, Mia, went to nursery with Jennifer's half-sister, so I thought it wouldn't seem as strange if I went with my best friend, who happened to be more directly connected to the family.

We parked as far away from the church as we could; I didn't want to be seen taking up spaces that the family could use, and Karen said it would be easier for getting away when the service had finished. We both had a few drinks before arriving, and I hoped it would be enough to steady my nerves and keep me calm for the duration of the service. There were not as many people as I had envisaged in the actual church itself. Jennifer's family sat at the front: her mother, Sue, sat with her head bowed, dabbing her face with a crumpled tissue. Her little girl was on her right, with her parents, and someone I didn't recognise, who, Karen told me in a stage whisper, was Sue's new boyfriend. On the left side of the church, I recognised Lee Haddison. He looked pretty much the same as when I had been to visit him. His grey shirt was crisp underneath an oversized black blazer. He was sweating, and his glasses kept sliding down his nose. I noticed, somewhat sadly, that he was alone. No matter how strange or different someone is, the thought of being alone at a moment like this seemed terribly sad to me; to not even have parents, or a friend who could play a supporting role at your side. For a second, I felt the urge to go over and give him a hug, or squeeze his arm and tell him that I was sorry for his loss, but in the same instant, I realised how utterly inappropriate that might seem to the rest of the congregation.

Amazing Grace echoed around us from all four corners of the church. I spotted Kristin Cliff with her husband, a few rows behind the family, her beautiful face red from crying. She noticed us, and managed a kindly smile, before burying her face in her husband's jacket. As the music crackled to an end, the vicar got solemnly to his feet and began to read some opening prayers and words of comfort. I clutched my pendant, and reached out for Karen's hand as his words seemed to dissolve around me. I could hear Jennifer's mother crying. I hadn't noticed it before, with the music playing over the church's sound system, but now, in the relative silence of the service, it was all I could hear: just loud, uncontrollable sobs.

'We are gathered together, on this day, for one reason: to pay tribute and respect to Jennifer Haddison and her family. Jennifer was taken from us, cruelly, and in a way that we cannot even begin to fathom. Not only have we grieved together, and shared our own personal feelings of loss since Jennifer's passing, but our hearts have been drawn toward her, and will continue to be with her and her family. We are all here today, to find and to receive comfort, and peace of some kind. It is with the deepest humility that we acknowledge that coming here today, and trusting in God, will aid us and give us strength. It is in our nature to want to understand everything, but in this, we must lean on God for support, to help us all through this difficult time...'

I had stopped listening. The vicar had said something similar at Michael's funeral; it all sounded the same, so impersonal and empty, so unrelated to the body in the coffin, the memory of our children. I had stopped believing in a god a long time ago, and had no wish to hear how 'He' could help me and Mrs. Haddison get through this 'sad time'. There was a scuffling noise from the front pew, and Mrs. Haddison got to her feet.

'My daughter, Jenny, was a lively and happy little girl. She would always make us smile. Her best quality was always to see the good in everyone, and everything. She would make us laugh and drive us mad sometimes, but she was our Jenny. She was our little girl, my first baby.' Her voice wavered, and she looked down, breathing hard, barely able to go on:

'I can't begin to face...' she stumbled again, her words silenced by sobs. The man that Karen had pointed out as her boyfriend got to his feet quickly, standing beside her and holding her up. He took the piece of paper from her, cleared his throat, and read:

'I can't begin to face a life without her. Good bye, Jenny.'

We filed out of the church, the same buzzing version of *Amazing Grace* playing loudly, and smothering the now hysterical cries of Jennifer's mother. I couldn't wait to get outside and breathe the fresh air. I didn't know how much it had helped coming here today and seeing the sadness first-hand, being reminded of just how difficult and unjust it was to have to bury a child. As we left, I caught sight of Paul Stone, standing by his car a few yards away. He was leaning on the door, the window wound down, his arms folded. I nodded politely to him. He returned the gesture solemnly, but didn't move.

'Mrs. Peters?'

I turned round, and felt my stomach lurch. Mrs. Stevens was standing there. Her loose dress hung off her slender frame, and I noticed her tights had a ladder in them. Her face was much softer than when she had been pushing me out of the way, telling me to leave her and her family alone.

'Hi.' She motioned to me to walk with her, and I did, until we were standing alone among the gravestones. 'I wanted to apologise for how I spoke to you, when we met outside school; I had no right to talk to you like that, and when I heard about them finding your son... I...' her voice faltered. I let her finish. 'I was just devastated for you. No mother deserves that.'

'Thank you, I appreciate that.'

'You must understand, I had no idea that that would happen; I thought maybe Michael had run away. I guess I wasn't thinking clearly, and I should never had said those things to you.'

I sighed, 'It's OK; you were protecting your son; I would have done the same.' Like hell I would, I thought to myself, but I remained composed, my eye on the prize.

'If there's anything you ever need, even if it's just someone to talk to, I'd be happy to.'

'Well there is something you can do.'

She looked at me. 'Anything!'

'I was telling the truth that day in the car park. I was not made aware of any problem between Michael and Billy, or any of his friends, for that matter. I genuinely came to you for help, trying to piece together what had happened to my son and where I might find him.'

She looked at me uncertainly, her smile wavering slightly.

'I need to know what happened between our children, and I need you to tell me what my husband did, or said, to you.'

Her eyes widened, and she glanced over her shoulder, as if she was worried about being overheard.

'Please!' I pleaded with her. 'I have to know what happened; if Michael was in danger, if he was scared about something or someone.' I could feel my voice breaking. She looked at me with such worry on her face.

'You have to understand that it wasn't easy for me,' she began. 'Billy is a handful, and I know he plays up at school, and tells a lot of lies about things; so when he came home and told me this, I thought that was just it, another one of his lies.'

I nodded. 'It's OK; whatever you tell me stays between us, and I won't tell my husband that I know.'

She sighed, her eyes heavy, and her hands gripping her leather bag tightly, as if for support.

'Billy came home with marks on his wrists. When I asked him how he'd done it, at first he wouldn't say. It took a few hours, but eventually he told me that he had sworn at Michael and so Michael had taken him to the toilets and bound his hands together with a belt, and left him there.'

I felt a cold sensation in my chest. I kept listening.

'I know this isn't easy to hear, and I'm not enjoying telling you.'

I nodded, 'That's OK, just carry on.'

'He said that after about ten minutes Michael came back, and said he forgave Billy, and untied his hands. And that was it, they carried on playing. I asked Billy why he didn't tell the teacher, but he said that Michael told him people do it all the time, that Miss Cliff probably did that with her husband, and that my husband also probably did that to me.'

'I see,' I croaked.

'Listen, it's none of my business what goes on in your house, but it is what goes on in mine, and I couldn't let that incident go unnoticed. And I certainly didn't want Billy thinking that that sort of thing goes on normally in people's homes, because it most certainly doesn't.'

'So what did Dave say to you?'

She went white, and looked at the ground.

'He convinced me to drop it, apologised and told me...' she stopped, and looked around again, with a terrified look on her face.

'He told you what?'

'Mrs. Peters, you have to understand, I had no idea what was going to happen; I was just trying to protect Billy and my own family.'

'What did he say?'

'He said he would take care of Michael, and that it would never happen again.'

Therapy with Doctor Blunt

Doctor Blunt was wearing a red blouse. She always wore red. I found this interesting, as red to me was quite a strong colour. I wondered whether she wore it to empower her patients, whether she believed that seeing the red would instil passion into a loveless marriage, force a silent housewife to speak up and fight back, or persuade a bereaved parent to accept the loss of a baby. But then again, she might just like the colour.

'So, Ann, how did you feel after our last session?' she asked me softly.

'Really tired, but then I'm tired most days anyway, now.'

'Not long to go now, is it?'

'Two weeks.'

'So exciting!' she smiled kindly. 'I think the hypnosis will really help you get a handle on your life. I think it can help you to accept and face your repressed feelings of pain. It can also help you to regain control in your life, perhaps with your husband or parents, maybe.'

'OK, whatever.' I was so tired, I pretty much was game to go along with whatever she wanted to do today; my mind lay elsewhere: on the dishwasher that I knew would not be emptied; on the nursery, which Dave had promised to get ready, and yet still had not even started painting; on my last ante-natal class, which I really wanted to make, as it was a tour of the maternity ward, and one of my huge phobias was giving birth before I got there, because I couldn't find the right place.

'Are you all right, Ann?'

'Yes, fine.'

'What's on your mind?'

I shifted uncomfortably in my seat.

'Eurgh! What isn't on my mind?'

She gave a polite little laugh.

'OK; well, if you have nothing further to add, then we will begin the hypnosis, the same as last time: now, relax... remove any tension... that's right, shrug your shoulders and let them go. Good, OK... now take a deep breath... and release...'

7 Months Gone

'I think you should bring Dave in for questioning.'
I was sitting in the café on the main street, staring gloomily into my muddy cappuccino. Inspector Stone sat across from me, rubbing his greying stubble between his finger and thumb.

'I think you may be right.'

We had met up with each other several times since Jennifer's funeral, and each time I knew that I would be seeing him, I applied lipstick, and took a little more care than usual over my appearance. It filled me with a combination of both disgust and excitement. Part of me wanted to believe that I deserved happiness on some level. That after all the years spent in a loveless and unconventional marriage, it was somehow my due to meet someone who looked at me with desire. It had been so long since I could win men over just by wearing a short skirt and doing my hair, a long time since I had felt it necessary to, but part of me also held back, for the sake of my son. Not only because I believed, in some strange way, that I was being disloyal to his memory, but also because I wanted, I needed, to remain focused on finding out what had happened to him. This was possibly the worst time to fall in love, even if, for the time being, it wasn't even that. We hadn't kissed again since the train station, but I could always feel his eyes on me, travelling over my body, meeting mine with a burning look, and a half smile. Paul was difficult to read; as a policeman, that was most definitely a good thing. He hid his emotions and often seemed hard and indifferent, but he was a man, after all, and men, whatever their other attributes, aren't that hard to read.

He had given me his card, with his address and phone number, in case, as he put it, I remembered anything else of significance, so I had phoned to tell him about the incident between Michael and Billy; it felt like the right thing to do, despite having made a promise to Mrs. Stevens that, even at the time, I knew I would be unable to keep. So here we were; he had listened silently, glancing up at me from time to time. I had tried to skirt around the issue of why Michael had done it, but the reasons were obviously self-explanatory, and I could feel the disappointment oozing out of him.

'You came to me, Ann.'

I said nothing.

'I thought you were being abused!' He shook his head.

'I *was* being abused!' I had slammed my hand down onto the table, impatiently. 'I have been abused throughout my marriage to Dave. He wasn't the man that I signed up to marry! He made my life a living hell.'

'But don't you see? A judge is never going to believe that now. For all I know, those videos you showed me were for your own personal pleasure.'

That had hurt like a slap in the face.

'Do you really believe that?' I had asked him, earnestly.

'I don't know what to believe any more, Ann. I thought I had you figured out. I thought I knew your most intimate secrets, but now it looks not only as if I don't; I'm not even close.'

'You have no idea what it was like,' I whispered.

'Then help me to understand.'

'It's all I've known,' I croaked, 'that life with Dave: the beatings, the sex, the booze. He taught me; all of it.'

'But you enjoy it?' He shook his head in disbelief.

'I don't enjoy it, but I need it; it's part of me. When I was younger, and somebody hurt me, I felt suddenly in control; as if I needed those feelings of force and humiliation to grasp control of my surroundings in different situations. When I met Dave, I was only twenty-one. He showed me the world: fancy restaurants, fine wine, wild sex, and eventually, his belt. It became something that helped us to function. It enabled me to regain control, whenever I felt like I was losing it, and yes, even though you don't want to hear this, sometimes it felt nice; it could be a turn on.' He turned away from me, as if he couldn't bear to discover this duplicity, but to me, it was the person that I had become.

'So why did you make the videos? Does he know about them?'

'I don't think so. Although even if he did, I don't think he'd care. Dave is a strange person. He wouldn't care about that being out for the world to see. He thinks I'm the sick one.' I took a deep breath; 'I made the videos because I couldn't see any other way out of that marriage. I have never felt unsafe with Dave; having seen him at his worst, it was hard to fear what had become the norm, but I was scared for Michael. I didn't want him to see what went on between us, and I sure as hell didn't want Dave ever to take his belt to my son. I've been in therapy for years now, and I was hoping that it would have given me the clarity and the strength to leave Dave and demand a better life, with someone who would show me that happiness and pain are not intertwined. I made the videos to help with getting a divorce from my husband, and to get sole custody of Michael.'

'OK, but even though I want to believe you, Ann, this changes everything. We may as well throw out the videos, because of the relationship that the two of you shared.'

'But we can't, don't you see? We have to get Mrs. Stevens to tell her story, and that means explaining what happened in our personal lives. If anything, I think it only reinforces what he's capable of.'

'And *you* don't mind it being out there for everyone to see? For your father to sit in the courtroom, and hear about how you love to be whipped with belts and tied up like an animal?'

'If it means obtaining justice for Michael, then, as hard as it would be, I would be able to bear it.'

*

After I had told Paul about the incident, and we had dissected all of it into the tiniest pieces, and I had bared my tarnished soul to him, Paul had agreed to investigate Dave. The first step was tapping his telephone, and because he was between apartments and hotels, this proved difficult. Paul told me that they had recorded a few suspect conversations between him and Helen Anderly, and something in particular that he had read back to me from a transcript had made my blood run cold:

Helen: What do you want to do?

Dave: About what?

Helen: You know exactly what!

Dave: Nothing! Wait to see what happens.

Helen: Have you seen her recently?

Dave: Jealous are we? You've got nothing to worry about; I haven't seen my wife since the last time.

Helen: Soon to be ex-wife

Dave: You *are* jealous! ***LAUGHS***

Helen: Maybe just a little. Hurry up and get the papers over to her.

Dave: All in good time, don't worry.

Helen: I wish she would just permanently get out of our lives.

Dave: Don't you worry about a thing; Ann won't last five minutes after our divorce. She's weak, she needs to be kept in line, she'll fall to pieces without me.

Helen: I hope so.

Dave: See you later. Wear something naughty! OK?

Helen: Always! Love you.

Dave: I know you do.

I had always known that Dave was a cold bastard, but hearing his words, listening to how casually he could toss me to one side as though I was nothing was hard to bear. That he obviously did not care for either me or our son scared me more than anything. His indifference to Michael's death and his excitement about our divorce were chilling.

As if reading my thoughts, and bringing me back to the moment and my cold coffee, Inspector Stone put his hand on mine. It was warm and soft. He had lovely hands, not coarse hams with bitten-down nails like Dave: lovely long fingers, all ring-less. I turned my own around and entwined my fingers with his. I felt hot all over my body, and a sense of safety that I had never felt in fifteen years with Dave.

'If Dave did this, then I'll find out.'

'I know; I believe you will.'

'But there's always a chance that he didn't.'

I looked up, 'I know, but it seems unlikely. Either way, I have to know. I thought I knew what he was capable of, but I guess not.'

He sighed, 'I agree that we have a pretty strong case, and if he confesses, or lets something slip during questioning, I think that it could be even stronger, but I just have this feeling...'

'What feeling?'

'I don't know. I can't seem to find any connection between him and Jennifer. And even if it does make sense that Dave killed Michael in some bid to control you and to ruin your life, why did he kidnap and murder Jennifer Haddison?'

'Who knows what goes through the mind of a sociopath, perhaps he's been doing this for years and we have never known. Perhaps there are kids all over the Home Counties that are dead because of him. I honestly don't know, but he is most certainly not blameless.'

'I'm not disputing that, Ann; he's a horrible man, by all accounts, but, and I've told you this before, the world is not just split into two kinds of people: good ones and murderers. There's a lot of grey in between, and I don't want to mess up this investigation because you have a vendetta against my prime suspect.'

He was right, of course. I had allowed my hatred and lust for revenge, perhaps, to overtake the need for real justice. It felt almost like a reasonable exchange: having

Dave locked up for a crime he didn't commit, because in my mind he was guilty of so much more. Did it matter if one bad man was unjustly imprisoned, if it meant saving more women and children from falling under his spell, and having to swallow his lies and bullshit? Paul was spot on: I did hate everything about him; I resented him for the life he had given me, and for the person that he had turned me into. I had believed that he was a good man, a man who would give me a perfect life, children and a future, not scars and self-loathing.

8 Months Gone

There was yellow graffiti along one side of Karen's block of flats. It was fresh and smelled of solvent. The words 'I woz ere' and 'Fuck u' could still be seen in blue and red underneath. I imagined some fourteen-year old, with dreams of winning street art competitions, standing on one of the burnt-out cars and preaching to the losers below; sucking on a joint, and spitting onto the pavement. The car park was empty now. The rain beat down, just for a change; still no sign of the sun. I pressed the buzzer for Karen's apartment again, to no avail. I hopped from foot to foot, trying to keep warm, and blew my hot breath onto my hands. The door to the building opened.

'Hey, Auntie Ann!'

'Oh, hi, Max.' Karen's middle child, Max, a tall and gangling thirteen-year old (perhaps responsible for the new graffiti), stood in the entrance. 'God, you've grown quickly,' I observed; he had shot up in a matter of weeks.

'Or maybe you just haven't been to see me for ages!'

'Also probably true,' I said, nodding, and ruffled his hair. Pain seared through me as I did so, a feeling of such longing, wondering what Michael would have looked like at this age. 'I've been busy, I'm sorry.'

He smiled. 'That's OK; I know about everything that's happened; I'm not a kid, you know!'

'You're not?' I said, in mock confusion.

'No, I'm in year 9 now. We have sex ed., and drug class, and all sorts!'

'Wow! That's, er, great!'

'Anyway, mum's not here.'

I frowned. 'But she told me to meet her here; did she forget?'

'I dunno, but she left about half an hour ago, didn't say when she'd be back.'

'And she left you by yourself? Where are Emily and Mia?'

'Emily is watching us.' He shuffled his feet awkwardly.

'OK, well, tell your mum I stopped by, and get her to call me. Nice seeing you, Max!'

I winked at him, and gave him a little hug, before running with my head down across the car park, back to my car.

As I pulled into my driveway, I could make out Dave's bulky figure through the rain, standing under the porch. I stayed put, staring at him. He waved both hands, in a kind of over-the-top way, to make a point of being seen. I ignored this, and held my phone tightly in my hand, ready to call 999. He came down the steps, with what can only be described as a swagger, which unnerved me. He bowed his head and gestured slowly, in an exaggerated dumb-show, for me to open the window. I did, but said nothing.

'Hey Ann, how's it going?'

'It's going. Can I help you?'

'Well this is still my house, I'm confused as to why my key no longer fits the lock.'

'You're not welcome here,' I said, icily, as he dabbed his face with some tissue from his pocket.

'Can we talk inside, please? I'm soaked.'

'I'm not staying. If you want to talk, you can call my lawyer, I have nothing to say to you.'

'We don't have to talk,' he said quietly, a disgusting leer creeping over his face.

'I'm not stopping, I'm on my way to see Karen.' Any excuse, I thought, rather than have to let him into the house. 'What do you want?'

'I wanted some of my stuff, but it's OK, I don't mind waiting.'

'Email my lawyer a list of what you want, and I'll drop it at your hotel, or at your girlfriend's, or wherever.'

'Oh come on Ann, don't be like that!'

'You know, you should probably stay away from me right now; it doesn't look good, and I'd hate for you to get arrested for stalking, or something more serious...' I waited for him to flinch or blush, but he did neither, just looked at me with a triumphant expression on his face.'

'Oh I wouldn't worry about that.' He stood up, and as I pressed the button to wind the window back up, he placed both his hands on the top of the glass. He was so strong, he could stop it closing. 'Oh, and Ann, just so you know, I have spoken with your boyfriend; so you might consider dropping this whole act.'

'You spoke with Inspector Stone?' My voice faltered only slightly.

'So we both agree he's your boyfriend?'
I ignored this.

'When was this?' Paul had promised to call as soon as they brought my husband in for questioning, but that wasn't what alarmed me: it was the fact that he wasn't locked up.

'Oh, last week, and I think he was very satisfied with what I had to tell him.' He began to laugh. 'You're shaking, love; are you sure you don't want me to come inside and fix that for you?'

I shoved the car in reverse and sped backwards, causing Dave to lose his balance. I fixed him with one final glare of hatred, before taking off to find Paul.

'What the hell, Paul?' I stormed in through the door. He closed it behind me.

'Come in, why don't you?'

His apartment was nothing like I had imagined: it was a sort of endearing mess. Magazines and newspapers littered every surface; the wall furthest from the door was covered, every single inch of it, with newspaper clippings, words, letters, plastic bags, a map of Bridehill, of the main street. Red circles and arrows covered papers, and yellow and orange Post-it notes with numbers and words that didn't match were stuck all over it. There were photographs, too: of the river, of my house, of Jennifer Haddison, and of Michael. So many photos of Michael, but not like the photographs in my house, not photographs of a smiling and happy child, blowing out birthday candles and bouncing on a trampoline. They were photos of a pale and sad child, unmoving, cold and still, a picture of a child without life, still wet and cold from the river, his lips blue, his eyes closed for ever. I stepped forward to take a closer look.

'I don't think that's a good idea, Ann.' Paul stood in front of me. 'Why don't we go into the kitchen instead, and have a drink; this is my personal space, where I work, and it's not really for anyone to see, let alone you.'

I found myself nodding, and being guided into the kitchen. He sat me down at the counter, and poured me a glass of water. We sat in silence for many minutes. I had not seen Michael like that for weeks now. I had almost forgotten the unforgettable, and I was surprised by how much that bothered me: that somewhere along this bitter journey, I had tried to blot out the memory of the cold, lifeless body of my little boy. It shook me to the very core.

'I'm sorry, I really didn't want you to see those; it's just when I'm working, it helps me to think clearly when I can see everything in front of me. I create a sort of timeline, and using the photographs reminds me of why I'm doing this, and just how dark this world is.'

I said nothing.

'Do you want something else: a cigarette, a beer?' I shook my head, and sipped my water slowly, my hands trembling.

'I want to know why Dave is not locked up. I want to know why it's been over seven months, and you are nowhere nearer to solving this than you were at the beginning.'

'That's not true, Ann.'

'Isn't it? How many more children need to be murdered, Paul, before you open your eyes?'

'I told you before that Dave may not be responsible for this. I need time to build a case, to have something concrete to go at with him with.'

'And what?' I stood up, my arms falling heavily to my sides. 'And... and, you just happened to forget to tell me that you interviewed him and let him go last week? I thought we were on the same side; I thought you understood.'

He reached out to touch me, but I recoiled.

'I thought you actually cared about finding out who did this?'

'I do!'

'I thought you cared about me,' I whispered quietly, feeling foolish.

'Of course I do! What's got into you?'

'Dave. He's now showing up at the house, taunting me, vandalising my car.'

He rubbed his forehead, and poured himself a drink.

'I tried to tell you before, I don't want to be part of this personal vendetta between you and your husband. I honestly don't know what the hell *is* between you two, but I don't want to be a part of any of it!'

'This is not a personal vendetta; you have seen what he is capable of. I believe more than ever, now, that my husband had something to do with Michael's death, and you don't seem to be taking me seriously.'

'Because Dave Peters is not responsible. I am a hundred per cent certain that he didn't do this. He has an alibi that I have checked and double checked, and that cannot be faked.' He avoided looking at me now. 'What, that he was with his girlfriend? And you think she's a reliable witness? They're having an affair; you can't trust anything that bitch says; hell, she probably helped him!'

'Ann, you have to trust me. I know for a fact that Dave didn't do this?' He continued to look down, and I felt a sick feeling building in my stomach.

'What do you know? What aren't you telling me, Paul?' He didn't answer, and I got to my feet. 'How do you know that he didn't do this, Paul?'

He shook his head, and looked up at me with a pained expression on his face.

'Dave couldn't have done this. He was at a doctor's appointment with Miss Anderly.'

I felt cold all over.

'A doctor's appointment? What kind of doctor's appointment?'

'An ultrasound. A 13 week scan for their baby!'

I took the train up to London that evening. I had stayed for a little while in Paul's apartment, trying to process the bombshell he had just dropped.

'Look, I didn't want to be the one to tell you!' He had stammered and stuttered and vomited out excuses, but none of it really meant anything; nothing he could say would change facts. 'Talk to me, Ann.'

'There's nothing to say.'

He had paced up and down the flat, smoking, and drinking, and wringing his hands, all the while telling me repeatedly how sorry he was, how devastating it must be for me, how cruel life had become, but I wasn't really listening, I wasn't really there. I don't know what had shocked me the most: the fact that Dave, a man who he himself had described as 'non-paternal' and 'cold', a man who I never really saw openly show love and affection for his only son, was going to become a father again, for the second time, within months of his first child being murdered horribly, or whether it was the fact that he could no longer be a suspect. Come to think of it, he might already be a father for a second time. There was not even a remote chance that he had anything to do with it, and the one other person connected with him who might have was actually with him. Short of paying off a licensed gynaecologist to give him an alibi, there was no way even I could see that he might be guilty any more. I had been so convinced that he had been involved, so hell bent on doing everything in my power to hold him accountable for taking my son's life, and now, nothing. We were back to square one: no suspects, no reliable witnesses, no case. I thought I was strong enough to bear anything that life chose to throw at me, and I have borne some of the most horrific things that I would not wish upon anybody, but I could not bear the thought of Michael's killer walking free, among us, every day: an invisible person, allowed to live life, without consequences. I think out of everything, that alone could destroy me.

But maybe in all of this, something else had surprised me: I had clearly misjudged Paul. Or rather, my relationship with Paul, if indeed there ever was one. I had believed that no matter how painful, he would keep me in the loop as best he could; if he made an arrest or found a viable witness, he would tell me. Something in his confession made me realise that perhaps I was nothing more than a voice in his head, someone to listen to his ideas and thoughts, someone close to the victim. I felt used and wronged in some inexplicable way, as if I had slept with the enemy, and was now paying the price.

'Ann, I'm sorry, I've told you before, when its official...'

'Then don't tell me again; I don't have the energy to hear it.'

'What do you want from me?'

'Absolutely nothing. I guess I misread the situation.'
'What does that even mean?'
'Nothing, it means nothing.'
'Oh come on, don't do that!'
I could sense his temper rising.

'OK, I thought there was more between us than just my dead son!' I spat, and got to my feet. I made my way to the door, but he had wedged himself between me and it.

'That's not true!' He looked livid.

'I don't care any more. I'm done; please get out of the way.'
He didn't move.

'Do you have any idea how hard it is for me? This is one of the worst cases of my career. I sit in here every night looking through those nightmarish pictures, wanting to find out who's responsible and lock them away for life.'

'Well, I'm sorry you're finding it difficult; I'll make it a hell of a lot easier for you. Now step aside!'

His hands grasped my shoulders roughly; he was breathing heavily now.

'I didn't know that it would go on for this long. I didn't know that I would end up feeling like this about it... about you!'

I said nothing, but continued to stare into his eyes. His face was now inches from mine.

'I think I should leave,' I whispered.

'I don't want you to.'

He kissed me. I could feel his frustration, perhaps with me, maybe with the case. His kisses were insistent, his tongue in my mouth. I kissed him back, feeling his warm breath, inhaling his smell. My fingers ran through his hair, while he tugged gently at mine. He pushed me a little and then turned me around so that my back was against the door. He took his hands away, but continued to kiss me, softly, with a sort of rushed need, as though he couldn't stop himself. He fumbled with his jeans' buttons, his belt buckle, my zip, until he finally freed himself. I could feel him hard, pressing against my hip bone, moaning softly in my ear. He lifted my leg easily and pushed himself into me.

And we were fucking.

Not the violent, painful, pleasure-less sex that I was used to, but a raw, emotional moment of earnestness, of wanting each other in the most carnal way. He groaned as he thrust into me again and again and continued to pull a little on my hair. I could feel him building up, biting my shoulder and growling my name as he came.

Afterwards, we lay naked on his bedroom floor; with his fingertips, he traced my shoulder, my hips, and my stomach, with its shiny stretch marks. My whole life, I had never felt like that. Almost as if the act itself had lifted some invisible weight from around my neck.

'I really need to go now,' I said, softly.

'Yeah?'

'Yeah.'

'Where to?'

'Alice,' I said, simply.

He nodded.

'Do me a favour and don't make any stop-offs in Wreathwood.'

I gave a half-hearted smile.

'I just need to see my sister.'

'I'll call you.'

'Don't. I need a few days to...' I stopped, 'process things.'

He held up his hands, as if to tell me that he wasn't going to force the issue, that my stubbornness was understandable, and that he would cease to try.

'I'll call you when I'm back.'

Therapy with Doctor Blunt

'Hello. You have reached Doctor Blunt. Please leave your name, number, and a message, and I will call you back shortly.'

'Hi, Jane, it's Ann. I'm afraid I'm not feeling up to therapy this morning. The baby's head is pressing on my sciatic nerve, and I haven't slept in days. Will call you to reschedule after the baby comes. Take care! Bye.'

9 Months Gone

'This is fancy!'

Paul removed my coat and handed it to the waitress. The restaurant was dimly lit; little red miniature lamps were in the centre of each round table, and red curtains draped over the walls gave it a womb-like feel. The tablecloths reached to the floor, and candles on giant cast iron candlesticks burned in every corner of the room. A menu was positioned against one wall, with the starters and mains written in barely legible chalk scrawl; I had to screw up my face, squinting against the dim lighting, the distance and the handwriting, to try to decipher the fancy words and recipes. Eastern European music played softly in the background, waitresses hovered around, wearing crisp white shirts, and pouring champagne, red wine, or vodka.

Paul had driven us out of Bridehill, and into his home town, a forty-five minute drive closer to London. The restaurant, 'Есть' (meaning simply 'to eat' in Russian), was a place that his parents used to visit all the time when they were alive. He had told me this in the car, along with other stories of his childhood town and its prestigious food.

'I feel as if you know so much about me, and I know nothing about you,' I said, as we sat down at our table and Paul ordered us a bottle of Russian red. I wasn't hungry.

'I'm a very private person.'

'I get that.' I leaned in, inhaling the fumes from the scented candles, my hand hovering delicately above the dancing flame. 'Sometimes, I think all you know about me is pain, and sadness, and death.'

He nodded. The wine arrived and the waiter tried to pour some into my glass for me to taste. I declined and covered the glass with my hand, shaking my head and looking at Paul. He tasted it, before nodding and asking the waiter to give us a few more minutes before we ordered.

'This place hasn't changed,' he mused, looking around him. 'I half expected to see my dad come in through that door, or my mother sit down and spill her wine. She was always doing things like that.' He smiled to himself, but didn't look at me. 'My parents were good people. They did a lot for me. What do you fancy eating?' he asked, suddenly.

I smiled slightly, 'I can't read the menu from here.'

He laughed, 'Would you like me to get the waiter to bring it over?'

'I'll just have whatever you're having.'

'You're not allergic to fish or seafood, are you?'

I shook my head.

'Good.' He beckoned the waiter over, 'We'll both have the Dry Diver Scallops, Sun-Dried Tomato, Mushrooms, and White Wine Sauce, but can I substitute potatoes for the seasonal vegetables? Thanks. Tell me about Alice,' he said.

I looked up.

'What do you want to know?'

'I don't know; she seems to be someone you care about a lot.'

'I do care about her; she's my sister.'

'But it seems more than that; like you want to protect her, you'd do anything for her. When I first met you, you were so sad. Your eyes were always filled with tears and you looked so miserable, but when you mentioned Alice, you had this tiny light in them, like the smallest glimmer of hope, of something positive. I don't know, I guess that makes me like her, or want to get to know her, in the future, maybe.'

'She's sick,' I said, simply. 'I have always felt this overpowering need to protect her, as she's my younger sister, but then she was diagnosed with MS, and it made me want to care for her, and be there for her, even more. It made me so angry, you know, when we found out.'

'About the MS?'

'Yeah; it was as if she was being punished for having a good soul, or getting all of the karma that should have come my way, rather than hers.'

'You're too hard on yourself.'

'Am I? Sometimes, I think I'm not hard enough. I think my mum's right: I wasn't there for Michael; I didn't save him; I couldn't help save Jennifer. It's as if I have all these opportunities to prove that I am a good person, and I never seem to take advantage of them.'

The food came, and we began to eat in silence. I couldn't remember the last time I had eaten a proper meal, had enjoyed the tastes and flavours of home cooking or foreign cuisine. I had been living off a diet of clementines, and prawn crackers from the Korean, occasionally rifling through my cupboards to find a tin of beans, or canned soup, but whatever it was that I was eating, it felt like cardboard: tasteless and chewy in my mouth. Food had once been one of my pleasures, my passions; it now became a stark reminder of the meals that I would never get to cook for my child, the packed lunches that no longer needed to be prepared, and the family roast dinners that were now unnecessary. I felt bereft, to think that never again would I need to hide the vegetables in the mashed potato, or pretend the parsnips were really roasted spuds, just to get Michael to eat them.

'We all have our failings, Ann,' he said finally, without looking up.

'I find it hard to believe that you have been unsuccessful in the way that I have.'

He ate a scallop, and took a sip of the wine.

'You should try this, it's excellent.'

'I prefer white, especially with fish.' I shrugged, and looked around the restaurant.

'We moved here after my sister died,' he suddenly said. I turned my head sharply. He drank some more wine, and continued:

'She was a great girl: shy, but vibrant. If you knew her and she let you in, she was funny and caring, creative.' He smiled at the memory. 'Not unlike Alice, I imagine.' He ate some more of his food, swirling his wine around in the glass, sniffing it, taking another gulp.

'I'm sorry, Paul. What happened to her?'

'The official police report said she'd fallen. She was found in a quarry near our old house. She used to go up to the hill overlooking it, read her stories, create her own fairy tales. Some local kids found her there, the next day. My dad had been out looking for her all night. Her body was wet through from the rain, and covered in mud; I remember thinking she must have been so cold.' He closed his eyes for a moment, as if picturing her. I suddenly realised how sad he looked.

'But you think she was…'

'Murdered? Yes. Pushed by someone, or several people. I had no idea; I was only eight at the time, and we moved here straight after. My parents couldn't live in the same house, with the memories of her all around. They sold the house and got a flat here. I went to the local high school and life went on as normally as it possibly could.'

'But…'

'But my father never recovered from it. He died of cancer a few years later and my mother ten years after that.'

'Paul, I'm sorry.'

'That's OK; how could you know? As I said, we all have our failings, our regrets. Mine will always be not being able to find who was responsible for Helen's death. It nearly killed me; for years, it was all I thought about, it ate away at me. So I decided to do something about it.' He looked at me finally, his eyes glossy, his face etched with sadness, the table lamp illuminating it with a pink glow from beneath.

'What did you decide to do?'

'Become a policeman; help protect people, especially women and children.'

I reached across the table and held his hand gently. He didn't pull back.

'You think if you can find out who hurt Michael, that feeling of obsession, of self-destruction and guilt will go away? That somehow if you help me, you'll feel better about all of it: about your childhood, Helen, your parents, Michael, Jennifer?'

'Yes,' he said, finally. 'You see, you're not the only one who failed to protect someone you love. I felt compelled to help you with this case, because I know how you feel on some level. Helen wasn't my daughter, but she was the closest thing I ever came to loving another human being in that way.'

'It's OK to be sad. You're allowed to break sometimes, Paul. It doesn't make me think any less of you.'

I finally took a sip of the Russian red wine. It tasted of elderberries and blackberries, and left a sweet, burning sensation on my lips.

He was right, it was delicious.

10 Months Gone

It had started to snow outside. The star-like flakes floated gracefully down, covering my driveway with the thinnest layer of silver glitter. I stood on my porch, watching it trying to stick, wondering whether it would, and if the river would freeze over. In winters when I was younger, with old boyfriends, I would skate down it, laughing carelessly, until my ankles gave in and my nose turned pink. I stuck out my tongue to catch the snowflakes, letting them dissolve the instant they touched my warm mouth, swallowing, and starting again.

Karen was late. Which was typical Karen and did not worry or unnerve me; in fact, I usually deliberately gave her a time thirty minutes earlier than what I had originally planned, just so that we would be on time. Even now, when I have no place to be, no appointment to keep, I still feel uncomfortable and selfish when I am late.

Dave always used to make me late for appointments, which not only wasted professionals' time but that of other patients, and clients. This, however, did not annoy me half as much as when he was late for dinner with my parents. To me, there has always been something so important, so crucial about being on time when it is someone else who is preparing food for you, someone else who has been slaving away over the stove all day, making your favourite dessert and buying your favourite wine. But Dave never believed that anyone's time was as important as his own. He had even been late to our wedding, as if to warn me: a little preview of what was to come.

He had been on a huge bender the weekend before, for his stag do, and again the evening before, with his friends. In fact, I remember him still smelling of booze, as my father reluctantly handed me to him, his eyes bloodshot, his face unshaven. I remember thinking defiantly at the time that none of that mattered to me, and later, in the toilets, drunkenly telling my mother and sister that I knew what I was doing, that Dave was the man of my dreams, and that nobody really understood or had any idea what happened behind closed doors. God, I'd got that right, at least. I thought back gloomily to that day, remembering some poignant words that Karen had used just before her first child was born: that no matter what was to come, her wedding day was the happiest day of her life. I had married Dave, had Michael with him, and any day now, would be divorced officially from probably one of the worst human beings I could possibly have chosen to marry. So many years had been spent with an oppressive, violent, but fundamentally insecure man, whose principal pleasure had been in destroying my sparkle and watching me disappear, little by little, until what remained was something quite tragic. I thought about the bitter times and the sweet, unable, truly, to distinguish one from the other, and realised that for me, no matter how great the champagne had been, how expensive my dress was, and how wonderful the food had tasted, my wedding was most certainly one of the worst days of my life.

As I stood there, catching the snow in my mouth and reliving the past, Karen's red Honda pulled into the cul-de-sac. I could see her desperately shaking her head from side to side and mouthing 'I am so sorry' through the window. I locked the front door and made my way carefully down the steps. They had always been incredibly steep steps, and I remember asking Dave when I first moved in if he would get rid of them, and replace them with something more practical, especially as I was hoping to have kids, and concerned that I might break my neck climbing down them in a hurry, to which Dave had responded 'the steps stay, then!' with a grim smile on his face. I never knew with Dave, whether he was joking or not. At the time, it seemed to be just very dark humour. He often criticized my cooking, asked me if I planned to lose weight, bitched about my close relationship with my mother and how he had married me, and not my parents, but I always just thought that it was his idea of sarcasm and taking teasing each other to the extreme. Looking back, I know now that he was in deadly earnest; Dave has always been, contrary to what my mother thinks, sincere. He's many things, but he's also quite honest: honest about his affairs; about his attraction, or lack of it, towards me; about not wanting a child, his disappointment on seeing the positive pregnancy test that I had popped into his champagne glass as a surprise; his outspoken political comments, his views on my friendships, on my family. Dave has always said what he thinks, and I realise now that he had only been half-joking about the steps.

Karen had got out of the car and was making her way up the path.

'No! No! Get back in, it's freezing!' I shooed her back into the car. I stumbled over the snow covered concrete and jumped in next to her. As usual, Karen had the heating on full blast and *Il Divo* blaring out of the speakers, a cigarette burning in her gloved hand.

'I'm so sorry, I've just had the worst morning ever. Seriously! Max didn't want to go to his dad's, Mia is suddenly on a food strike for anything except chocolate, and I'm up to my ears in work.'

'It's fine, honestly, I know how busy you are.' I didn't look at her.

'Obviously, it's nothing compared to how stressed you've been and everything that you've had to do recently. I shouldn't complain; I'm just so tired, and the kids are, well, not making it easy.' She inhaled deeply on her cigarette, 'Sorry, do you mind? I'll smoke the e-cig, if you do.'

I shook my head.

'Smoke away!'

She drove out of the cul-de-sac, and inched down the hill slowly, the wheels skidding slightly on the steep slope.

'Be thankful you have them,' I murmured.

She stopped the car, and the engine cut.

'What?'

'The kids, Karen, just be thankful that they are there to annoy you, and run rings around you. I'd give anything to be sitting here bitching about Michael.'

She bit her lip, and reached over, touching my shoulder gently.

'I know you would. I'm sorry. It's so easy to take things for granted. I didn't think.'

She set off again and we finally reached the bottom of the hill. We continued in the direction of the main street, music still blaring, Karen occasionally joining in with her attempts at Spanish. I smiled. Being with Karen always made me remember what it was to be normal. Sitting in the car with her, feeling her friendship, made me almost forget the misery of most of the last year. It could have been just the two of us on a road trip, or going to collect the kids together from school, or going for a girls' night out on the town. For that fifteen-minute car ride, I could almost forget the excruciating pain of the last ten months. Almost. But that feeling of happiness and frivolity never seemed to last longer than a car journey, than an *Il Divo* song, than a cigarette. Sooner or later, I was always pulled back into the grim reality that had become my life.

'So what's the latest with Dave, then?' She asked casually, eyes still fixed on the road.

'We're meeting with the lawyers in about three weeks, I think. I can't remember the actual date, but he's signed the papers. Only a matter of days now, until I can use my old name, and get rid of that man forever.'

'Does he know that you know about...' her voice trailed off.

'The baby?' She nodded. 'I don't think he even cares.'

'Cold bastard!' She lit another cigarette.

'He is!' I agreed. 'And you know, it's not even that he's having a baby with someone else. It's not about jealousy, or about the fact that he can get back something which I can't, and can replace someone who is so completely irreplaceable; it's not about how I feel.'
She nodded her head knowingly, 'Yeah.'

'It's the whole thing! As if he never wanted a baby in the first place. He didn't want one with his first wife, or with me, yet now he's having one with this woman.'

'Slut woman!'

'Slut woman, yes, although in a way, I don't even blame her any more.'

She looked at me, wide-eyed.

'Are you sure you are feeling OK?' She felt my forehead in mock concern, and we laughed a little.

'It's him, he just gets under my skin, into my nervous system. I just want him as far away from me as possible. And I certainly don't ever want to see the baby, although don't get me wrong, it's not the kid's fault; but I just can't do it, especially now.' I could feel the anger and frustration that I had first experienced when Paul had told me about Dave and Helen's unborn child, and began to feel the fire start raging again. It was not good for me.

'I know exactly how you feel. When Tom first left me, I was fine with it! Well I was broken, actually, because Tom was...'

'The love of your life,' I finished, quietly.

'Exactly! But I accepted it; I tried to be the bigger person, for the kids. But when he got with that blonde slapper from down Langdale End, I knew...' She was talking animatedly, and leaving longer gaps in between drags, 'I knew that I could never forgive him, or even be like how we used to be, ever again. It just changed everything.'

I took a cigarette from her half-empty pack and lit it. It made me queasy, and sent a strong rush through my body. I only smoked cigarettes with Karen. It made me feel fifteen again, smoking them round the side of her parents' caravan while they were at work. Three shots of vodka, and half a stolen ciggie, and we were away. The memory made me feel warm and fuzzy.

'Men!' I breathed.

'Fuck men!' Karen hissed.

'Fuck men!' I repeated.

We had arrived at our destination. I took one last drag and stubbed out my cigarette, as Karen turned up into the driveway of Sue Haddison's house.

It had stopped snowing by the time we stepped out of the car. Mrs. Haddison lived right on the outskirts of town, opposite Bridehill park and the old school football field. Both looked deserted now. I had never personally known Sue Haddison, Susan Brown as she had been back then. She was several years below me at school, and our group certainly never mixed with the younger girls.

Back when we were teenagers, Karen and I would sneak out to meet boys at the park. It was the centre of the universe to us back then, our shirts tied into crop tops, skirts rolled over once or twice to make them even shorter, sucking on apple sour lollies. I remember my school boyfriend, Joshua Brindley, pushing me on the swings; every time I swung back towards him, he planted a horrible wet kiss on my lips that I pretended to enjoy. It had been a place where girls in our year had lost their virginity, or so we'd heard. In fact I vividly remember how one girl would give out blow jobs in exchange for cigarettes. The thought made me wince, now. As if reading my thoughts, Karen nudged me, looking over at the old changing rooms.

'Do you remember Jason Barnes chasing us back up there?'

'Only because you dumped his best mate!'

'Ha, ha! Yeah, you're right! Well he was hardly boyfriend material was he?'

'He never left us alone after that! Every break time, I had to duck from their water bombs in summer, or snowballs in winter.'

Karen burst out laughing, 'I'd completely forgotten about that!'

'I hadn't! I distinctly remember taking a lot of shit for you, because of something you had done, or someone you had upset!'

'God, I was a bitch, wasn't I' Karen sounded almost wistful.

'You were the best friend I could have wished to have.'

There we stood, lost in the moment, reliving old memories, and smiling at the past, when the front door to the house opened, and Sue Haddison stood there, arms folded, almost like a stern headmistress punishing us for talking in assembly. That wiped the nostalgic grin off my face, and I looked at the ground.

Sue was a tall woman, her jet black roots pushing through the dyed blonde on top. She had the look of someone who had aged a lot over a short period of time, yet she was still attractive, despite her lack of make-up, greasy hair, and general unkempt appearance.

'Sue!' Karen was walking up the drive to greet her; she gave her a big hug. I stayed behind, and nodded awkwardly.

'Come in,' she mumbled, and we both followed her inside, and sat on the dining chairs she had drawn up in the centre of the room.

Her house reminded me instantly of her ex-husband's: very tidy and neat, clean and in order, but whereas Mr. Haddison's house had an oddly cold feel to it, this was personalised and homely. Pictures hung on the walls, and a fire crackled in the grate. Photographs of Jennifer and her sister lined a bookshelf and the window sill, photos full of laughter, of happiness and of family. Jennifer had been the cutest little thing: pale skin and bright eyes. With her little black bob and rosy cheeks, she looked just like Snow White.

Mrs. Haddison took a seat by the open fire, her little girl jumped up onto her knee, and she continued to look at us, a sort of glazed expression on her sad face.

'So,' began Karen, looking from Sue to me, to the fire, then back to me again, raising her eyes and shifting uncomfortably in her seat. 'How have you been, Sue? Keeping busy? How's Ella doing?'

'She keeps asking me where Jenny is.' she replied, solemnly, holding her little girl closer.

Karen leant forward on her chair, 'Children pick up on everything! Even Mia knows something's not right; she sees that I'm upset about something; keeps asking me what's wrong.'

Nobody spoke. I felt extremely uneasy, as though we shouldn't really be here.

'You having trouble sleeping, too?' I suddenly asked, avoiding eye contact.

Sue looked from Karen to me, and nodded.

'Every night.' Her eyes were shiny with tears. 'I know Jennifer's not coming home, and I know that somehow, I need to find some strength from somewhere to keep going, for Ella, but...' her voice trailed off, and she looked lost for words. 'I keep hoping that if they find out who did this, I'll be able to sleep again. But what if I never will?' I nodded, closing my eyes. 'What if this is my life, from now on: just sadness and sleeplessness, and trying to get through the day as best I can?'

'I feel the same,' I murmured. 'Ever since Michael went missing, I've not been able to sleep. My therapist prescribed me some sleeping pills, but I'm too afraid to take them; scared of missing something, or not being able to wake up for something really important!'

'Have a couple of glasses of wine, or the whole bottle; it works wonders for me!' Karen said, trying to lighten the mood.

Sue smiled wanly, and I leaned back in the chair. Ella got down from her mother's knee and waddled off to play in the next room.

'Karen said you wanted to talk to me,' Sue said, finally.

'Yes. We came to the funeral together,' I began, choosing my words carefully. 'I didn't know your daughter, but Michael did. I felt the need to share some of my grief with you, if that makes sense.' She nodded. 'But I also want to find out what happened to our children.' She looked up. 'The thought of not knowing, of never knowing exactly what they went through; I can't bear it.'

She got up suddenly, and moved over to close the kitchen door; the voice of her boyfriend and Ella's laughter became muffled murmurs; she returned to her chair.

'Karen said you have met my ex-husband,' she began slowly. I nodded, careful not to give anything away. 'And what did he tell you?'

'Not that much really. Just about the day that Jennifer went missing: what they did together, and where he was when she disappeared. He seems a very private person; didn't really give too much away about anything...'

'Eerie, isn't it?' she said, with wide eyes. 'I should never have married him,' she paused, 'but then I wouldn't have had Jenny, and she was the best thing ever to happen to me.'

'I certainly found him a little different from other people, but then who am I to judge? My mother came round to clean the house last week, and there was green hair growing on my loaves of bread.' Karen made a gagging noise. 'Anyway, George Young confirms his story. He saw Jennifer get taken.'

'Oh, faithful old George!' She laughed sarcastically. 'What a surprise that he had to stick his oar in, and what are the chances that the one witness who can vouch for Lee just happens to be his best friend, his only friend?'

'I went to see George, too. I think he's credible enough, and I don't see what he'd get out of lying for his friend. He's just an old drunk.'

'Exactly. He's drunk all the time. Probably got his days mixed up. He's not really what I'd call reliable.'

'So you think Lee had something to do with what happened?'

She sighed and closed her eyes, a pained expression on her tired face.

'Every time that I dropped Jenny off, she'd have these panic attacks. The night before going to her dad's, she'd nearly always wet the bed, and wake up several times in the night. She'd beg me not to take her; it was getting so bad, she'd even seen the school counsellor, on Mrs. Cliff's recommendation, and that seemed to help, for a while.'

I looked at Karen with a horrified expression. I had never got as far as that with Dave and Michael, but could only imagine having to part ways with my son every couple of weeks, to leave him with that sociopath and his girlfriend.

'I tried to explain to her that she had to see her Daddy; that it was important she spend time with him. It was all unofficial, anyway; Lee didn't fight me for any more, and didn't seem interested in setting up something more frequent and in writing.'

'Well then, that doesn't give him much of a motive, does it? If you were stopping him from seeing her, or asking for supervised visits, or threatening sole custody, I could maybe see some kind of motive, but if he was fine with the way things were, then why would he have killed Jenny?' Karen interjected, blunt as ever, sounding as though she badly needed a cigarette. Her e-cig had run out of battery on the way here, and she looked tired and pissed-off.

'She was frightened of her father; I don't know why, and I don't know what happened, but as a mother, you know when something's not right. I should have stopped her from going, but I've had so much on my plate recently. I'm working two jobs, just to pay for this place, and with Ella starting nursery, it just all got on top of me. I should never have let her go. I'm a terrible mother!' She held her head in her hands, and burst into tears, the same loud, heart-wrenching sobs that I had heard at the funeral, and that had haunted my dreams ever since. I moved over and knelt down beside her, putting my arm around her.

'This has nothing to do with us! I blame myself every single day for what happened to Michael, as if trying to make sense of it all will bring him back, give me some peace, or make me think I did OK, that I didn't let him down, and that I'm a good mother, but I've come to realise, and you must too, that nothing we could have done would have changed the outcome. This wasn't something that we could have prevented. You'll only make yourself ill believing that it was!' She mumbled something, in agreement or appreciation, and I decided that it was time to leave. 'Come on,' I said to Karen, who got to her feet, almost a little too quickly. We started to make our way to the door, then Sue's voice stopped me in my tracks.

'Something very bad happened to both of them, Ann. When Jenny found out that Michael was never coming home, she was even more scared of going to her dad's. I'm certain that he had something do with it; a mother always knows.' She continued to cry helplessly into her hands. I could hear her sobbing as we walked back down the drive, all the way to the car.

Therapy with Doctor Blunt

'So you're a mother now!' Doctor Blunt smiled warmly as she greeted me for the session. 'Glad you could make the time, in between nappy changes and breastfeeding.'

I laughed. 'It's certainly not been easy.'

'Motherhood never is,' she faltered, 'or so I'm told.' I felt a pang of guilt and could sense her silent suffering. 'I'm very happy for you, Ann.'

'Thank you.'

'And I'm so proud of how far you've come.'

She got up, and went over to a white dresser that stood alone in the corner of the room. She withdrew a shoe box from one of the drawers, and returned with it to her chair.

'What's that?' I hoped that she wasn't going to start bringing out mementos of her pregnancies that had never come to full term, as I would feel incredibly uncomfortable.

'This is my sensory box,' she explained, 'a box that contains different objects from my life that have good connotations and happy memories.' Thank goodness for that! I thought; there's no way it would have been appropriate to reveal a selection of bootees and bonnets for babies that had never got to wear them. 'This is an exercise I do with a lot of my patients; it's a sort of practical homework that you can do over the next few weeks, if you don't have time to come in for a session.' I nodded.

She retrieved a champagne cork, a perfume bottle, a golden frog ornament, a silver ring, a birthday card, and a sea shell. She placed the items in a row on the table and pointed to the cork.

'This was from a bottle of champagne that my father opened at my graduation. I was the first in my family to go to university, let alone get an MD. My parents were so proud of me. When I see this, I remember the emotion of pride, and what it felt like for someone to believe in me. This is a bottle of the perfume that my mother used to wear: *Diorissimo*. When I smell that scent of jasmine and boronia, I remember seeing my mother preparing for a night on the town: styling her hair, applying her lipstick, asking my opinion. The little girl in me loves this memory. This is an old ashtray that my grandmother would use; look!' She lifted the frog and showed me the open mouth where you flicked the ash. 'I have actually always been fervently against smoking, and cannot bear the smell of cigarette smoke, however, it's here with these other items, because it is the memory that I associate with it, rather than the smell itself. I loved my grandmother very much. And this, this was my wedding ring.'

'Was?' I interrupted before I could prevent myself.

'Yes, Ann, as you can see, I no longer wear it. A marriage without children was not something that we were able to survive,' she said, sadly, 'but that doesn't mean that I regret the marriage itself, or the wonderful eight years that we were married, or the glorious wedding, that I had dreamt about since being a little girl. When I touch this ring, I remember the church, my long wedding train, pink champagne, violins, canapés and all my friends and family coming together in happiness. My wedding day was perhaps the happiest day of my life, as we truly believed we had the future to look forward to, together. I have only good memories of that day.

'This is a birthday card from a dear friend, my best friend actually. We don't speak often, but when I read this, I am reminded of all the years of solidarity and friendship that we shared; of laughing until we couldn't breathe, or getting drunk together; of driving round our university campus in her car, singing along to old songs.

'And this last one,' she paused, and held up the sea shell to the light, its speckled finish glimmering and shining. She smiled, reliving the memory, I supposed. 'This used to be on my bedroom window sill as a child. When I was sad, or bored, or lonely I would put it to my ear and listen to the sea, and imagine that I was in one of my favourite places, at the seaside with my family. All special objects to me, all wonderful memories.'

She returned the objects lovingly to the shoe box, and sat back in her chair, crossing her legs and looking at me intently.

'So, Ann, I have shown you my sensory box, the memories and souvenirs that I hold most dear. What I would like from you, is for you to go home today and find some of your own.'

'OK.'

'They can be anything, from mundane objects around the house: forks, cups, fridge magnets, pressed flowers; or things that are more personal and significant, like photographs, letters, jewellery; anything that you can find that comes with positive connotations from all different areas of your life. And when we next meet you can show me them, and tell me all about what you have chosen and why.'

'How will this help me?' I asked.

'I believe that in order to move on from the painful experiences of our past, and, in your case, to change the way that you live your life, we have to be surrounded by positivity and happiness. It is vital to embrace the good times in our lives, in order to make room for other and equally positive moments to come, and new memories to be created. By focusing your memories onto physical objects, you can collect them, and, like me, place them in a box, and access them whenever you are feeling insecure, low or lost. If you choose the objects carefully, I truly believe that this can make a difference to your perception of positivity, and it can help find the key to your own destiny and personal happiness.'

This sounded a little far-fetched and highly convoluted. I could imagine the expression on my mother's face, and her scoffing at the idea of this exercise, but I was a hoarder, and I had enough objects and items in my house to do car boot sales every week; there were certainly things that I could connect to happy times in my life.

'OK.'

She placed the shoe box back into the drawer, and locked it.

'Jane?'

'Yes, Ann?'

'Does it help you? Do you feel any less sad about never having a child because of the good things that you have done and accomplished in your life?' She flinched, only slightly, as if she was becoming accustomed to my rather frank, and, at times, intrusive questions.

'Some people keep a diary, some people keep photo albums. I keep objects from times in my life that I was most happy. I am thankful to have those memories, to be in good health, to be alive. Not everyone can say that. And I think just believing that has slowly helped me to accept the course that my life has taken.'

'Thank you for your honesty.' I found myself saying; and then feeling the rush of my milk coming through, and a burning sensation in my chest, I got up and left.

11 Months Gone

I woke abruptly, almost as if somebody had shaken me awake. I immediately felt regret over the night before, and yet, at the same time, was completely unaware of what I had done. My hands were trembling, and my breath smelt distinctly of cheap Chardonnay. My phone was ringing relentlessly.

'Yes, hello,' I mumbled; my lips felt swollen and sore.

'Ann, it's Paul Stone; are you OK? You sound, er, tired.'

'Fine. Yes, I mean no, not tired; I'm just... not feeling myself.'

'I'm sorry to hear that. Listen, could you possibly come down to the station this morning? There's something I need to tell you, and I'd rather do it in person.'

And just like that, I was awake, alert, sitting up to attention, listening intently.

'You have a lead? Something new?'

'I really would prefer to discuss it with you here, in person; and also I wanted to pick your brains, if I could.' Disappointment.

'No problem, I'll be there as soon as I can.' I hung up the phone and tried to focus on my surroundings.

Each time Paul called my house, it was like an alarm going off in my head. The urge to get to the police station as soon as possible was almost overwhelming. As a child, it was the same feeling of impending doom that washed over me at the thought of being late to a friend's birthday party, or waiting for my friend at the end of the road to walk to school, and knowing that we would be late; as a student, sleeping through and missing a lecture. These little things always worried me, growing up, as though my time was always less important than that of the person waiting for me. And even now, as a 37-year-old woman, I feel compelled, ashamedly so, always to keep my appointments, always to make it as quickly as I can, no matter how many speed limits I might break, and people I might crush in the process. I will be on time, I must be on time.

I reached over and picked up my watch, a horrid, gold, expensive thing. It was an anniversary gift from Dave, that no matter how much I hated, both for aesthetic and sentimental reasons, I couldn't bring myself to bin. It was reliable, and kept my haphazard life in check. It broke up the day for me, the hours representing different jobs to be done, the hands ticking away, reminding me of how long I had left. Time: an incredibly patient and trustworthy friend, and one that had kept me in line all these years. 9.20 am. I had overslept, and this in itself sent chills down my spine. I reached for the glass by the side of the bed and slugged down the last of its contents: warm white wine, acidic and dry in my mouth. It helped to calm me a little, and I started to look around the room for some clothes.

Everything about my house seemed so unfamiliar now. Perhaps it was due to the absence of love and laughter, or even of fights and raised voices. It felt so lonely now, in this big house that I couldn't bring myself to leave. The bedroom was large and had once been organised and well-maintained: beautiful silk underwear filled my drawers, and perfume bottles, smelling of jasmine and of rose, lined my dressing table. It had been a place of breathless, clothes-tearing sex, of revealed infidelities, of fights that drew blood, but also a place of forgiveness, soft kisses and fresh starts.

It had been where we had conceived our first and only child, Michael. I remember sitting on the edge of the bed and reading the positive pregnancy test for the first time, and being so relieved, so elated finally to be growing a life inside me: something that was mine and mine alone. It was a place that had welcomed the incessant screaming of a new-born baby, swaddled in blue, who demanded the breast every hour, until he would fall asleep with it in his mouth, milk dribbling down his little chin. A place where he sat up for the first time, laughing his toothless laugh and playing with whatever he could get his hands on.

And later, as a toddler, and then a child, he would run the length of the hall and jump ferociously, like a wild animal, onto our king-sized bed. I would scold him with mock disapproval, and we would both collapse in a heap of giggles onto the soft quilt, holding on to each other. I could never stay mad, or even get mad really with Michael, one of my many faults that Dave liked to point out during his brief interactions with our relationship. Michael was so perfect, so lovable, and so innocent. Everything about him was so pure, and untouched by the imperfections and lies of the world, and I felt that I would be able to protect him from all of that for as long as I could.

I was wrong: he never made it to his sixth birthday. The room disgusts me now. I know only hate, only the injustice and desperation that sleep with me every single night.

When I got to the station I was met by the secretary, who informed me that I'd just missed Inspector Stone, and that he was already on his way to the river. I didn't know why he was going back there this morning, but I knew it couldn't be for anything good.

'Ann!' I put up my hand to shield my eyes from the sun. Paul was already down by the river; he was waving frantically from below, as I stood at the top of the bank.

'Down here, Ann.'

I nodded. 'Thanks, I think I'll stay up here.'

We were at the lower reaches of the river, not where my Michael had been found. This was a part of the river more accessible from the town. Children often came to play here at weekends. In fact, I think I remember Dave bringing Michael here once or twice to go fishing. Dave didn't fish, but it would have been an activity he would have pursued to make it look like he had a healthy relationship with his son. It was cooler here; the trees provided shade, and allowed a gentle breeze to tease the skin. I drove to the river almost every day, usually in the evening, to feel closer to Michael, but I never really came to this stretch. It hadn't occurred to me before just how peaceful and beautiful it was. The silence was the first thing I noticed. It was so quiet: not even bird song, just deathly silence, broken only by the faint murmuring of the river below. How could anyone turn such a lovely spot into a place of horror and death.

'Ann!' Out of breath and sweating heavily, Paul Stone grabbed one of my shoulders. I jumped in surprise, grazing my ankle on a bramble.

'Ouch!'

'Shit! Sorry, Ann. I'm clearly too old to be clambering about on river banks.' He sat down on the muddy earth and took a swig from a water bottle. I took a seat next to him, my skirt riding up as I did so, exposing some leg.

'So?'

'So. Would you like some?' he offered me the water. I hesitated.

'Er, no, thanks, I don't drink, er, water.'

He smiled grimly. 'Neither do I!'

I caught the whiff of vodka, strong and clinical. I considered for a moment, and then thought of Michael.

'No, thanks, I need to try to keep a clear head. At least for part of the day.'

He smiled again and put the bottle away.

'So why are we here, Paul?'

'For two reasons: firstly, a fact, and secondly, a question.' He pulled out a basic map of the area, covered in notes. 'Michael's shoes were found here.' He circled the area of wood that I knew intimately; I clutched my pendant, pressing the rough metal into my skin. 'His body was found roughly a mile upstream, here.' Again, he indicated the two places on the map, both of which I had seen and visited more times than I could remember. 'And Jennifer's shoes were found here.' He pointed to a spot not far from where we were sitting. 'Her body was found down there, where I was standing, which is about fifty metres away; it's not far. Both children were killed where their bodies were found, but their shoes were discovered in separate locations, and in Michael's case, quite a way from where he died.'

I suddenly felt extremely tired; we were going over the same facts, again and again; this was nothing new. I had already been over these scenarios time and time again during the last year. All sorts of ideas had come to me, all of which had been dismissed in turn by the police. I struggled to grasp why this was important now, and what Paul could possibly be thinking, by coming back up here in search of answers.

'We have been through this; I just don't know.'

I had bought Michael's shoes for him the weekend before he went missing. They were cobalt blue and white, and he loved them. I'd taken him to the local shoe shop. His old trainers were grubby and tattered, and one of the soles was peeling away. His little eyes had lit up when he saw those trainers, and he wanted them immediately; he wore them all that weekend to break them in, even though they gave him nasty blisters on the heels of his little feet. I remember blowing onto the broken skin and giving him a plaster, showering him with hugs and kisses and ruffling his chestnut brown hair, as he complained about the pain. I clutched my pendant and closed my eyes, reliving that weekend, seeing his happy face, glowing with pride, pride in his new shoes.

'He loved those shoes,' I mumbled, in barely a whisper. I opened my eyes, which were brimming with tears. Paul held my hand.

'I know he did. Please humour me.' He got to his feet and started pacing to and fro. 'Why would the killer remove the children's shoes, take them to another spot and then kill them? What is significant about the shoes? I kept asking myself this question; Jennifer's mother told me that hers were not new, nothing special. They weren't her pride and joy like Michael's. I think our focus has been all wrong here. I don't think the shoes are what connects them, or are even that important. It's why they were removed that we need to find out, and what happened between their removal and where the children were murdered!' He seemed on a roll, and I had no idea where he was taking this. I just kept thinking about the new rubber smell of those trainers, the trainers that my son had loved so much. 'Then I had this idea. Michael was good at sport wasn't he? That's one of the reasons you bought him the trainers.'

'Well, I mean, he's a kid. And he was a boy, so I always bought him boy things, but he did love football and running...' I had flashes of Michael on school sports day: first prize, running through the ribbon, collapsing by the side of the race track and drinking from a bottle of water. I smiled to myself. I was so proud of that boy.

'Yes, Ann, running!' Paul cut through my thoughts. 'We always thought that they were brought up here in a truck.'

'Well there were tyre marks at the top of the embankment, so that's a reasonable assumption. And Michael, if he knew he was in danger, wouldn't have come quietly on foot. It would have been easier to transport him in a vehicle.' It made me feel so cold, talking about him like that.

'He was running, Ann!'

I felt a pang of both pain and of encouragement, the thought that Michael had perhaps run away, fought until the very end to get away, get back to me.

'But what does it mean?'

He cut through me again. He had obviously been thinking this over and over, and knew exactly where he was going.

'Jennifer had asthma. I remember when she first went missing, and her mother was so worried, because she didn't have her inhaler. It would have been dark, and cold, and she couldn't breathe; she would've only made it about...'

'Fifty metres,' I whispered.

He nodded.

'So,' I began slowly, 'they both tried to escape, barefoot? That doesn't make any sense.' But even as I said this out loud, I finally understood what Inspector Stone was thinking. It sent a cold shiver down my back. 'They were made to try to escape?' I looked at him desperately. He handed me his water bottle, and I took several gulps. I'm sorry Michael, I whispered to myself; I needed this to help me see it properly, to understand exactly what Paul was telling me.

'I think they were both made to run, to see how far they would get, how fast they would run, how desperately they wanted to escape... and Michael, he was a runner, even if he was tired and afraid, he made it nearly a mile, a mile upstream! But Jenny, well, she had asthma; she was a little girl, alone in the dark, without her mummy. I think she ran a little way but had to stop. She couldn't make it any further because of her asthma.'

We both stood there in silence, processing his words, trying to make sense of it. I could just see my son running blindly through the woods, calling my name, or maybe silently, to avoid being found. And then another bitter thought occurred to me: perhaps if Dave had brought him up here more often he would have known the way, would have been able to escape, or make it across the river, and back to the main road. I could see his face, lit by moonlight, running until he couldn't move any more. I violently vomited up the Chardonnay and the vodka, and every sick thought and feeling that was inside me. When I'd finished, I looked grimly at Paul Stone, who rubbed my back and continued to stare at the river bank.

'But there were tyre tracks, and they were at the top of the hill, where Michael was found, so I ask you, Ann, what do you think that means? Why would a killer let a child escape and then drive to the top to wait for him?'

I had no idea, but I watched him, hanging onto his every word.

'Well, to me, it means one of two things: either the killer removed their shoes, and followed in the car until they stopped, and then got out and finished the job.'

'That doesn't seem likely, or?'

He pondered for a second or two.

'Or?' I repeated, desperately.

'Or there were two of them!'

Therapy with Doctor Blunt

Doctor Blunt was not in her office when I arrived for our session. I sat in the empty waiting room for ten minutes, alone, looking at the freshly painted white walls, and the aquarium, which I only just noticed had fake fish in it. Not that I minded the quiet, and the sense of non-existence. With a screaming baby and equally demanding husband, it was nice to escape for an hour, and I took full advantage of the sound of my own thoughts, my breathing; it was pleasant just to be alone. The space was calming and reassuring. I flipped through a lifestyle magazine, thinking about how I could update and redecorate my living room, whilst simultaneously acknowledging ruefully that Dave would never go for it. He refused to pay for anything that was not a necessity.

'Ann, I'm so sorry!' The door burst open, and Doctor Blunt came running in, out of breath, her arms laden with shopping bags. 'Please forgive me; it's been a very stressful morning. Come in, come in.' She unlocked her office door with a tiny gold key from around her neck, and pushed it open with one toe of her stylish black stilettos. She continued to apologise profusely, and I continued to revel in someone else's excuses. I let myself almost fall onto her couch. She noticed. 'You look exhausted, Ann, is everything OK?'

'I don't think you'd make very much money if I was,' I joked.

She laughed, 'Coffee?'

'I'm not supposed to.'

'Still nursing are you? That's wonderful. I have decaf, if that's OK.'

'Decaf would be great, thanks.'

She removed her coat, and despite her wind-blown hair and frazzled initial appearance, her clothes beneath were, as usual, immaculate.

'Again, please accept my apologies.' She handed me a coffee and sat down facing me. 'How's Michael?'

'He cries, a lot!'

She smiled, 'Well, he is a baby, I'm fairly sure that's normal.'

'It's non-stop! I keep feeding him, thinking he's hungry, and then, I think: what if he's having too much?'

'Yes, that's one of the things I remember about Lucille. I had to give her a bottle every three hours, but at least we knew how much she was getting.'

'Who's Lucille?'

'My niece; my elder sister's child. It helped, you know, after my losses.'

'God, that must have been so difficult, and how brave of you!' I said, awestruck. I could barely bring myself to feed my own screaming baby, sometimes.

'It was very hard, but also very rewarding.' We sat in silence for a few moments. 'Enough about me. Let's talk about how your relationship with Dave has evolved since the arrival of Michael'

'Pfft!' I snorted.

'Pfft' is not an emotion that I am familiar with,' she remarked, 'please expand.'

'He's even more distant, if that's possible, and because I'm so involved with the baby, I feel like I'm deliberately pushing him further away.'

'Maybe because you are... deliberately pushing him away. You said yourself that you were not sure how you felt about him: he was a means to an end, so to speak.' She turned back several pages in her notebook and read: 'Staying married to Dave is what I have to do, to get the baby I know I want.' She removed her glasses and looked at me. 'Would you say that you still feel this way?'

'Probably even more so, now.'

'Why?'

'Because I have Michael, now; I have this other human being who needs me to survive. He needs my food to live, my touch to feel protected. I have never felt like that with

Dave. It's a brand new feeling of happiness and warmth that I never knew existed until now.'

'You know what we call that?' She leaned forward, scrutinising my face: 'Love.'

12 Months Gone

When I was a child, I used to dress up my Barbies in extravagant outfits, plait their hair and act out weddings to Ken, with Cindy as a bridesmaid. As I got a little bit older, but not too old to enjoy the land of make-believe and the possibilities of the imagination, I would colour their hair with blue or green hair mascara, piercing their plastic noses with a needle from my mother's sewing kit, and bending their toes to fit into shoes that were too small for them. Eventually I chopped their hair off altogether with toenail clippers, and made Barbie have an affair with one of my uglier dolls, a frizzy-haired, flat-chested, bendy doll, named Pearl. She never had any children, but one Christmas my father had bought me a Barbie that came with a newborn baby and a pram. I lost the baby a few weeks afterwards and though I never knew what became of her, I would have Barbie pushing round her empty pram, singing lullabies to a baby that wasn't there any more.

With hindsight, maybe I was subconsciously predicting my future, and the Barbies and other dolls were all just metaphors for how fucked up life truly could become, due to the choices and decisions that we make. My life had become frighteningly similar to that of my old Barbie dolls, who now lay covered in dust, amongst the baby clothes and old photographs in my parents' loft. What wouldn't I give to be eight years old again, a little girl with her whole life ahead of her, to be unaware of the failings and inevitable disappointments to come.

I remember always feeling very loved, by both of my parents, and although my mother wasn't clingy or suffocating, the bond between us was very powerful. I found it increasingly difficult to sleep away from my parents' house, and my stomach would twitch instinctively when friends used to ask me over to theirs for a night of popcorn and slasher flicks that we were too young to watch. I loved my house, my bedroom, my life. I never felt any inclination to search for a deeper meaning to things. And I could be carefree, careless even, and often unappreciative of my easy and comfortable life. How I wish I could speak to my younger self and warn her: that life wasn't always going to be cups of tea, cuddles and friendship bracelets, hot dogs, pizza and school trips, Barbies and kittens. It would be full of disillusionment, constant disappointment, and more recently, never-ending, mind- numbing pain.

'Ann, love?'

My father's voice floated up the spiral wooden staircase, and I could hear voices, and the sounds of shoes and coats being removed. My head was resting on the small baby-blue pillow that was propped up against the wall, just as Michael loved it. He had always hated lying flat. Even as a baby, he would scream the house down when I tried to lay him down gently in a Moses basket, or a cot, and later, before he would go off to sleep, he would always beg me for an extra cushion, or his favourite knitted blue throw, rolled up into a ball and shoved underneath his pillow, so that he slept with his head slightly raised. I turned my face into it, smelling my son's ever-present scent: children's strawberry shampoo, sweat, comic book paper, dried plasticine, and then his own unique smell, which I loved so much, and wished I could inhale forever.

I had left his room untouched. It was quite small, with his little blue bed in the corner, underneath the sloping ceiling. His crumpled duvet, with aeroplanes and fluffy clouds, was half on, half off the bed, and underneath, on the floor, were books and comics: 'Tin Tin', 'We're Going on a Bear Hunt', 'The Gruffalo' and 'Peter Rabbit'. His carpet had the usual stains: milk, chocolate and talcum powder, that I unashamedly couldn't bring myself to remove, all a painful reminder that somebody had lived in this room, and a year ago had spilt a full glass of full-cream milk all over the floor. Leaving it there made it feel real, made me think that he was still there. A wardrobe stood in the right-hand corner, with Bob the Builder stickers and Blu-tac, and magnetic letters that Michael had stuck to the door with sellotape. A wooden train set threaded its way between the bed, a little desk and a toy chest, some of the carriages broken, some of the little wooden people missing arms and legs. The toy chest was open, and crayons and plasticine and paper lay next to it, as if a child had just been playing, before being called away to the dinner table to eat.

I would never change the perfectly ordered chaos of this room.

The door opened, but I didn't jump, I remained motionless, with my eyes closed, savouring every second, still breathing in my son, and feeling his covers, his teddy bears, his presence.

'Ann?'

Eventually, I opened my eyes and slowly wiped away the tears. I sat up and tried to smooth my hair, although having not washed it in two days, that was fairly pointless. Slowly, my father's face came into focus. He sat down on the edge of Michael's bed.

'Hi, Dad,' I said, numbly.

The past few weeks had been particularly hard, and more emotional than usual, which, in itself, was difficult. In fact, I surprised myself at just how much worse I could feel, and how desperate my life was becoming. Tracking Michael's murderer, questioning people who might be connected, visiting my sister, embarking on an affair with the policeman in charge of the case; all of these things had created a distraction from something so horrible. Keeping myself occupied, even though it was difficult, had overshadowed my need to talk about my son, to mourn, to grieve for him; just as playing detective, and revisiting my teenage relationships, had somehow caused me to forget a little that I still hadn't visited Michael's grave; that part of me had never really let him go, said goodbye to him, told him how sorry I was for letting him down. Something inside me was perhaps still clinging on to a lost hope, a hope that if I could somehow make things right, none of it would hurt any more. This made me feel increasingly angry at myself. Michael deserved more than that.

'Shall I open the curtains?' My father's voice brought me back to the present, and I nodded, dreading the sunlight that would expose all the cracks, dust, and other failings. He opened them in one swift movement, and sunlight fell into the room, lighting up my son's belongings. My father stepped over the train track and came back over to me. He didn't mention the mess, or the smell of stale milk. That was one of the wonderful things about my father: he could be very critical of everyone else, point out their weaknesses and shortcomings, but for me and Alice he would always make excuses for them, turn them into our strong points, our attributes, our successes. He believed in us to a fault, and when there was nothing positive to say, like now, he said nothing.

My relationship with my father had always been a good one. His tolerant, open minded ways balanced well against my mother's cynicism and sarcasm. They fitted perfectly together, and growing up, I felt assured that always at least one of the two could help me, whatever it was I needed.

'You'll never guess who I ran into last night at The Goose?'

'Who?'

'Nigel Jennings'

'Really? Goodness! I've not heard that name for years; what on earth is he doing back here?'

'Oh, his parents are in the new nursing home on the Greensworth road, and he visits them once a month; said he wanted to see if the pub was still the same; if the Guinness was still as good as it used to be!'

'How are Sara and Elise?'

'Both doing well, apparently. Sara is married and has two daughters, and Elise is studying to become a doctor up in Leeds. He asked after you and Alice. He knew about what happened.' For a moment, neither of us said anything. 'Nigel and his wife were two of the first people who came to see you when you were born.' He smiled a sort of wistful, lop-sided smile. 'You were such a beautiful baby: big dark eyes, a little tuft of soft hair. I fell in love with you right away.'

'That's not the way mum remembers it!' I smiled a little. 'A horrific forceps birth, I wouldn't latch on for five days, and then I screamed the place down with colic!'

'Oh, your mother does like to exaggerate,' he said, good naturedly.

'Or maybe you like to look back with rose-tinted glasses,' I reminded him.

'You were perfect,' he repeated, 'perfectly ours. I'd never known that kind of love before. I'd had girlfriends before your mother, and goodness me, I loved her so much. I was a bit apprehensive, you know, about you coming and mixing things up. I liked the way things were. But then you arrived, and you were so little and helpless. The feeling of love that rushed through me when you grabbed onto my finger and held it so tightly, I knew then, that I'd never known real love before. You changed how I felt about everything: about life, about the man I was, the husband I had been and the father that I wanted to be.' As my father talked, I found myself leaning into him slowly. He smelt of wood varnish and nails, coffee and home. 'People say they never really know what they have until its gone, but I don't think that's true. We know it all along. We perhaps don't say 'I love you!' enough, or talk about how great someone is, but we feel it; and I knew that my girls were the most important things in my life.'

'Oh, Dad!' I turned my face into his shirt, rubbing my nose into his chest.

'We all miss Michael, every day, sweetheart,' he whispered, kissing my forehead, 'no-one more so than you. I can't even begin to imagine waking up every morning without you and Alice, and all the things that I'll never get to say, or do.' I began to cry silently, my tears muffled by my father's fleece waistcoat. 'You do whatever needs to be done.' I stopped and looked up at him, my cheeks sore from the tears. 'I would have done for you,' he said, simply, and hugged me even closer.

13 Months Gone

I had fallen asleep on the train up to London. If I had expected the ticket officer or a fellow passenger to wake me, I was obviously mistaken, and I awoke with a start, dried saliva stuck to my cheek, my eyes sealed shut. It took me a few moments to realise where I was. I had gone one stop too far. Annoyed, I checked my watch; it was gone ten, and by the time I had caught the train back to where Alice lived, it would be at least half past.

'Excuse me!' I shuffled past the other commuters, all of them seemingly unaware of my existence: typing emails, answering phone calls on their flashing, hands-free sets, animatedly talking to the back of the seat in front of them, applying a last coat of lipstick before arriving at their destinations, savouring the last dregs of cold coffee. I pressed the button angrily, and when the door opened, practically fell off the train onto the busy platform.

The taxi rank was crammed full, as usual, and by the time I joined the queue there were only two taxis left. Irritated that nothing seemed to be going my way this morning, and feeling helpless to rectify it, I stood behind the people in front of me, tapping my foot impatiently, and inhaling someone's illicit Marlboro Gold cigarette smoke.

The taxi driver dropped me at Alice's building and I didn't tip him. I was wet, cold and beyond politeness. Slamming the door, I marched up the path, and stood, for what seemed like an age, with my finger resting on the buzzer, as if to convey my mood via the intercom.

'You look happy!' said Alice drily, as I helped myself to coffee, and finally sat down.

'Forget it!' I grumbled.

Alice, I noticed, looked very pale. The shadows under her eyes were darker than usual. We had both inherited the hollow circles from our mother's side, but today she seemed even more tired, exhausted, and washed out. As if reading my face, she smiled her usual brave, courageous smile:

'I'm fine, Annie.'

'You look tired.'

'Well, nothing worth having in this life is easy or free.' She raised her eyebrows.

'Meaning?'

'Meaning, I have not slept, and I am now broke and living off pot noodles. But...'

'But?' I felt a little rush of excitement, and set my coffee down on her dark, polished wood coffee table.

'But, I have news: very important, possibly life-altering news!' She smiled at me triumphantly and picked up a brown envelope from the sideboard, running her delicate fingers along it as she did so.

'What is that?'

'Last time you were here, we talked about the other little girl that was missing: Jennifer. I waited until I was sure that she wasn't coming back before doing some research. There was something you told me about it that didn't sit right with me. We have been going over and over Michael's abduction and finding no leads. Everything is a dead end, everything just burns out, so I thought I'd take a look and do some digging on Jennifer Haddison and her family, instead. I wasn't sure exactly what I'd find, but like I said, I didn't feel right after you left last time, and I really wanted to do something to help.' I nodded, listening to her intently. She often babbled when she got a good story to publish, when she had finally found proof of corruption or fraud. I felt confident that I was going to believe whatever it was that she was about to tell me. 'I hired a private investigator,' she said, simply, as she took a sip of coffee, 'James knows someone; he tracked down his birth mother; good, but expensive.'

'I never asked you to do that, Alice.' My sister already had so many problems, I couldn't bear the thought of my despair becoming yet another burden to add to her load.

'Listen to me!' She pulled a chair closer and sat down, resting both her hands upon my knees. 'Nothing is more important than finding out who did this. Do you understand?' I nodded. 'I would sell my flat, my car, quit my job, split up with James; whatever it takes to get to the truth, I am prepared to do; for you, for Michael, for all of us.'

'I love you!' I whispered.

She closed her eyes and reached over for my pendant, squeezing it. She handed me the brown paper envelope. I continued to hold on to her, unsure if I wanted to see what was inside, unprepared perhaps for the life-changing news or revelation linked to the death of my son. I opened it, and a photograph dropped into my lap; it was a mugshot, in black and white, but even without the eye colour, sporting a long mop of unkempt hair, Lee Haddison was still immediately recognisable. I stared up at Alice, not really understanding the significance. She got up, and went into the kitchen.

'Just read it,' she said quietly, when she came back, as if sensing my confusion.

I placed the photograph on the table, and withdrew several other pages. The first, an investigative report, followed Mr Haddison's movements over the past month, but brought up nothing suspect. The second was information on his various jobs since living in Wreathwood. The third, details regarding his separation from his wife, and the unofficial custody agreement of seeing his daughter every other weekend. The last page had the same photograph as the first picture. Lee Haddison's hard face, solemn and devoid of any feeling, stared into the lens. However, this was not a close-up, but the original, I guessed. He was holding a sign between his hands. I had to look at it again, to ensure that I had read it correctly, that my eyes were not deceiving me, as they so often did at the prospect of unearthing something new and credible. It read: Alan Wells. I looked at Alice in disbelief, my heart pumping faster, my fingers trembling, as I held the piece of paper. Looking back down, and taking a deep breath, I read aloud:

'Name of the defendant: Alan Wells. Date of birth: 02.12.1970. Case number: 0356789. Arrest date: 04.02.2004. Original charge: Statutory rape. Plea information: Plea of not guilty on 21.08.2004. Sentenced on 15.10.2004. 7 years in prison.'

I finished reading and dropped the papers to the floor. I felt sick, excited, afraid, unsure how to proceed. I wanted to call Paul, in fact my first impulse was to call him and fill him in immediately, but I imagined his stern face when I revealed Alice's involvement, his disappointment that I had continued to go about solving the case on my own, behind his back, and then the patronising manner in which he would tell me not to worry, that he would personally see to it that Lee Haddison was questioned. Part of me felt betrayed by the earlier promises he had failed to keep; his dismissive attitude when I had told him of my suspicions about my husband making me doubt his belief in me, or at least in whatever information I might manage to obtain. I wanted to have something more concrete, something that could tie Mr Haddison to Bridehill on the day that Michael went missing, a link between the children at school, anything that could prove this wasn't something to be discredited and ignored; this was serious.

I thought back to when I was inside Mr Haddison's house, remembering the clinical cleanliness of the living room, the almost sterile environment and the lack of photographs. I remember thinking it strange that he lived like that, but accepting, at the time, that people have their reasons. What if the truth behind the lack of emotion and personalisation was because he had started again with a new identity. There were no pictures, because prior to his living in that house, he had gone under a different name, worn a different mask. I felt a chill slide down my spine, ever so slowly.

'Bastard!' I muttered, looking down again at the blank face that stared up at me from the page.

Alice slammed a hand down on the kitchen top.

'Right under our noses the whole time!' She exclaimed. 'And what exactly has your boyfriend been doing through all of this, hmm?' She looked livid.

'Hell if I know!' I got up and paced over to the window.

'This took me all of three weeks to find out. Surely the police have access to this kind of information. Why hasn't anything been done? It's ridiculous!'

'I know! I don't know what to think.'

She came over to me and put her arms around me,

'Never doubt your intuition on this, Annie! Honestly, I know that you have a soft spot for that policeman, but...'

'I do not have a soft spot for anyone!' I spluttered indignantly.'

'Oh come on! Mum told me that you've been out for dinner, that he keeps calling the house asking where you are, and how he can reach you.'

'We're friends; he's helping me find out what happened to my son.' For some reason, I felt as if my sister was accusing me of something. It made me feel strange, hostile in some way, and I felt the need to protect my relationship with Paul, or at least to defend it.

'Annie, don't be dishonest.'

'I'm not being; god, what is it with everyone having an opinion on this?' I could feel anger and frustration bubbling under the surface.

'That stung!' She looked hurt. 'I didn't think I was just anyone. I'm your sister, and I care about you.'

'Well, I'm fine!'

'You're not fine, and I'd be extremely worried if you were.' She pulled me to her, 'Listen, Annie; you can be honest with me; you know that I, of all people, would never judge you. I have always had, and continue to have, your back; Just don't insult me by lying to me!' She looked at me, her big dark eyes sad and tired. She kissed me on the cheek; her lips felt cold. I sat down, Alice's point made, and the fight going out of me.

'This thing with Paul, it's tearing me apart. You know, at first, I think we were drawn to each other because of Michael. He was interested in me from the start, and I was interested in using him to find out as much as I possibly could about the case: updates, progress, clues, everything. The more I spoke to him, spent time with him, the more I couldn't shake off the feeling that we both felt something else; something more.' She nodded, but didn't say anything, listening to me, like she always did, without judgement, without criticism. 'When they found Michael's body, he tried so hard to protect me; it almost made me angrier. I thought at first, he was doing it for the obvious reasons. He said that no mother should ever have to see her child dead. Just remembering Michael's face, his little eyes closed, his hands all wet and cold...' I closed my eyes, and began to feel the memory of my son stealing over me again. 'I have never, ever seen anything that can compare to that.' I shook my head and blinked back tears. 'At first, I thought Paul didn't want me to experience that, you know, he's a policeman; he must have seen his fair share of death, but I think he wanted to preserve something of what I was before...'

'How so?'

'Before I saw his body, Michael was just missing; he was missing, but I had hope. They found his shoes, but I still felt unbelievably hopeful that nobody would hurt him. Before I saw him, I was still a mother, and I had memories that were not final chapters. I had dreams and projects and ideas for the future, of all the things that I would do when Michael was found, and we were back together again.'

'Oh, Annie!'

'I think, looking back, that Paul wanted me to be like that always; that he had begun to see me in a different light, but still as a mother, as a woman who had hope, and who had not yet been destroyed by tragedy. He was trying to protect me from so many things.' I shook my head and began to cry, leaning into my sister and feeling her warmth. She wrapped her arm around me, her hair falling onto my cheeks, absorbing the tears that began to stream down them. We sat there like that for a few moments, before I began wiping my eyes with my sleeve.

'And now?' she asked.

'Now, I feel I don't deserve to be happy any more. I feel some attraction towards Paul, but I don't feel good about it. Every time I see him, I feel like a traitor. That I'm somehow betraying our family unit in some cruel, unnecessary way; that if Michael was watching over me, he would be disappointed in the person that I have become.' I shrugged, still dabbing at the tears and looking at my sister, who had such compassion and understanding on her face.

'Listen to me,' she said sternly, 'whatever you do with Paul Stone is your business, your problem. It's probably not the best way to fall into a new relationship, and I'm sure you know that the timing is not ideal either, but never think that you owe an explanation to anyone. Michael would be happy that his mum was happy. And anything beyond that isn't important.'

I nodded, and moved back over to the brown envelope and the papers now littering the floor.

'Do you think I should tell Paul about all of this?'

'It's your choice.'

'I can't believe that we may have found out who hurt Michael. I honestly can't thank you enough.'

She waved her hand dismissively, 'Don't be stupid, it's fine! Whatever you do next is up to you, but just be careful OK?'

I stayed for dinner. Alice made pancakes, which we ate with golden syrup and strawberries. It was the best thing I'd had to eat in ages.

*

I only stayed at Alice's for one night. The revelation of Lee Haddison's true identity made it impossible for me to stay any longer. I had wanted to call Paul, then thought better of it, afraid that he would only scold me again for looking into things myself, and continue to warn me to leave the investigation to the professionals. He didn't have any children, so he couldn't possibly begin to understand the urgency and motivation that drove me. I felt compelled to discover who was responsible for hurting Michael, with or without his help. I felt that our relationship, or rather us sleeping together, had altered the way in which Paul looked at me. I was no longer just the victim's family: he cared about me, about my feelings, and as nice as that felt, in a way, I also believed that he was holding back. I could see the way he looked at me. He was unwilling to tell me about developments, or nervous of saying what was on his mind, for fear that I might break down, or even worse, break it off. It had begun to feel as though he was keeping things from me, in order to keep me in his life the way things were; as if lying for my protection would make me cling to him. But he could not have been more mistaken. I didn't need Paul Stone to feel safe, and however nice it was to fall asleep next to someone, feel the warmth of his body, the weight of a man on top of me, my eyes were constantly fixed on the far horizon; the journey with Paul was just the means of getting there.

The train was empty. I took a seat next to the window, carefully moving the empty Styrofoam coffee cups, ignoring the middle-aged woman opposite who continued to stare, a confused look on her face, as if she was trying to place me. Was I a celebrity? Had she seen me on the news? Finally, it came to her, and, horrified, she looked down and pretended to be extremely interested in her magazine. I took out my tablet and started typing up the latest developments. I had already highlighted Lee Haddison as my new number one suspect, and with the fresh evidence that had landed in my lap, I felt convinced that he had done something to his daughter, and possibly to Michael too. My phone vibrated in my pocket, and Paul's name flashed at me from the screen when I took it out to look.

'Yes?'

'I thought we'd agreed that you were going to leave the detective work to me.'

I sighed, not even bothering to question how he knew where I'd been, and if he knew what Alice had discovered on my behalf.

'I thought we'd agreed that you were going to trust me, and stop following me.'

'Please, don't embarrass yourself!' he snapped. He sounded extremely out of sorts, and for the first time since I'd met him, livid.

'What do you want?'

'I don't understand you, Ann.'

Exasperation.

'I'm not having this conversation with you; it's not the right time.'

'It's never the right time.'

'Fine. Come to my house in about an hour; I'll be home by then.'

He grunted, and hung up the phone. I felt a mixture of anger at constantly being questioned and tested and at the same time, a frisson of excitement, that my actions meant something to someone. His anger could only stem from either his annoyance over the case, or his feelings for me. I relaxed back into the seat; the lady opposite me was staring again, but she quickly looked down as soon as I noticed. The train was cold. I wrapped my scarf around my mouth and blew into it, feeling the warm condensation spread up my face. I turned my head into the seat trying to get comfortable, but it smelled of stale coffee, b.o., grease, and the tiniest hint of urine. I gave up.

Paul was already outside when the taxi pulled up to my house. He looked furious. His duffel coat was wet from the snow. He clearly hadn't shaved in a few days, and his grey stubble added to his ruggedness. The twenty year old in me blushed as I got out of the taxi.

'You said an hour.'

'I'm not explaining myself to you!' I snapped, defiantly, and rummaged around for my house key. He followed me up the steps and into the house. It was freezing, but then I never bothered lighting the boiler these days; I flicked the switch, hoping that he wouldn't notice the cold, and praying that the thermostats would kick in, and breathe some life and warmth into the place. The lounge was a mess of papers, photographs, drawings: my own personal memory board. Surprisingly, Paul's face softened a little, as he stepped over my timelines and my endless scribble.

'Quite the Miss Marple we have here!' he drawled sarcastically, as I began collecting my things into a pile. 'No, don't do that.' He put his hand on mine. 'I can't stop you from doing your own research at home. There's nothing illegal about that, yet.' He sat down wearily. I continued to pick up my things.

'I don't need them any more.'

'Really? Why? Have you decided to stop all this nonsense?'

'You really don't know me at all, do you?' I said, without looking up. 'I'm not about to just give up. Whether you like it or not, I have to do this. You don't have any children, you wouldn't understand.'

'That's a cheap shot!' He sat up. 'Don't you remember a few months ago? I thought I had helped you to realise that, contrary to what you believe, I do understand how much this hurts, how determined you are to find out who killed Michael.'

'Helen was your sister, not your son.'

'She was everything to me.'

'OK, so you do understand. And you tried to find out what happened to her.'

'The right way, Ann. I went to school, I trained, I studied, I became a policeman; I didn't just watch a few episodes of Midsomer Murders or Poirot, and start questioning witnesses or suspects.' I ignored him, and continued wildly clearing the floor of all my work, as if the more he talked, the more I was determined to destroy all of it. 'Will you just stop!' He was on his feet, his voice louder. 'What are you doing?'

'I don't need it any more, because I know who did it.'

'What?' He lowered his voice and came closer towards me.

'OK,' I took a breath and looked up at him, 'you're really not going to like this, but Alice hired a private investigator.' Paul groaned, and stumbled into the kitchen, re-emerging with a bottle of vodka, which he took a large gulp from. 'That's not a good idea,' I cautioned.

'It's the only good idea.'

'I thought you were sober.'

He shook his head and lowered the bottle to the floor.

'So tell me what you and Erin Brockovich have discovered, then!'

'Don't patronise me, Paul.'

I handed him the file that Alice had been given by her boyfriend's private investigator and explained, as best I could, what we had found out. I stumbled over my words and found myself apologising and rambling somewhat, while Paul listened and continued to swig from the rapidly-emptying vodka bottle. When I had finished, and after what seemed like an eternity, Paul closed the file and returned it to me. He leaned back in the chair and sighed, rubbing his temples with his fingers. I stayed where I was, sitting on my freezing cold lounge floor, surrounded by papers, waiting for a reaction, for something.

Eventually, Paul put the bottle down, and slid off the chair onto his knees, joining me on the floor. He continued to look at me, his eyes a little red from the drink and fatigue, but also less angry than before. He reached over and tucked a strand of hair behind my ear. I said nothing. He moved a little closer and unbuttoned my shirt, stroked my neck with his hand, then moved it down, caressing me, one thumb circling my nipple, his other hand feeling my jawline. I leaned in and kissed him. I could feel my eyes filling with tears, but I didn't care. All we had done was argue, and shout. I didn't want to be angry any more, I wanted to feel safe with someone, and for someone to be kind to me, for once. He kissed me back, passionately, holding my head with his hands. He unbuttoned the rest of my shirt, and unhooked my bra, his hands travelling across my body, searing my skin. I felt myself crying, letting him continue, as if I needed this release, this merging of pain, and sex and sadness; as if bringing them all together would help in some strange way.

Afterwards, we lay together, with me resting my head on his chest.

'You haven't said anything, since I told you about Alice.' He didn't reply. 'I know you are angry with me.'

'I'm not angry with you, Ann. I suppose I'm more angry at myself. I tried to push you away, rather than let you in. I should have stopped fighting it and always been honest with you, no matter how it made you feel.'

'About what?'

'You have to understand, we get a lot of cases where parents want to help. It's natural to want revenge, to try to figure things out on your own. I see it a lot. But grief is not a good component when investigating a murder. It clouds your judgement and makes you try to rationalise things.' He kissed me again, hard, on the lips. 'But that isn't the case with you.'

'No?'

'You are one of the strongest women I have ever met. You let me in to your darkest moments, without being ashamed of them. I didn't want to involve you, officially, because I wasn't sure how you felt, how I felt, about you...' he trailed off. I sat up.

'So be honest with me now.'

'Two things,' he began, and lit a cigarette. He didn't ask, and I didn't scold him. 'Firstly, Lee Haddison has been our prime suspect for some time now. We're waiting on a warrant to search his house.'

'And secondly?'

'I'm in love with you!'

14 Months Gone

The news of Lee Haddison's arrest spread quickly around Bridehill. Wherever I went that week, whispers, words of sympathy and knowing looks followed.

'It's a small town; people talk,' said my mother, reasonably, as I sat having tea with my parents. Alice had come down for the weekend, and we all felt strangely united, for the first time since Michael's disappearance.

'I don't mind them talking, I just wish they would say whatever they need to say, to my face.'

It had been an increasingly difficult week. On the Monday, Paul had called to let me know that they had got the search warrant for Lee Haddison's house in Wreathwood. I had been waiting, with bated breath, for that moment, convinced, more than ever, that Mr.

Haddison was responsible for my son's and his daughter's deaths. That evening, Paul had turned up at the house. He looked like hell, and clearly hadn't slept. He seemed torn between an instinctive reluctance to be there, and his promise to be open and share everything with me.

'You look sad.' I closed the door behind him and led him down the hall into the kitchen. I had been making dinner: an apple and a gin and tonic.

'It's not good, Ann,' he mumbled.

I immediately began wondering about all the possible outcomes of the search that could not have been good. Was he referring to the lack of an incriminating discovery, or the opposite? I felt sick in the pit of my stomach. Paul sighed, and took a seat at one of the bar stools. Back when Dave and I had been just a couple, we used to use this part of the kitchen as a bar. Dave would make cocktails; Mojitos, Cosmopolitans, Daiquiris, and we would invite over his lecturer friends, sometimes his students, women that he was sleeping with, that at the time I remember finding nauseatingly over-friendly. The memory disappeared as quickly as it came.

'Tell me,' I said, anxiously.

'The team were in there all day. Found nothing at first. Nothing much to search through, really. You were there, you saw how minimalistic that place is.' I nodded, listening intently. 'They were pretty much done. One of the guys was just examining the toilet under the stairs. He checked the tank. It's pretty routine. Most people hiding something, usually bottles of alcohol, hide it there. I should know,' he added, bitterly. I swallowed, suddenly aware of how dry my throat felt. Saliva stuck to the roof of my mouth, and the sinking feeling in my stomach grew stronger. I was powerless to stop it. Paul rested his head in his hands, avoiding my eyes.

'What did they find, Paul?' I realised that I was trembling. After several moments of excruciating silence, he lifted his head.

'Photographs!' he said, finally. He looked as if he was about to cry.

'Of what? Of Michael?'

'Of children. There are hundreds of them, the guys are still going through them at the station, trying to identify as many children as they can.'

'But Michael...' He cut me off:

'I didn't see any pictures of Michael.'

'What is it Paul, what's wrong? What did you see?'

'Oh my god!' he muttered, and rubbed his eyes with the back of his hand. 'I thought I'd seen everything in this job; turns out, I haven't. But I wish I could un-see that.'

'What? What did you see?'

'Photographs of Jenny, and her father, together: explicit photos.' I turned and vomited gin and chunks of half-digested apple into the sink, all over the unwashed pots and the sponge. I stood there, breathing deeply, trying to get a grip on myself.

'That bastard! How could he do that, to his own daughter? How?' I turned around, looking towards Paul for some kind of answer. He simply shrugged.

'I have no idea. I have to go back to the station; I said I'd help finishing up.'

'Paul, you haven't slept, you should stay.'

'Do you really think I can sleep, after the day I've had?' he asked me, in disbelief. 'I'm only here because I promised you that I would fill you in, and I didn't feel like having this conversation over the phone.'

'I appreciate that.'

Paul had gone without another word, and I had been left alone in my kitchen that stank of vomit and despair.

On Tuesday, he had sent me a text informing me of Lee's arrest, warning me not to get involved any further, and to trust him, and that he would take care of everything from now on. They had not found any photographs of Michael, but I figured it was only a matter of time. In fact, I didn't actually know what was worse: there being no photographs, but the killer still being out there, or the reverse? And the lack of photographs couldn't actually erase what had happened, anyway. The whole thing left me feeling nauseous, and extremely anxious. Paul had not been to see me since then, and although I guessed he would be busy questioning Mr. Haddison and building a case against him, I felt nervous without our contact. When he had told me that he loved me, it had been the first time in so many years that I actually believed those words, said out loud to me.

My mother set down some scones on the table. They were warm and soft and smelled of currants and spices. As we sat there in our family kitchen, the four of us, I suddenly realized that it was a week until Michael's birthday, what would have been his seventh. His absence from the table made the lump in my throat grow more solid. No matter how many days, and weeks passed, it still never seemed to get any easier. He would have come out with some mispronounced word or adult expression which would have made us all laugh. I wondered if I would ever truly feel happy again, laugh with genuine laughter, or feel hopeful about the future. I wondered if I would ever forget Michael's face, or if we would recognise each other, when we were finally reunited after so many years apart. I needed strength now, more than ever, for him.

There was a knock at the door, and Paul, without waiting for someone to answer it, walked into the kitchen. He looked his usual harassed self. I wished he would come over to me, stand by my side, stroke my arm, but he kept his distance, leaning instead against the kitchen counter.

'Would you like a scone?' My mother offered him the plate, her face unreadable.

'No thank you. Ann, can we talk?' he said, without looking at me.

'Anything you need to say to me, you can say to my family,' I replied, irritated by his lack of emotion and warmth.

'Fine!' he said, bluntly. 'The press is outside, and at the house too. Please don't give them any comment. I have asked them to move back to the end of the street, but I doubt they will be that respectful. Is there somewhere you can go, where you feel safe, where nobody will think to look for you?'

'Karen's, or yours?' He looked at me angrily, as if he thought I was playing some kind of game with him, daring him to say yes. He didn't take the bait.

'Karen's is fine; I've stationed an officer outside; leave the details with him.' My parents and sister looked back and forth between us, as though it were a game of tennis. Eventually, I said to Paul:

'Actually, I don't really mind the press. I'll just go home, if that's OK.'

'Ann, please don't start...' but I cut him off.

'Legally, can I go home?'

'Yes, but...'

'Then I'd like to. I feel safe there. I don't mind photographs being taken. I have nothing to hide.'

He shrugged, almost as if he had given up.

'Fine.'

'Sorry to interrupt this, this... whatever this is!' interjected my father's voice. 'Inspector Stone, if you don't mind my asking, what exactly is happening? Have you charged Mr. Haddison yet?' Paul's gaze shifted from my defiant stare to my parents and his entire demeanour changed. He became polite and respectful again.

'I was just about to get on to that, Sir, yes. Mr. Haddison has no alibi for either murder.'

'George Young saw someone else take Jennifer,' I interrupted, angrily.

'Thank you, Ann, for your contribution. As I was saying, he has no concrete alibi for the times of either disappearance. We have found photographs implying an abusive father-daughter relationship, amongst other horrific images and videos. I can't tell you any more than that; he will be transferred tomorrow to somewhere more permanent; again, I can't give any details…'

'Thank you, Inspector,' I found myself saying, 'I could have saved you a trip down here, and read that information tomorrow morning in the paper!'

'Ann!' my sister warned, but Paul shook his head.

'It's fine, you're right; I'm sorry to have just turned up unannounced; I should have called first.'

'Yes, do that next time!' I could feel the build-up of anger and frustration growing again. I got up, and left the room, without seeing him out.

Therapy with Doctor Blunt

'Today I want you to share something positive with me.' I listened. 'We spend a lot of our lives concentrating on the negative, and although that is how I make my money, it is not always the most helpful way of moving forward. I want you to choose a positive memory, something that made or makes you really happy. Now, I'd like to begin by sharing something positive with you about my life, if you are interested, that is.' She smiled.

'Of course,' I nodded.

'One of my favourite memories is going to the theatre with my mother when I was a child. We would often go up to London on the train, my mother dressed to the nines, and me wearing a pretty dress, so excited, so happy to accompany her. And I loved the theatre; there is something so fascinatingly overwhelming about it for a child: the intricate costumes and sets, the orchestra, the seats, the crowds; I loved it. My mother was a fan of

Shakespeare, but we would see anything that was showing. I think it was more the fact of the outing, rather than the specific play itself, the sense of occasion, which has stuck in my mind. Whenever I think of that memory, it makes me smile. Getting the train up to London with my mother was such a happy time for me!' Her eyes glazed over, dreamily, as she re-lived the experience, as if she was being taken back there, to those times spent with her mother. Then, as if she had just noticed my presence, she cleared her throat: 'So, what about you? What happy memory do you want to tell me about?' I thought for a moment:

'Well, when I was a little girl, my parents would take my sister and me for walks at the weekend. My dad never got a lot of time off work, but on Sundays he was ours. We would set off in the car, and stop off for sweets at this sweet shop. It smelled of stale smoke and strawberry bonbons.' I laughed at the memory. 'My father always let us choose one thing, and then we would carry on, and go to Epping Forest. It was such a beautiful place: so quiet and wild; full of birds and flowers. I remember these big rhododendrons that lined the path; I remember my sister hiding behind them and jumping out at me; waving sticks around, running, weaving in and out of the bushes, my parents holding hands and walking a little way behind us, happy, in love. I remember thinking that I was so lucky to have this family.' Jane was staring at me, an unreadable look on her face. Was it pity? Jealousy? Understanding? I couldn't tell.

'That's a wonderful memory, Ann. How do you feel when you think back to it?'

'Safe.'

'Safe?'

'As if no-one could hurt me, could break up our family. As long as we were together, everything would be OK.' She checked her watch and scribbled something down.

'Excellent work today, Ann, well done. We will continue next Tuesday.'

'Oh, about that, Jane, I'm taking the car in next week, so I'm afraid I'm going to have to cancel.'

'Are you sure? I am available for house visits in special circumstances. Of course you would have to feel comfortable with me being in your private space.'

'Oh that's brilliant! I had no idea. And no of course not, that's absolutely fine. Hang on a second, let me just give you the directions.' I scrawled a quick sketch of Bridehill on a piece of paper and handed it to her. 'See you next week, and thanks again!'

15 Months Gone

It was 2pm. on a wet Wednesday. I had not left the house in what seemed like weeks, and when I did emerge, I dared the reporters to catch me in an unwashed drunken stupor, but they had seemed to lose interest after the first few days of nothing. I hadn't been 'available for comment', and my father had sneaked me into my house by the back door. I was apparently a mundane disappointment, in an otherwise red-hot case. Paul phoned occasionally, apologising for not dropping by, not wanting to draw attention to me, or to our relationship. I wished he would come. I felt extremely lonely without his visits, but on the other hand, we seemed to disagree on so many levels that it felt nice to miss each other, for once. He filled me in when he could, paranoid at times that someone might be listening in on our conversations; he wasn't always able to talk about the case, or about Lee Haddison. He did confirm, however, that he'd been charged with both murders, and had been refused bail, but other than that, our exchanges were brief and dull. He was often tired, working late at the station, going back and forth to Wreathwood, and liaising with lawyers. We rarely talked about us; about what would happen when this was finally over. The thought hadn't really occurred to me, until it became clear that there might actually be an end to it all, and I wasn't sure whether I had seen Paul, in some sick kind of way, as a means to an end, a tool, to catch a killer so that I could sleep again at night, or did I genuinely feel something for him.

Michael; I hadn't stopped thinking about him since I had woken up that morning, although there was nothing unusual about that; most days I spent remembering specific things about him, episodes from his short life: a picnic in the local park, fighting over the last Babybel, Michael falling from the swings, blood trickling from his knees; combing nits out of his beautiful hair, explaining that it had to be done, and to please sit still. Sticky lollipops in summer, and candy floss at town fairs; I had enough memories to keep me going for now. What worried me was what would happen when I had used them all up. Michael, my eternal five-year old, would never get to create any new ones.

I decided to drive up to the river. This was a strange ritual, and one that Paul had always advised me to stop doing. I would often go up there at night, imagining Michael's terror at being there alone, wandering aimlessly through the trees, trying to find him, sometimes calling his name. I would often get drunk up there, lie on the river bank a few metres from where he had died, crying into the mud, wishing my life away. Other times, I would take a snack up there: a carton of juice, and some strawberry muffins that were Michael's favourite. I would eat in silence, listening to the sound of the river, until the wind had numbed my cheeks and I could no longer feel my fingers. It always struck me hard, that Michael had been so close when he was taken from me. A seventeen-minute drive and I would have been there, my arms wrapped around his body, my kisses covering his face, my warm breath on his frozen hands. I would go over and over this scenario, as if there were some possibility that I could make it happen; that there might be a chance I could go back and change facts, bring back my son, do a little more.

I took Dave's old Beetle that he had left in the garage, to avoid being followed, but the reporters seemed to have all finally disappeared. As I turned the key, Natalie Imbruglia's *Torn* sang out from the one working speaker, and for a couple of minutes, I sat and listened, thinking this was a CD I had made for him years ago, and wondering why it was in the car. I closed my eyes and hummed a little, before a DJ's voice ruined the end of the song, and I realised that it wasn't a CD, just the radio. How could I ever have believed, even for a moment, that

Dave would have been even the tiniest bit sentimental? Naivety still got the better of me, even now.

The grass was slippery, as always, as I made my way up the embankment. The path that led to a shortcut through the trees was muddy, and littered with loose rocks and stones. I stayed on the grass, feeling the ground soft beneath my feet. When I reached the top, the first thing I noticed was just how quiet it was. The last time I had come, with Paul, there had been a storm. The river had overflowed its banks, and the noise had been deafening, but today was like the day after, the calm after everything had been washed away. There was the faintest trickle of water and the occasional murmur of birdsong, but other than that it was hushed and tranquil. I started off in the direction of the trees, bending to avoid the spiky branches, and holding on to the trunks to stop myself from slipping. I sat down, my back against the trunk of a fir tree, the rank smell of the damp, of mud and decaying vegetation overpowering me. I sat there for several minutes, staring ahead of me, down to the rocks below, to where my son's little body had been discovered, where he had met his end.

'Well, baby boy, it's been a busy couple of weeks,' I sighed, picking up jagged stones and tossing them into the water below. 'Auntie Alice came to see mummy, and I've been spending a lot of time with Grandma and Grandad. I wanted to come last week, but it was Mia's birthday, and Karen wanted me to make a cake. She knows it's the only thing I can bake, and I think she wanted me to feel useful, as if there was something I was still good at. Mia had all her friends over, some from your class too, and there was a clown, who, come to think of it, you definitely wouldn't have liked: in fact I'm not even sure any of the children liked him. There was red jelly and vanilla ice-cream, and mini pizzas and hot dogs and turkey twizzlers and loads of other junk that mummy never let you eat. I would have let you eat it all today, though, my sweetest boy. There were games: pass the parcel, pin the tail on the donkey and musical chairs, although some of the kids were way too competitive, so you probably wouldn't have liked that either. Your teacher, Miss Cliff, came along, too. She talked about you, about how you had been coming on in Maths, how you were the fastest runner in the class, and how you always made her smile.

'It's nice that I'm not the only one remembering you. It feels good that other people have these wonderful ways of keeping you with them. Mummy's friend, Paul, that I told you about, has found out who did this to you. There is no actual proof connecting you and him, but apparently he did some awful things to your friend Jenny. Maybe Jenny's with you right now. Anyway, this bad man is going to go to prison for a very long time. I think that will make things a little bit easier for mummy, but we are not completely sure that he did this. Oh, Michael, I wish there was some way for you to reach out to me, to tell me who hurt you. If I could just see him, or know his name. I would do anything. I don't know how much more I can take. The not knowing, and now the knowing but not being sure is killing me. Come on, baby, my handsome little boy...' I stopped, mid-sentence, remembering a phrase that Lee Haddison had used, when I visited his house after Jenny went missing:

'Handsome, blue-eyed, innocent little boy. It breaks my heart.'

My body went cold.

'I'll come back, Michael; mummy's got to go somewhere!'

I scrambled back up the hill, through the trees, and ran down the embankment back to the car, slithering and sliding, losing my balance and skidding to the bottom on mud-covered knees. I got in the car and drove as quickly as I could to the police station, hoping and praying that Paul would be there. I tried calling his mobile, but it went straight to voicemail. I pulled up by the entrance, oblivious to the reporters outside, who appeared excited by my sudden arrival and abandonment of my still-running vehicle.

'Paul!' I shouted, as I ran into the station. A few people looked up, but most ignored me. I could see Paul in his office; he was talking on the phone, the door ajar. 'Paul!' I tried to catch my breath, leaning on the desk for support, wheezing. I was so unfit.

'Ann? Er, Stuart, I'll call you back, OK? Ann, are you all right? What's happened?' I suddenly realised how I must look: two long mud stripes down both legs, my hair wet and full of leaves and grass, my face flushed and tear-stained. He came out from behind the desk. 'What on earth's happened? Are you OK?'

'Paul, you have to listen to me! We are looking at this all wrong; Lee Haddison did not kill Michael, in fact he probably didn't kill Jennifer, either!'

'What are you talking about?'

'He thought Michael had...' I tried to breathe, suddenly aware of the lack of oxygen, feeling my chest close and my head becoming incredibly light. I took a deep breath, and another, trying with every ounce of energy that remained to stay calm, to keep it together. 'He thought Michael had blue eyes.' Paul looked at me as though I was on crack. He blinked and shook his head.

'Ann, have you been drinking?'

'No, Paul, you don't understand. When I went to see him, he said something about how sorry he was that my handsome, blue-eyed boy had died. I just thought he was being sympathetic; I didn't really pick up on it.'

'Ann!'

'Anyone who knows Michael, the first thing they notice about him are his eyes: his dark, warm, round eyes!' I looked at him pleadingly, 'Paul, Lee Haddison has never seen Michael. He's never met Michael.' Paul Stone closed the door to his office gently. He had a strange, patronising look on his face; it incensed me.

'Ann,' he began.

'Why are you not listening to me?' I could feel the frustration mounting, my voice breaking.

'Honestly?'

'Yes honestly, honesty would be great!'

He frowned. 'Because I don't think you are thinking straight.'

'Not thinking straight!' I tried to contain myself, to keep from exploding.

'I think you're only seeing what you want to see.'

'Want to see! Want to see? In what way do you think I would ever want to see this? Any of this!'

'You wanted Dave to be responsible, and you were disappointed when he wasn't.'

'You bastard!' I began, but he continued:

'You are the one who came to me about Lee Haddison, and only after you and Miss Marple had overstepped the line, yet again!' My protests fell silent as he went on: 'And now this! I did everything you asked me to do; I dug as deep as I could possibly go, I finally found the person responsible, and you're still not happy!'

'What on earth are you talking about?'

'You are never going to be satisfied with any answers that you get, any answer that I give you. Even if Lee Haddison confessed to killing your son, you wouldn't accept it!'

'MICHAEL! His name is Michael!'

'Maybe you don't want this to be over after all; maybe you want to feel some purpose, and if it ends, then everything else ends too.'

'Fuck you!' I whispered, unable to look at him. He bent down, his face level with mine.

'Don't you see? Of course you remember Lee Haddison saying that, because it's convenient that he did. The truth is that you have no idea whether or not he met Michael. And so what if he got his eye colour wrong? That's pretty thin, don't you think?'

'He's a paedophile, for god's sake, he targets children, he likes how they look, the colour of their hair, their eyes, the way they dress. He would have known that Michael had brown eyes. He would have seen them, he would have looked into them.'

'I'm afraid I'm going to have to ask you to leave. You need to go home and get some sleep. Take a shower, eat something.' He didn't look at me.

'I thought you cared about me; I thought you had my back.'

'I do, Ann.'

'You don't even know what that means. I honestly thought that you were different. God, how stupid have I been? You are just like the others, another Dave!' I turned to leave and he grabbed my wrist, pulling me back round to face him. I stared at him defiantly: 'Go on, prove me wrong. Or don't. Hit me, if that's what you really want to do.' He leaned in, his eyes sad and angry at the same time.

'Be careful, Ann,' he warned.

'Or what? God I thought I could trust you.'

'So did I!' he spat. 'But I am done protecting you.' He let go of my wrist and moved back to his desk.

'Protecting me?' I repeated, 'Protecting me from what?' He sighed.

'Do you remember where you were when Michael went missing, Ann?'

'What are you implying?' I stared at him, bewildered.

'Do you? Because Dave does!'
I stared at him, my heart pounding.

'What are you talking about?'

'All this time, you want me to be honest with you, when you can't even tell me the truth: where you were when it happened. Jesus, are you even honest with yourself?'

'I was in the living room, watching him play in the front garden...' I began to repeat the same story that I had learnt off by heart. He held up his hand to stop me:

'You were unconscious, drunk on the floor. Dave found you like that, before calling the police.'

'How dare you!'

'Me? How dare I? I have clearly misjudged this situation. I should have charged you with neglect, at the very least! But I protected you, because I believed you, that you were a good person, who only wanted justice for her son.'

'I do want justice for Michael, that's the only thing I want.'

'Then maybe you should start telling the truth.'

I fell helplessly into a chair, shock completely overwhelming me. I tried again to pin a memory to the minutes after I had stood at the window, watching Michael playing outside, but it just went black, every single time. I had to be strong, I could not give in, I had to come clean, call his bluff.

'Fine! Charge me! And another thing: you'll probably want to test every single bottle of alcohol in my house for drugs, because I had a few sips of a drink and then, yes, I must have passed out. So perhaps you should start expanding your list of suspects to include people who might want to drug me, or better still to make me look responsible for something happening to Michael. Don't think it's something that isn't eating me up inside, because it is; If you think for one second that I'm in denial about it, that I could possibly have done something to hurt him, if you really believe that I'm capable of that, then you don't know me at all, and you never did!'

Therapy with Doctor Blunt

'OK, Ann, we are going to start straight away with hypnosis today. Last time we made such progress, and I want to try and get to a specific memory that is making you hold back, something painful or difficult that happened to you, that your brain is forcing you to forget. With trauma, our brains sometimes do not allow us access to these memories, they try to protect us.'

'So is it important that I remember, if my own brain wants to protect me from it?'

'It depends on the memory. I am a firm believer in tackling the problem head on, and getting to the root of the issue, talking about it, healing together, but only, of course, if you are open to this.'

'I am,' I replied.

'Excellent! Now, just like last time, close your eyes and begin to relax. Take a deep breath... and release, and another, breathe and release... allow yourself to relax even more... wonderful, you are doing just perfectly...'

16 Months Gone

Winter merged slowly into spring, yet the weather remained wet and grey, an ongoing metaphor for my unchanging mood. I sat curled up on the sofa at my parents' house, flipping through photo albums, plunging into old memories, trying to pass the time. My parents had never redecorated their house. Bad news, if they ever decided to sell, or when they invited friends for dinner, to be met every time with the same sixties décor: patterned sofas, thick carpets, garish wallpaper. On the other hand, good, in that it was unchanged from my childhood: a constant, and ever-present reminder of the life I had been brought into and the happiness I had known as a girl. Everything was so familiar and homely, everything carried a scent, a memory. A dark stain in the corner of the lounge, partly covered by a ceramic pot, showed where Alice had spilt ketchup as a toddler while watching *Noddy* on TV. The sofa sagged in the middle, its cushions reminding me of all the pillow fights I had had with my sister when we were small. The photographs on the wall showed the happy family that we were, how close, how united. Coming back to my parents' house made me remember all the good times that I had known, and made me forget a little about the pain that had since ensued.

I picked up a large cream-coloured album. My mother, meticulous as ever, had written in ball-point pen along the top: 'Ann and David's wedding 16.09.06'. I turned the page to see my own happy, smiling face looking back at me: 'Eyes and teeth down to the footlights!' as my old choir mistress used to say. There I was, getting ready with my bridesmaids, Karen and Alice, my make-up artist brandishing the tools of her trade, attaching false eyelashes here, straightening or crimping hair there. I remember how, ten minutes before we had to leave, I ran upstairs with Karen and we scrubbed off all the make-up: layers of fixing cream, foundation, powder, blusher, eye shadow and a heavy coat of lipstick, merged together on a baby wipe, dirty and smudged. I remember half-panicking, half-laughing, as Karen tried to redo something simple: just foundation, eye make-up and lip gloss, giggling at how much Dave's mother had spent on that make-up artist, high-fiving each other at our deception.

And here was my father, walking me down the aisle, a mixture of pride and uncertainty on his face; proud of the woman I had become, uncertain as to the kind of life I was about to embark on with Dave. Here were the two of us leaving the church, Karen showering us with confetti, her now ex-husband, Tom, at her side. Karen looked so different, so fresh-faced and in love. Tom really had been her soulmate, her life. Back then she didn't need to drink or smoke to take away the pain of not being with him. They held hands, kissing in the background of other photos, looking at each other with such respect and love. I wondered if Karen had kept any of these pictures, or if she still sat up sometimes at night, drinking her way through bottles of wine and staring sadly at the life she had once had, and the person she missed so badly.

The next page showed the two of us in our wedding car, cream and purple flowers attached with mauve ribbons to the bonnet. In the first picture, we were both waving and smiling to the cameras; even Dave looked excited, happy to be my husband. The second picture had been taken as we were driving away, as if we no longer thought the camera was rolling. I was looking down, perhaps at my manicure that Karen had done for me the night before. Dave was looking out of the window, not at me. It was a foretaste, a premonition, perhaps, of what was to come, I thought, continuing to turn through the pages of our old lives.

Then came the drinks reception, with pink champagne and canapés; our first dance: Lionel Ritchie, *Endless Love*, how ironic! Cutting our three-tiered wedding cake. Speeches. The end of the night, and Dave carrying me up the staircase to our wedding suite. I closed the album. It wasn't especially painful to see the past, just incredibly sad; to remember that day, knowing what had come after. If I had been watching a film, or looking at somebody else's wedding album, I would have believed that here were two people in can't-live-without-each-other love. I would have imagined a fairytale marriage, beautiful children, holidays in the south of France, a future. I realised just how much of a disappointment my life with Dave had been.

'Ann?' My mother's face appeared at the door. 'You OK, my lovely? Oh, looking at the old albums?' She came in and sat down next to me. 'I've kept all of them; they're all in here somewhere.' She put her arm around me and kissed my cheek. 'What are you feeling?'

'Regret,' I replied, simply, putting the albums away, and I turned to take the cup of tea my mother had brought me. 'It's an emotion that I never thought I could relate to. I've always said, no matter what I have done, that I take responsibility for, and accept, that every experience I've had has been part of the learning curve of life.'

'Well, that's true, sweetie; we all make mistakes, or do things that we maybe wish we hadn't, or could change, but that's life, and it doesn't always do any good to regret them.'

'But I do, mum; I regret so much. I regret meeting Dave, regret marrying him, quitting my job, even deciding to have children with him. I regret all of it. All it's given me is pain and suffering, and feelings that I never even knew existed before. I regret a lot of my life, mum.' She pulled my head towards her, and stroked my hair.

'You know, when you and Alice were very little, your father and I went through a bad patch. We were always arguing. It's hard having babies that are close in age. You cried a lot, and then when you were a bit older, Alice would scream with colic, and we never got any sleep. It made your father work a lot more; he would be gone for days on end, on business trips, or staying sometimes with friends. I was often alone here with the two of you. I remember thinking one day: is this it? Is this my life? What happened to the girl I was and the person that I dreamed of becoming? Why wasn't your father there for me? What had I done wrong? How was my marriage and my life failing so badly?'

'You never told me any of that!'

'Because a parent's job is to protect their children, not burden them with their own problems.'

'So what did you do?'

'I spoke to my mother, like she always said I could, and like I have always said that you can. She never judged me, always understood me, and listened, when it seemed that no-one else would. And she gave me some very good advice. She told me to pull myself together; that life was hard. Marriage, and bringing up children were the hardest things that we ever have to go through. That I should understand how hard it was for your father, too, and I should try and set aside one day a week for the two of us, to reconnect, to remember why we fell in love. She told me that I was not a failure, and that I had to just suck it up and move on. That abandoning my marriage was not an option.' My mother looked at me with tears in her eyes. 'And I did just that; I got on with it, and I've been getting on with it ever since. Your life is what you make it. It doesn't do to dwell on the regrets that you have, but rather the wonderful things that came from those bad decisions. Through your marriage you may get to keep Dave's house, through the wedding you got to keep all the presents and these beautiful photographs of you in a size 8 wedding dress, and through deciding to have children, you had Michael. And however painful it is for you now, knowing that those choices resulted in these events will make it easier, with time, and you will look back with happiness at the wonderful years you had as a mother.'

I placed my head in her lap, as she continued to stroke my hair, the two of us holding on to each other. I closed my eyes, and for the first time in several days, slept.

*

I must have slept for several hours, because when I finally woke up, it was dark outside and my father had lit a fire in the lounge. My mother was gone, and I had the old family patchwork throw covering me. I felt warm, and comfortable, and at first, extremely hesitant to leave the safety of this cocoon. I reached for my phone and saw that I had several missed calls from Paul Stone. I sat up, rubbing my eyes, my body guilty from the extra hours of sleep it thought I didn't need. There was a faint knock on the door, and my father came in, carrying some more logs for the fire.

'Hello, love,' he said kindly, putting the logs down by the fire and giving me a squeeze. 'Can I get you anything: tea, water?'

'No thanks, Dad.'

'Right, well, I'll leave you to it then.' He was about to leave when my mother's voice echoed down the hall. She appeared at the door, worry clouding her face.

'Ann, I'm really sorry, I couldn't turn him away; he says it's really important!' she garbled quickly, and before she'd even got the sentence out, Paul was at her side.

'Ann.' He nodded politely at my father and came into the room.

My eyes followed him as he took a seat next to me: a rather brave move, I felt, considering the last time we had seen each other he had been talking of charging me with neglect, and I had called him a bastard. But this seemed to be the course our relationship had taken. He would try to tell me what to do, I would defy him, we would argue, then we'd make up and have sex and the cycle would start again. It was almost as if the sex erased all of the bad stuff and gave us a clean slate, although somehow, I didn't think we'd be doing that this time.

'How have you been?' he asked, stiffly.

'Fine, you?'

'Busy.' He certainly looked it: the usual dark circles underneath his eyes were even more pronounced today, and he looked as if he hadn't shaved since the last time I'd seen him.

'I tried calling you, to let you know I was coming. This really couldn't wait, I'm afraid.'

'Oh?'

'There's been a development: Mr. Haddison won't be facing trial.'

'I see.' It took every ounce of energy in me to stop myself from adding 'I told you so'. I wanted Paul to see a different side of me, one that could be tamed without violence or anger. He seemed surprised by my reply, and looked round at my parents, who were still hovering in the doorway.

'Ann, Lee Haddison has hanged himself. He was found this morning. There had been talk of putting him on suicide watch; it had not been easy for him so far, as you can imagine, given the nature of the charges.' I stayed put, processing what he was saying, a part of me wondering why I didn't feel relieved, or happy. After all, regardless of whether or not he was guilty of hurting Michael, he had committed so many other horrific crimes. Those children and their parents deserved some kind of justice. When I didn't reply, he ploughed on: 'He left a note, a letter of sorts, and he mentions you in it.' Again, he waited for some kind of explosive reaction. I held back, refusing to give him what he seemed to expect. He took out a plastic evidence bag containing a single sheet of white paper and handed it to me. 'You can read it, if you like; I think you should.' I looked down briefly, before handing it back to him. He raised his eyebrows. 'You don't want to read it?'

'I don't need to, Paul. I'm pretty sure I know what it says. He confesses to the sexual abuse of his daughter and other children, but he denies killing his daughter. He wants to apologise to me, if he misled me, and to promise me that he never touched my son. Is that about right?' Paul looked again at my mother, who shrugged apologetically, and then he nodded.

'Yeah. How did you...?' I stood up.

'It doesn't matter, Paul. Perhaps now we can put all this to one side and concentrate on finding out who's really responsible for murdering Michael. I'm not sorry that Mr. Haddison took his own life; judging by what you told me, hell is too good for him, but I don't want to be distracted from finding out who is really to blame.'

He seemed confused, bewildered almost, mixed with maybe a little awe. He had clearly expected me to blow up, to blame him for wasting time while a killer continued to prowl the streets of Bridehill looking for another victim, but I hadn't, and honestly, I didn't blame him at all.

'Oh, and Paul, about arresting me... did you test any of the bottles at my house?'

'Ann,' he began, but I interrupted him again,

'It's fine, I should have known Dave would try and screw me over one last time. The sooner you can rule it out, the faster we find Michael's killer. Honestly, it's fine.'

'I was just angry, Ann. This case is eating away at me, and there never seems to be an end to it...' He looked downcast. 'Anyway, we tested the bottles in your drinks cabinet, like you asked, and all came back negative for possible drugs that would have that kind of effect. If you were drugged, then the person responsible obviously came back and removed the evidence. It's kind of a dead end really.'

He got up and moved over to the door. My father shook his hand and my mother gave him a warm smile. I could tell that she approved of Paul, despite our differences. I led him down the hall to the front door.

'Thank you for coming and telling me in person,' I said.

'I don't think I've ever heard you say 'thank you' before!' His face was inches from mine.

'Thank you!' I said again, and kissed him.

Therapy with Doctor Blunt

'OK, now that you are in a peaceful place, we are going to try and reach in and remove any block to your memory. It is important that you stay calm, and relaxed, and any time you feel the block coming back, take a deep breath and the block will melt away. Remembering is now a priority for you. It is no longer a battle to remember; it is easy and natural for you to remember. OK, let us begin. Where are you, Ann?'

'I'm at university halls, in my room.'

'Are you alone?'

'No, my new boyfriend is here; he is cooking carbonara; it smells good.'

'What is your boyfriend's name?'

'Dave.'

'How did you meet Dave?'

'Working at the Italian restaurant; he's a regular; he asked me out one day.'

'What happens after you have eaten the food?'

'Dave is talking to me while I wash up. He is telling me all about Italy, how he wants to take me there.'

'And then?'

'We are sitting on the floor, playing cards. He tells me how beautiful I am. I know this, but I pretend to be all shy. We are playing whist. It's my favourite card game. I always win, and this makes Dave angry.'

'Does he often get angry with you? Does he have a temper?'

'Just sometimes, usually when we play cards, or I say something that he doesn't like.'

'I see. What is happening now?'

'We are kissing. Dave is very passionate; he tells me I'm sexy; he wants me to do things to him.'

'Like what?'

'I can't say!'

'Ann, what's wrong; you seem afraid?'

'He's angry now. I don't want to stay. I can't remember, it's all black, I don't want to see...'

'It's OK, Ann, you are safe. You have access to the memory, but only if you want it. You can melt away the block and see what happens, but only if you want to.'

'He's taking off his belt. He tells me to bend over. He is whipping me, hard; the buckle of the belt keeps slapping my bare spine; it's so painful.'

'Don't cry, Ann, you are safe, you are with me, you don't need to go on, if you choose not to.'

'I'm bleeding; he throws some tissues at me; then we have sex. It's exhilarating, exciting. I'm in pain, I'm bleeding, but it feels good.'

'You find the pain enjoyable? Sexually exciting?'

'Yes. It's not something I know, but he does.'

'He's done it before?'

'Not with me. With his wife.'

'He's married?'

'Yes. Please, no more.'

'That's OK, Ann, listen to my voice, now, it's time to return to the present; back to reality. I am now going to count from five up to one, and when I get to one... you will be back in the present, in this room with me, OK... 5... 4... 3... 2... 1!'

17 Months Gone

I'd been for drinks with Karen. I had wanted a distraction, and Karen didn't need much persuading to rant about Tom's new girlfriend. If I thought she couldn't possibly be any more cynical, or drink any more alcohol, I was mistaken on both counts; she surpassed my expectations. I sat listening, while she vented about how Tom had lied to her. He'd said their marriage had fallen apart because of circumstances, his job, growing apart, not about another woman, only for Karen to find out that he had been seeing someone for a while.

'It's not about the fact there is someone else,' she'd repeated after her fifth gin and tonic, 'it's the fact that he wasn't honest.'

'Hmm.' I had nodded, humouring her as best I could.

'You know, take Dave, for example: there's a man, about as low as you can possibly find, I mean, no offence, Ann.'

'None taken.'

'But at least he's open about it! There's no bullshit with Dave. He doesn't pretend to be a Romeo to your Juliet.'

'I can't argue there.'

'But Tom sold me the dream, Ann, and I bought it! Every bit of it!'

'It must be hard letting him go.'

'Hard? No! I'm strong; as women, we have to be, don't we? But I just can't take the lies. That's hurtful. That. Is…' She had stopped, as if searching her brain for the appropriate word, and smiling once she had it. 'Wrong!'

'You're right,' I agreed.

'Same again, please!' she shook her empty glass rudely at a passing waiter; the ice cubes rattling against the sides had not even begun to melt yet. I could sense that she was in self-destruct mode, but I knew better than to say it. 'And you know, these women who break up families, they don't care. They don't think about the children left behind, the ex-wives, the families. But I said to Tom, "if you think that I am going to let my children be raised by another woman, you can think again." He wasn't so full of it, after that.' Karen had begun slurring her words, now was a good time to make an exit. I raised my glass:

'Fuck men!'

'Fuck men!'

When I arrived home, it was to find that my front door was unlocked. I distinctly remembered locking it. As I pushed open the door, a memory flooded over me. I was standing in my lounge, by the window, watching Michael outside. He was riding up and down on his bike, collecting dead leaves in his yellow bucket, laughing. Suddenly, the phone rang. I answered it, and a voice floated down the line: a sentence, words, but I couldn't piece them together, they didn't make any sense. I fell to the ground, unable to move, aware that I wanted to, but paralysed, incapable of doing anything. I closed my eyes, and when I opened them I was standing in my doorway, back in the present, trembling from head to toe. The memory had felt real, Michael had seemed so real that I could have reached out and touched him, could have called out to him to come in, saved his life. But it was just a memory, just a faint glimmer of what had happened. I had had a similar one a few months ago: I had remembered that the phone had rung. This time I knew that whatever had been said to me had upset me enough to make me collapse in shock. But what could that person have possibly said to me, to have such an effect? I felt helpless, and frustrated that I couldn't unlock the memory further, find out exactly who had called me, what had been said, and finally, what had happened after I had lost consciousness.

I could hear the kettle boiling in the kitchen. Thinking it was perhaps Paul, I made my way into the back.

'Hi, Ann.' I pulled up short at the sound of his voice. My husband stood there, a mug in each hand, a grim expression on his face. I hadn't seen him in months.

'What are you doing here? And how did you get in?'

'It was open.'

'Don't lie to me; I know it's second nature for you, but please stop it.'

He smirked, and put the mugs down on the wooden counter top.

'I don't want to fight with you.'

'That makes a change. What do you want?'

'To talk.'

'It's a little late for that, don't you think?'

He looked at me for a few seconds and then reached into his bag. He pulled out a folder and passed it to me.

'What the hell is that?'

'The divorce papers. It's official. You are rid of me.'

'Thanks. But you could have posted these. I don't need a sentimental goodbye.'

'Don't you?' he asked, genuinely surprised.

'Not from you.' I said curtly, taking the folder and opening it. There were more papers underneath the initial divorce ones. 'What's this?' I asked, shoving the file back to him. He pointed at the papers, without looking down at them.

'My way of saying sorry,' he said, simply.

'I don't understand.' I was confused.

'The deeds to the house. With your name on. My gift,' he paused, 'to you.'

'And what do you want in return?' I demanded, completely caught off guard by the ease with which he had handed over this house, a house that he had bought thirty years ago with his ex-wife, a house worth a lot of money. Why would he give it to me, no questions asked?

'Nothing.' He smiled at me, but I took a step backwards.

'I don't believe you. Nothing is free with you.'

He took a step towards me.

'I promise. I don't want anything from you. Just to talk, and for you to listen.' I looked at him sceptically.

'I'll give you five minutes, and then I want you out of the house, or I'll call the police.'

'Fair enough.' He shrugged, and pulled up a bar stool. He took a sip of tea. Mine remained undrunk. He was rubbing his hands together, and for the first time I could ever recall, he looked nervous. Nervousness and stress were not characteristics that went hand and hand with Dave's narcissism, but today he looked a little softer than usual. Something else too: he looked sad. 'This isn't easy.'

'You'd better get on with it then. Four minutes.' I said, flatly.

'Jesus, Ann. OK.' He took a deep breath: 'I don't know how our lives became like this,' he began, looking anywhere but at me, 'honestly. I know you think in some weird way I deliberately seduced you, with the intent to destroy you on some level, but that isn't true. When we were first together, I was in love with you. I'm not proud of the things I have done to you, the way I treated you. I can't apologise for the person I am, and I cannot change the past. I like things a certain way, and in the beginning with you, I thought you were the same, like me. But then, as we got older, I realised that you wanted a family, and perhaps I'd made a mistake in marrying you. I couldn't give you what you wanted. I know that, now.'

'So, why are you doing it again, with someone else? Don't you think you should be having this conversation with Helen, explaining to her the kind of man you are, and what you will do to her, eventually.'

'It's just who I am, Ann. I like women. I like new relationships. Helen is young, hopeful. She reminds me a lot of you, when we were first together. And the baby's here, now, so I'm going to try and do the right thing.'

I suppressed a sob.

'We had a baby, Dave!'

'I tried, so hard, to love Michael; honestly, I did. I tried to bond with him, as best I could.'

'You don't try to love your own child!' I shouted across the kitchen at him 'You just do it!'

'I wanted to be his father, and for him to be my son, but I just couldn't be that vulnerable. It's not in my nature, Ann. I tried, so hard.'

'Not hard enough!' I spat, tears blurring my vision. 'And now? Now he's gone, and he's never coming back, and

I'm alone, with nothing. You did this! All of it! You may not have been the one who took him from me, but you sure as hell didn't prevent it!'

'Ann, you're right. I'm here to tell you that you are right. I know all of this.' He was shaking his head from side to side.

'Have you ever cried for him?' I took a step closer, my eyes boring into his.

'What?'

'You heard me. Have you ever been to his grave? Or up to the river, to the place where he died. Have you ever done that?' He shook his head. 'I have nothing to say to you. You disgust me!' I pushed him with both my hands, as hard as I could; he swayed back a little on the stool, but recovered quickly. 'Get out!' I hissed at him.

'I wanted you to know that I'm moving to London with Helen and the baby.'

'I don't care; I don't want to listen to anything else that you have to say.'

'You won't see me ever again. The house is yours.'
I stared at him in disbelief:

'Do you really think that makes it OK? That giving me this house will somehow erase the last fifteen years?'

'I'm trying to make amends.'

'It's not good enough, and it never will be.'

He started to move towards the front door. He looked almost disappointed. Had he expected me to forgive him, welcome him with open arms; a kiss, sex, perhaps?

Nothing was free with Dave, and I couldn't help but wonder what the punishment would eventually be for not accepting his apologies and waving him off to his new life with my blessing. He opened the door and turned towards me, his arm outstretched. He dropped a key into my hand.

'My key. When I found out you'd had the locks changed, I stole one of yours last time I was here; made a copy of it. That's the only one. You don't need to worry about me sneaking in here, or dropping by unannounced.'

'Some honesty. Finally. A little too late, unfortunately.' I put the key on the table, and looked up. He genuinely did look remorseful. 'Oh, and Dave,' I called after him, as he made his way down the steps to the drive. He turned back, looking almost hopeful. 'I won't worry. I'm in a relationship with Inspector Stone, so I believe you when you say you won't try anything.' I smiled a nasty smile at him, before slamming the door, and locking it.

I went straight back to the kitchen, and poured the cup of tea down the sink.

Therapy with Doctor Blunt

'You never told me that you were a masochist, Ann'
I was sitting in Doctor Blunt's white office, feeling sick to my stomach. My reservations about hypnosis had been both confirmed and contradicted at the same time. I had been hopeful that hypnosis was simply psychobabble nonsense, and wary at the same time that it might reveal my deepest secrets unintentionally. This was, in fact, what had happened, and now, sitting here with my psychiatrist, I felt guilt, guilt for not being honest with her about my initial reasons for coming to her, and ashamed of what she must think of me.

'It's not something I talk about,' I said, simply. She nodded.

'Ann, we all have secrets, some greater than others. Some are just that, secrets. They are there to be kept, and only visited when they can be useful. I'm not interested in your sexual activities with your husband. I don't care that you had an affair with a married man; I am not here to judge you, and those details are unimportant to me. What is important is unlocking the door to the past, in order to help you move forward. We wanted to identify why you have such low self-esteem, why you feel unhappy in your marriage, and how you have struggled since becoming a mother. Those were the initial issues that we were supposed to focus on together, and by exploring the past and the events that created it, you can be helped, to change the future if you want to.'

'Of course I want to. It's just... that side of me, it's something that nobody knows, except my husband. I just don't understand how discussing it can help me to change.'

'We all have vices, Ann. There are things that we all know we shouldn't do, and yet through excitement and pleasure, we indulge. I believe that on some level, you do these things with Dave because that is all you have ever known. At the age of twenty-one, you don't necessarily know your own sexual preferences and turn-ons. Had you met a romantic, sensitive man, perhaps you would never have even known that that side of sex existed.'

'So what are you saying?'

'I'm saying that masochism doesn't have to define you. There are ways that you can overcome it, make yourself a better person, a happier and pain-free person.'

'Is that really possible?'

'Of course it is. Your feelings may never truly go away, but the act itself can. You see, masochists need someone to help them pursue their sexual fantasies and pleasures: a sadist.'

'Dave!' I whispered.

'Exactly! Eradicate the sadist in your life, and you can turn everything around. Pain works both ways, and is usually something that requires two people: the giver, and the receiver.'

'So... you think I should leave Dave?'

'I think you have to be open to choices, for yourself, your health, and most importantly, for your son.'

18 Months Gone

I felt a strange sense of freedom and independence following Dave's departure, and although I wasn't taken in by his apologies and excuses, they did give me some form of closure. I wasn't angry with him any more; I guess I had become indifferent to the life we had shared. He had been right: he was incapable of changing the person he was. I should have known that getting involved with a married man in the first place was never going to lead me to a happy ending, and perhaps my mother was right, marrying Dave had given me experiences that I would not have had otherwise.

I spent the following weeks busying myself as best I could. Alice came down for a weekend, and we went shopping together. Her boyfriend had moved in with her, so we had been looking for furniture for her new flat in London. Several days a week, I visited Karen. We would meet for drinks at our local pub, or have sleepovers at mine, when Tom had the kids. We would spend the evenings drinking cheap wine and laughing at old photographs: us at thirteen years old, eyebrows drawn on in thin lines, bright blue eye shadow caked onto our eyelids, and two strands of hair twisted into gelled snakes coiling down our faces; us at the school netball game, and later, at our year eleven prom. We reminisced about our failed marriages, life before the children, and after, and about Michael.

I'd finally gone to Michael's school to collect all his work, that Mrs. Cliff had been saving for me. I had not felt ready to take it home with me; there had never seemed to be a right time. My heart ached as I turned through page after page of paintings, drawings, letters and numbers, the words to a song they had been learning in class, and at the back of the book was Mrs. Cliff's evaluation:

'Michael is a wonderful student, who uplifts and motivates his classmates. He makes everybody laugh, and has a sweet nature. He works hard in every subject, and plays sensibly during break time.'

Underneath in a different-coloured ink it read: 'Michael's warm smile will be sorely missed by all of us here at Bridehill Primary - Kristin'. I hugged the book to my chest; images of Michael working at school, and playing with the other children, flashed before me. I wondered what he might have achieved, had he got to continue his life.

During the last week of April, I went to the theatre with my mother. It was the first time I had been in years, and it felt good to do something other than wallowing in my misery. Afterwards, we went for a cocktail and some food, and then went home, and I slept over in my teenage bed, in my familiar room. I wasn't losing sight of finding out what happened to my son, but rather adjusting to the inevitability of life without him. I had seen Paul a few times, but today he had sent me a rather urgent text, asking me to come over. I never hesitated with Paul, I jumped in the car and set off in the direction of his flat.

When I got there, the door was open, and I found Paul on his hands and knees on the floor of his lounge. The place was an absolute mess. He beckoned me over when I entered; he looked different, excited almost.

'I got your message, what's up?' He was bent over a map of London and the surrounding towns. He pointed to two different locations, I squinted down to read, Roachford and Standen. He was tapping them both with his finger. I looked down at him and shrugged. 'Have you ever been there?'

'Nope,' he replied, 'but I'm going to!'

'Why? What's in Roachford and Standen?' He passed me two sheets of paper that he'd printed off from the local library. They were both short newspaper articles, with similar headlines: 'Girl, Five, in Accidental Drowning' and 'Boy, Five, Found Dead in River'. I skimmed them briefly, and handed them back to him. 'What is this?' I asked, confused. He got to his feet and began pacing back and forth.

'This is a connection.'

'To what exactly? These children's deaths were accidents. What are you getting at?'

'I got to thinking, why did whoever took Michael, take him specifically? Why Michael? It obviously wasn't personal, because he took a girl as well. Serial killers usually don't stop at two, and if the killings were random, then I thought there might have been other cases, in this area, around London, that we weren't aware of.'

'But Paul, these are both confirmed accidental drownings, it says so!'

'And I have to disagree. I've already made some preliminary calls; I'm going to go along there tomorrow, and see what I can find; interview the parents, find out exactly how the children died, and what the circumstances were.'

I considered for a moment.

'I think you're way off here. I think it's great that you are looking for other connections, but this just seems so unlikely!'

'I said I would keep you informed, on what I was doing and where the investigation was taking me. I'm going to go up to London tomorrow and do whatever needs to be done. If there is a link between the four deaths, then I'll find it.'

'OK,' I said, holding my hands up in defeat. 'I'll come with you; I said I'd visit Alice; you can drop me off on your way.'

It was the first time that I had been in a car up to London. I usually took the train, sometimes a bus from Wreathwood, but I had never driven. It was a slightly longer journey, but also more pleasant. Paul took the scenic route, and it was nice to drive through the villages and hamlets that were gone in a flash of colour on the train. When I was a girl, my parents had often brought Alice and me to places like these, for village fêtes, flower shows, cricket matches. I had not been in years, but could still remember the distinctive scents of flowers and Pimms, sun cream and sweat. They were good memories of my childhood summers.

'Ann!' Paul's voice broke into my thoughts.

'Sorry, I was just daydreaming.' I apologised.

'It's a nice drive isn't it?' He turned to look at me quickly, before switching his eyes back to the empty road.

'Beautiful.' I murmured. He reached over and clasped my hand.

'I know you think that you'll never be happy again, Ann,' he began. I didn't reply and he continued: 'I remember several years after Helen died. My mother was so, so sad, every day, as if nothing anyone did could make her smile. We tried, all of us, you know: my father would take her on cruises, and buy her gifts; I knuckled down at school, wanting to make her proud and impress her, for her to see that even though one life had ended, another still thrived, and I was determined to make something of it.' He paused. 'But she never seemed to get over it, it really did break her heart.' I didn't say anything, picturing a young Paul coming home with report cards, bouncing up and down, waiting for a reaction, only to get nothing. 'A part of my mother died with Helen, and it destroyed everything: our family, my parents' marriage, and all my mother's relationships. She went to her grave never finding out who was responsible.'

He stopped talking and wound down the window a little. He lit a cigarette and blew smoke through the crack. Cold air rushed around my neck and I pulled my coat closer around me.

'What are you getting at, Paul?' I asked, eventually.

'Merely that you are nothing like my mother,' he said. 'You're so much stronger than she ever was. Even though all of this is killing you, you are fighting it, which is something she never could do.'

'Does it seem that way to you?'

'I believe it is. I think on some level you know that life has to continue, even without the person you have lost. My mother could never accept that.'

'I don't blame her.'

'But you need to be prepared...' he said, cautiously.

'For...?'

'We might never find out who took Michael.'

'I believe that you will!'

'All the same, Ann, it's a possibility that you have to accept. I'm doing everything I can, everyone is doing everything that they possibly can, but sometimes these things go unsolved. I just want you to know that there is a chance we may never catch him, we may never know...'

I looked away, out of the window, as thatched roofs and church steeples merged into green fields.

'I know,' I whispered.

'I want you to promise me something: that if we don't catch him, if we fail, that it won't change how we feel about each other. That you won't let it destroy the rest of your life, like it did my mother's. That we can be together after all this is over.'

I turned back to him, my eyes shiny with tears,

'I have to know, Paul, I have to...'

'I know, I know you do; but if you don't, if you don't find out, please promise me that our lives will go on...'

'I don't know whether I can.'

I looked at his face, disappointment etched all over it. He stared determinedly at the road, and turned up the radio. I knew he was frustrated with me. He wanted something from me that I couldn't give him. Even now that we were so close to the truth, my focus was solely on that, and nothing else. Paul would always come second.

He had to know that. To avoid any further awkward conversations, or questions that I simply didn't have the answers to, I closed my eyes and pretended to sleep. The car journey made me feel nauseous, but I remained that way until we pulled up outside Alice's new apartment. I stepped out of the car, and Paul leaned over to say goodbye.

'Shall I call you, when I'm coming back?'

'I'll probably just get the train back, I don't know how long I'll be staying.'

'I'd like us to go back together, Ann,' he pushed.

'I'll call you.' I lied, knowing full well that I wouldn't, and we both knew that I would be getting the train back to Bridehill when I was good and ready. I waved as he drove off, walked up the path into a small court, and pressed the buzzer to Alice's apartment.

'So what's the story with you and the handsome detective then?' Alice put the kettle on, determined, after that one lapse, not to give in to my ever-present need for alcohol, unlike Karen, who would inject me with heroin if I asked her to. Alice was much more of a 'tough love' kind of girl; she never humoured my problems, because she had very real ones of her own to deal with. Her MS was a battle that couldn't be won by willpower alone, unlike my drinking, my dark thoughts and my masochism. She was very like my mother in that way. She had no time for weakness or pity, and believed firmly in getting better, as opposed to wallowing in your problems.

I remember when we were children and we both got stuck in a snow drift. We were only little, perhaps seven and five, at the time. We couldn't move, and I remember this overpowering feeling that we were going to die there. Of course I had no real understanding of death as such, but I felt desperate. I knew that if help didn't come, we would be left there all night, in the freezing cold. I had started to cry, to tell Alice that I loved her, that I was sorry for stealing her dolly, that I had hidden it in a purple storage box under our parents' bed. I told her that even though I called her ugly sometimes, I didn't mean it, and that I thought she was beautiful. Alice, on the other hand, despite being younger than me, had told me to be quiet, to pull myself together. She had then screamed and screamed until a farmer had heard her. He helped us out of the snow drift and took us home. We were only a few minutes from our house, but at that age, it had seemed so far, and I had been so frightened, but Alice, she never gave up hope, and she certainly had no time for sentimental goodbyes and last words. That was the amazing thing about my little sister, that no matter how dark and hopeless everything seemed, she managed to see the light at the end of the tunnel, and to fight her way out of any situation.

I think this was one of the reasons that I had felt annoyed by Paul's request for a promise. By asking me to promise that I would move on, if he failed, he was in fact already letting me down. Alice, on the other hand, had said to me that she would do whatever it took to find Michael's killer. She had spent some of her hard-earned savings on a private investigator, she had used her contacts at the newspaper to track down phone numbers and addresses. She had essentially done all the things I had expected Paul to do, and yet here he was, asking me if I could just get on with my life, as if it had all been for nothing. How could he expect me to make that promise, to forget the one role that had meant the most to me in life, the role of a mother?

'What do you mean?' I replied. Alice handed me a cup of tea, strong, but milky, just how I liked it.

'Annie, I know you better than anyone! Mum has told me all about his visits; she said you are always together these days.'

'Did she? I suppose I do see him quite a lot. We are working together on the case.'

She laughed, 'Is that what you call it?'

'I have no reason to call it anything else.'

'Oh come on, give me something; I've been with James for eight years! The most romance I've had this week was James having the courtesy to close the bathroom door while he had a pee! Come on, I'm dying to know some details!' We both giggled, and I sat back on the sofa, sipping my tea.

'OK, fine.' She clapped her hands appreciatively, and sat down next to me. 'We're sort of together, I think. I don't even actually know what we are. We don't really talk about it like that.' She nodded, still listening, hanging off my every word. 'Paul is very discreet; he doesn't really want people to know about us, especially while the case is still open; he thinks it looks...'

'Tacky!' she interrupted, nodding. 'I agree! So, have you slept with him yet?'

'Alice!'

'Oh don't pretend to be coy, we both know you weren't with Dave for his sensitive side!'

'Yes, and yes.' I replied, not looking directly at her.

'And? Good, or bad?'

'Good! Very good. Very different from Dave.'

'Well, Dave is a caveman, anyone can see that!'

'It's very complicated at the moment. We fight a lot, and disagree about almost everything. I want to be open and honest with him, but I feel as if I owe it to Michael to keep my distance. He asked me to promise him that whatever happened in the case, we'd still be together and we'd still feel the same way about each other...' my voice trailed off. Alice held up a hand to stop me.

'Wait a minute, I thought you guys were just having sex! I had no idea this was anything serious!'

I didn't say anything. 'Annie, do you love him?'

'He told me he loves me,' I said, my voice barely audible.

'Oh, my god!' She got to her feet, and began pacing around the room, over-dramatising, as usual. I regretted telling her anything. 'This is huge!'

'It's really not!'

'I had no idea, Ann, honestly; mum just mentioned that you were close. Is your divorce even final yet?'

'It is, actually, for your information. Dave came round the other day with the official paperwork. Not that that would have made a difference anyway. Paul told me he loved me months ago!' I suddenly felt defiant, a need to defend a relationship I hadn't even wanted to admit to.

'Annie, don't you think it's all a little fast? I mean, Paul sounds like a great guy, and a wonderful influence on you, but is it the right time?'

I was aware of feeling incredibly let down by my sister. She, of all people, knew the hell I had been through with Dave, and I found her reaction to be both disproportionate and disappointing.

'I thought you would be happy for me!'

'I am!'

'It doesn't feel like it!'

'I'm always happy and supportive whatever you do, Ann, you know that. I'm just worried that this relationship will cloud your judgement.'

'How so? I haven't taken a minute off the case, not even a minute. I'm more focused than I have ever been! I resent that, Alice!'

She moved back over to the sofa, and took her seat again next to me.

'I'm sorry; I just want you to be aware of what you're doing. Sex is sex, but a relationship is so much more complicated, and I don't want you forgetting what's important.'

'I would never forget my son!' I choked.

'Of course you wouldn't.' She stroked my cheek with her hand.

'I think I love him, Alice; I've never felt that way about anyone before, even Dave, not even at the beginning.'
She hugged me, and we stayed like that for several seconds.

'OK. Let's crack on with things!'

I watched Alice get to her feet and disappear into her office. The new flat she had bought with her partner, James, was a lot bigger than the old one, although it lacked the homely, cosy feel to it that I had loved about her old place. Alice had never been someone who wanted or needed money to be happy. As long as her health care was paid for, she always said that never really needed anything else. She never wore make-up, rarely bought new clothes, and drove the same old car that my father had bought her after she passed her driving test, nine years ago. Her old flat was full of reminders that 'simple was enough': IKEA bookshelves, a second-hand sofa, no TV. Her lounge had always been full of newspaper clippings, her laptop always open, and half-drunk cups of coffee in random places around the room. She would order a Chinese whenever she was hungry, and often went to bed after midnight. In a way, I had always envied her carefree, unorganized lifestyle, perhaps because it reminded me of just how uncomplicated and easy it was, and how difficult yet predictable mine had become.

The new flat was flashy, and expensive; I guessed James had chosen a lot of the up-market décor: a plasma screen plastered to the far wall, a white lacquered bar in the corner, a drinks cabinet full of decanters and expensive liqueurs, that Alice didn't even drink and certainly wouldn't appreciate. There were still the odd touches that showed Alice had contributed, I noticed, looking around: half-burnt candles on the window sill, her University of Liverpool graduation photo, and fluorescent Post-its on every surface. I smiled to myself; it was nice that my sister's personality still showed through the glamour and grandiosity of the new place.

I knew that she only had my best interests at heart. Her questions were not based on anything other than genuine concern for me, and I never doubted her love or her loyalty, to me or our cause. She emerged with a blue ball-point between her teeth, her glasses pushed up on her head, loose strands of hair framing her face. She set down two espressos on the glass coffee table.

'Oops! Let me just get some coasters; James hates it when I leave water rings everywhere!'

'I bet he does!' I muttered, bemused by how my sister could let any man tell her what to do.

'Don't look at me like that,' she said, her back to me. 'I know what you are thinking. I'm making an effort. Compromise is important in a relationship.'

'I agree,' I smiled, taking a coaster from her, and carefully positioning my espresso on top. 'Just don't compromise who you are, that's all.'

She blinked, looking for a second as if she had something to say, then thought better of it, and set her papers down on the table.

'Since you were last here, I've been doing some more work on finding connections between Jenny and Michael. One of my friends at the paper, Rick, an excellent tech guy, in fact he was a hacker before he came to work with us, bit of a geek really, but lovely, and very good at what he does; he's been cross-referencing dark-coloured Land Rovers that were spotted in the area, on both days that the children went missing. Now it's a long list, especially if you bear in mind that Mr. Young said that the car could have been navy or dark green, but I'm fairly confident that it was black; I mean, who would buy a navy-coloured Land Rover, seriously?' She handed me the list.

'These are all the owners of dark-coloured Land Rovers that were in Bridehill and Wreathwood on both days. He then cross referenced those with people with criminal records, which I've then highlighted in yellow. So we are left with a shortlist of thirteen people. Rick is now working on phone records; it will take some time, as he can't do it through the normal channels, for obvious reasons, but he is getting there. We want to see who made phone calls around the time of Michael's disappearance, and if any of those phone calls were made to you. Like I said, it's going to take a little bit longer, but I have complete confidence in Rick.'

'Alice, that's amazing! You have done so well! Paul hasn't even mentioned any of this to me. I mean, I know I don't know exactly what goes on at the station, but this is all really good work; thank you so much, I really mean that!'

She blushed a little, Alice was never one for compliments, and despite being entirely deserving of them, I could tell she was uncomfortable and changed the subject.

'I brought you the pictures that you asked for,' I said, and went into my bag to retrieve several photographs that Paul had taken at Jennifer Haddison's and Michael's funerals, 'although I don't know what you'll find, exactly.'

'Paul just let you have these?' she asked, wide-eyed.

'Oh, god, no! He'd go absolutely mental if he knew I'd taken them. But then again, what he doesn't know...'

'Honesty: good basis for a relationship!' Her voice dripped with sarcasm, but I took it good naturedly.

'Ha! Ha!' I drawled. 'So, tell me, what exactly is it you are looking for?'

'Well, you said that Paul believed the killer might have been present at both funerals, that serial killers enjoy seeing the reactions to their crimes etc. I thought we could have a look and identify people at both funerals, and cross reference those with the Land Rover owners; again, it might not be helpful but it's worth a try!'

I stared at her with a mixture of awe and disbelief,

'You really are incredible, you do know that!'

'You're welcome!' she said, without looking up.

'I seriously don't know what I'd do without you. I...' my voice faltered, 'You were such an incredible Auntie to Michael. He loved you so much. The fact that you want to help me like this, I don't know how I can ever repay you!'

She looked up at me, finally.

'Do you remember when we took that road trip to Leeds? How old were we? I think I was about nineteen.'

'I'd completely forgotten that trip!'

Flashes of open motorway surfaced in my head. We'd stopped for a McDonald's at a service station. I remembered not wanting to go, as I'd just started seeing Dave. He had been angry at me for leaving him that weekend, but I'd gone anyway. Alice wanted us to let our hair down, do something crazy, have some fun. We had stayed at a cheap hotel, visited the German markets, got wasted on a pub crawl, doing shots and drinking cheap rosé, then staggered back at three in the morning. Dave had left me thirty missed calls, and angry voicemail messages. I remember Alice confiscating my phone and refusing to give it back.

'Make him suffer!' she'd laughed, as we grabbed a taxi, and prepared to dance the night away.

'Bitch!' Dave had growled at me the next day. 'Your sister is a fucking bitch!' I should have dumped him then, as soon as he began to give me a glimpse of his true colours, but hope had prevented me.

'What makes you think about that road trip?'

'Well, I don't know whether or not you remember, but on the way home the next day, we were so hungover, probably still a little bit drunk actually! We were talking in the car and saying what we wanted to do with our lives. I said I wanted to be a writer, that I was sure I wanted to write for a newspaper or a magazine. Do you remember what you said?'

I thought back, trying to visualize the car journey, our conversation; it suddenly came to me:

'I wanted to be a mother.'

'Yeah, you did, so much. I got to be a writer, I got to make my dreams come true, and be exactly what I wanted to be. I feel as if you got cheated out of your dream, and I want to make that right!'

'Oh, Alice!' I hugged her tightly, 'It's not your responsibility to do that! You don't owe me anything, and I'm so pleased and proud that you got the life that you wanted!'

She flicked through the photos, occasionally peering at the unsmiling faces, the black clothes and pointless hats.

'There's that bastard, Haddison!' she muttered, leaning in with her magnifying glass. 'Not a tear to be seen.'

'I'm serious, Alice, don't feel like you owe it to me to find out who did this!'

'I don't feel like that at all, Annie, I promise! Oh look at Jennifer's little sister, she's Mia's age isn't she?' I nodded. 'God, no child should ever lose a sibling that young! How do you even explain to her that her sister isn't coming back?' She continued looking through: 'Where is Dave on these? I'm pretty sure I remember seeing him there.'

'He left straight after the service. I had asked him not to be at the house afterwards.'

'Good call! But honestly, Annie, I'm doing this because I want to, you know, Mikey was my little nephew, and I loved him to pieces. I'm doing this because I can, and I want to help.'

'I can't even remember half the people who were there!' I said, looking down at the almost unrecognisable photos of Michael's funeral. 'I'm sure I thanked all these people, but I can't remember; everything was so blurred, so confusing!'

'I think people understood; I mean, you had just lost your son, your priority wasn't sending out thank you cards - oh, my goodness! What on earth's she doing there?'

She had stopped at one of the photos, leaning in with her glass, looking at a face in the background of one of them.

'Who?'

She tapped the photograph with her finger and passed it to me, I looked down, squinting at the tiny face, the blonde bobbed haircut, the immaculate make-up.

'It's my therapist, Jane Blunt. What's wrong Alice, why are you looking at me like that?' Alice's face had paled, and her eyes were wide. 'Alice. How do you know my therapist?'

'What did you call her?'

'Her name's Jane, Jane Blunt; why are you shaking your head?'

'I'm sorry, it's just that I haven't seen that face in a long time. Her name isn't Blunt, Ann, its Bridge, Elizabeth Bridge. She used to be the psychiatrist attached to the children's department at Barts, before she lost her licence.'

'What on earth are you talking about? She's been my therapist for the past seven years.' Alice was frozen to the sofa, staring at me, a look of the utmost horror on her face. 'What are you saying? Why did she lose her licence?'

'Her daughter died, she became unfit to work. One day, she just stopped showing up completely; it was the talk of the hospital.'

I began to feel extremely sick.

'Alice, what do you mean? How did her daughter die?' Alice stared at me, a look of sheer terror in her eyes, and said, in a voice barely above a whisper:

'She drowned.'

*

'You have reached Inspector Paul Stone's phone. Sorry I can't take your call at the minute; just leave me a message, and I'll get back to you.'

'Fuck!'

I had been calling Paul's phone since leaving Alice's, to no avail. I crossed the road blindly, in the direction of the railway station. I tried him again; straight to voicemail:

'Paul, listen to me very carefully. You need to find out if the other children, if the other children who died, or their parents, had been having therapy of any kind. It's of the utmost importance. Please call me back as soon as you get this message!'

Shit! A car swerved, narrowly missing me; I wobbled, one foot on the pavement, trying to regain my balance. It was about 5 pm. I didn't know when the next train back to Bridehill was, just that I needed to get there as quickly as I possibly could. It had started to pour with rain, and I was already completely soaked. I didn't know what we had discovered. I couldn't explain what any of it meant, but I knew that it involved Doctor Blunt, and I knew that if I didn't see her, confront her, get to Paul in time, then another child might be taken, another family's life destroyed.

So many memories and thoughts were flashing through my brain, I felt as if it was going to explode. Jane had been recommended to me by Karen. She had a reputation as a good therapist, but Alice said she had lost her licence nine years ago, two years before I started my therapy sessions with her. This had to be a misunderstanding, there was no way that she could be responsible for hurting those children. She had been to my house; she had loved Michael, *like a son*. The thought made me go cold.

'I had three miscarriages.' She had admitted this to me when I had been pregnant with Michael. God, we had bonded over pregnancy symptoms; she had confessed to me her darkest secrets in the hope of understanding mine. I had believed her; believed that she had never carried a baby to term, had never held her own child, had never felt that mother-child love, but I was wrong, she had done all of those things. What had happened to her daughter? My phone vibrated in my pocket, and, thinking it was Paul, I answered quickly.

'Ann, do you have your iPad with you?' Alice.

'Yes, why?'

'Rick has found an old newspaper article about Elizabeth Bridge, sorry Jane Blunt! I've scanned it and am sending it to your email now.'

'OK.'

'Where are you? Did you get through to Paul?'

'No, he's not answering. I'm waiting for the next train to Bridehill, I'll text you when I get there.'

'Be careful, Ann, don't do anything without speaking to Paul first,' she warned me. I hung up the phone, and logged into my email. I had one new message from Alice's address, with an attachment.

I opened it.

Jane Blunt's face stared back at me from the screen. Her hair was wavy, and a darker blonde than it was now, more natural. She still looked the same, but a sort of less well-groomed version. She didn't have any make-up on, and wasn't wearing her glasses, but it was still definitely her. If I had not spent an hour almost every week for the past seven years in her presence, I perhaps would not have made the connection, but I knew her face by heart: her cool, grey eyes, her small nose, thin lips, usually outlined in red. There was no mistaking her face. I read the text underneath.

Five-year-old girl dies in hospital after falling into swollen river

and being dragged downstream for SEVEN miles

A five-year-old child has died after falling into the Thames earlier this afternoon, in what witnesses described as a horrific accident. The youngster, Lucille Bridge, fell into the upper reaches of the Thames near Standen at around 1pm. A major search and rescue operation was launched and the little girl was recovered from the river, some seven miles downstream, and airlifted to hospital but was declared dead shortly afterwards.

A pupil at Standen Primary School, Lucille was the only child of Doctor Elizabeth Bridge, Resident Psychiatrist with the Paediatric Department at St. Bartholomew's Hospital, London.

It is unclear as to how the child fell into the river, but onlookers said that they were alerted by Mrs. Bridge's cries, as her daughter was swept downstream by the strong current.

Dr. Bridge and her husband have been unavailable for comment, but a source close to the family has said that they are completely devastated. Lucille was an IVF baby, after Dr. Bridge had been told that it was impossible for her to conceive naturally.

A spokesman for the Community Search and Rescue said that this was the ninth case of accidental drowning in the Thames this year alone, and begs the question as to whether or not there are enough safety measures in place. A full investigation into the exact circumstances of the drowning is underway, however it is not being treated as suspicious at this time.

The article continued but I didn't read any more. I was still reeling from the revelation that Doctor Blunt had in fact had a child; a last resort after failed pregnancies and unsuccessful IVF attempts. She had been so happy for me when I had told her that I was pregnant with Michael; she had advised me on how to proceed, had encouraged me to keep the baby. Why? To seek out some kind of warped revenge, to make me suffer the same loss as her? I couldn't make sense of any of it. My phone rang again; this time, to my relief, it was Paul's name flashing on the screen:

'Paul, thank god!'

'I got your message; what's happened, what did Alice find?'

'Listen, I can't tell you everything over the phone right now. Did you do what I asked?'

'About the children?'

'Yes!'

'The first girl, Laura, drowned in the bathtub while her babysitter was downstairs asleep.'

'Asleep?'

'Passed out! They found no drugs or alcohol in her system. She was only young: eighteen, and her parents told me she was extremely stressed about her upcoming A-level exams, so stressed that she had actually been in therapy about it, and had spoken to school counsellors. She had been staying up late and revising. The detective in charge of the case said that he believed that she had just been excessively tired and had fallen asleep. There was no other evidence to contradict that, and he ruled the death as accidental. She had been giving Laura her bath, and had gone downstairs to answer the door, thinking the parents had returned. They found nothing suspicious about it; it was just a tragic accident.'

'And the little boy?'

'The little boy is more complicated. He was missing for a week before the police found him drowned in the river. He loved to swim, and was often at the local pool. It also emerged that he had run away from his parents' house before. The police concluded again that it was accidental. He had run away, and wanted to go swimming. It was a particularly hot summer, he often went swimming with friends and family at the river, apparently.'

'And were they having therapy?'

'The little boy's father saw a therapist once a week; her name was Felicity Sutton. She gave a statement to the police, shortly after his disappearance. She then relocated to the Greater Manchester area. She was never a suspect, so they never followed her up.'

'And the girl, Laura, what about her?'

'No, she had not been in therapy, but she did have more than her fair share of health issues. She had problems with recurrent lung infections, and apparently had a lot of trouble sleeping. She was treated at several different hospitals for obstructive sleep apnoea, a sleep disorder.'

'Where, where was she treated?'

There was a pause, and I could hear him rummaging through his notes,

'Great Ormond Street Hospital, and...' I held my breath... 'St. Bartholomew's'

I said goodbye to Paul, leaving him still in the dark about where I was going, and what I was going to do when I got there, although even now, I wasn't sure myself exactly how I would handle the situation, or what I would find. He seemed edgy, asking me repeatedly to give him a time to meet, an address where he could pick me up so that we could go together, that under no circumstances was I to act without his approval, his go ahead, but I knew, as I made promises that I couldn't keep that, having come this far, I had only revenge and retribution in mind; nothing else mattered, not even Paul.

I was trying to rationalise what was dawning on me as the truth. My therapist, Jane Blunt, my friend, my diary into which I had poured my soul, my very being, for the past seven years, could be a killer! What could she possibly want with my son, with Jennifer Haddison, with the two children that had died before them? What was she looking for? What was her motive? My blood ran cold as I remembered her at my house, fussing over my son, tickling him, complimenting him on his birthday outfit, eating dinner with us. I thought of all the secrets I had confessed to her, all the things we had discussed. And I thought of her always discreetly writing down little notes here and there.

My head suddenly began to throb, and I felt like I was being sucked into a vacuum; lights and colours flashed before my eyes, as I began to see, for the third time, the day that Michael had been taken. I was standing again in the lounge, watching my son playing, listening to his laughter. The phone rang, just as I had remembered the previous times, and I had answered it. I still couldn't make out the voice, or what was said. I tried to listen, to hear the words. It was short, like a poem, perhaps, or a riddle, or the words to a song, maybe. I tried, but could not decipher it before I collapsed, as usual, to the floor. This time, however, I stayed conscious, my head turned towards the plasma screen on the wall that was turned off. Before my eyes closed, I saw a reflection: a car, a big, dark-coloured car. I saw a door open, heard high heels on concrete, and tinkling laughter, then Michael's voice, a door slam, and nothing.

I opened my eyes, and was back on the train. My head felt like I had had one too many of Karen's generously-dosed margaritas, and the memory continued to pulse repeatedly within my brain. This was the first time I had remembered anything after falling to the floor. It made me wonder whether I had really witnessed it, or whether now, knowing what I knew, my brain wanted me to put a name to a face. The memory sent chills down my spine. I looked at my watch, fully aware that I had another three stops until I was back in Bridehill, and then I had to pick my car up. I couldn't concentrate. My hands were clammy and sore from rubbing them together nervously. I wanted a drink, I wanted a cigarette, and I wanted more than anything to get to Greensworth as quickly as I possibly could. The memory had already started to fade; it felt like a *déjà vu* moment; at the time, it had seemed concrete and so real, yet in a matter of minutes, it was floating further and further away from me. But there was something incredibly real about the memory; something which I could not have mistaken or made up. It was the high-pitched, tinkling laughter, laughter that I had heard every week, sitting on a white leather couch, being made to look into a mirror. Laughter that belonged to Jane Blunt.

*

The train pulled into Bridehill station a little after 7pm. It was drizzling now, and I ran with my hood up, as quickly as I could, across the empty car park. It was so cold, I could barely feel my fingers to turn the key, and each time I tried, the car made a choking sound. I tried again: three, four times; perhaps this was some kind of warning: the universe telling me that I really should wait for Paul, that going anywhere after dark in search of a killer was a horribly bad idea. But if that were true and the universe or God was trying to send some kind of message, then they could both go to hell! Where was their protection, their warning when Michael was taken, and killed? Where was their help then, when I really needed it? No, this was something that I had to do alone. I had nothing to lose. What more can someone take from you, when you have already lost everything that you hold dearest?

On the fifth turn of the key, the car made a growl, a bark, and finally woke up. Smoke billowed from the exhaust as it started up, and Barbara Streisand's voice belted out of the speakers. I hastily turned off the stereo, and pulled out of the station car park. As I drove along the main street, past Suntae's place, past the police station and the school, I could see my son running behind me, waving. This was it! He knew it, and I knew it!

I turned off my phone, and removed the sim card and threw it out of the window.

Gone

It was a road that I knew by heart. Blind, I could find my way. The twists and corners seemed natural, naturally etched in my memory. My hand knew how to turn the wheel, which gear to use, my foot when to brake. My heart achingly remembered the way. Over the past year I had driven maybe twenty times, fifty, a hundred. I lost count, along the expanse of grey concrete. I never found solace coming here; it became more of a ritual, a rite, a date in my diary that must always be kept. As if returning to the place where Michael died would bring him back somehow; would fill some part of the gaping hole in my embittered heart; replace pain and loss with some form of memory and love. And each time I sat in my car, making the seventeen minute drive to the end of my world, the answer seemed cruelly so much further away. Seventeen minutes, seventeen lonely minutes between truth and lies, seventeen minutes of asking myself what I could have done, how much my baby suffered, for what cause, and at whose hand. Until tonight. Tonight I'm going to find out everything. If it breaks me, if it kills me, I will know what happened to my son, and this will be the last time I make this drive.

Instead of continuing on to the river, I turned right, in the direction of Greensworth. The houses eventually faded away against the black backdrop of invisible fields and country lanes. The rain had started to pick up again, and I could barely see the road. Not that it mattered. I knew exactly where I was going; the only real question was, what would I find when I got there? I became increasingly aware of the minutes ticking away, knowing that I was so close to the answers that I had been seeking for nearly two years. Why me? Why Michael? Why had our lives been selected to be ruined? What possible reasons could there be for wanting to hurt somebody so gentle, so sweet as my lovable little boy. I wanted to do him justice, I wanted to face his killer, and to make that person pay for doing this to us; but not before explaining why.

When Michael had been about two years old, he had toddled out onto the road. Our front garden did not have a fence or a gate and the cul-de-sac was never busy, or particularly dangerous, but the steps were steep. I remember shouting out for him, my heart dropping into the pit of my stomach, when I realised he wasn't where I had left him. I had been in the kitchen making ice lollies for the two of us, and I ran out and down into the road after him, terrified of what could have happened and what I might find. I always imagined the worst-case scenario, and I remember feeling so relieved when I discovered him just sitting on the pavement, playing with stones and stroking the neighbour's cat. I remember vividly thinking to myself how lucky I was that he had come to no harm, and that I would never take my eyes off him again. Yet here we were, nearly two years since Michael's life had ended, and I finally understood the reason I couldn't move on, the reason that I couldn't forgive myself for letting what happened, happen.

Michael hadn't asked to be born. He didn't necessarily want to be here, but I had made that choice, alone, to bring him into the world, on the condition that I would do everything in my power to make him happy, to give him the most perfect life that he could have. I had quit my job, and stayed married to a horrific man, in order to have a child and become a mother, but it wasn't enough; I simply could not protect him from the inevitable. I finally realised that this wasn't a random incident that could have been prevented by getting a locksmith in, having a police patrol car outside the house, or enhanced vigilance on my part. It couldn't have been stopped by us moving away, changing our names and living anonymously. Michael's death had already been decided. Like Jennifer Haddison's. Like Laura Booth's, and Thomas Bailey's. We never stood a chance, and just as I finally understood that terribly crushing but vitally important fact, I pulled into Jane Blunt's driveway.

The outside light clicked on as soon as I stepped out of the car. Inside, the lounge light was off, but I could see the flickering glow of a television set. I rang the doorbell. Jane answered the door immediately, her glasses on, her lipstick in place. Had she been expecting me?

'Ann!' She looked somewhat confused. 'Did we have an emergency appointment?' She opened her diary and moved down the page with a long, French-manicured fingernail.

'No,' I said, unsmiling. I had a sudden urge to scratch her eyes out. 'I was just in the area, passing by. I've been thinking a lot about Michael, and I really wanted to talk to someone. You seemed to be the obvious choice.'

She smiled her usual Jane Blunt smile, although in light of what I now knew, it seemed plastic, artificial, and incredibly cruel, and just for a second, it faltered, as if she sensed that something was wrong; but in the flash of headlights from a passing car, the look had disappeared, and she had recovered her sphinx-like expression.

'Of course, please come in.' I followed her down the cream hallway into her black and ivory tiled kitchen. 'I'm sorry, it's a bit of a mess; I wasn't expecting any visitors at this time. Not that I mind you dropping by, at all; you are always welcome here, Ann.'

I didn't reply; I couldn't take my eyes off the room; My glance took in every piece of furniture, every bowl, every picture, looking for some kind of evidence of Michael's presence. How long had he spent here, I wondered? How long had this woman kept my son from me in this place? How many days had he suffered here, while she continued to see me weekly in our therapy sessions? What had he seen? What food had she given him? What had they talked about? I felt cold; sick; unable to look her directly in the eye, for fear that she would read what I was thinking.

'Are you all right, Ann? You look as if you have seen a ghost?' Her soft voice bounced off the walls, and she continued to fix me with the same eerie smile. 'Coffee, tea? I can't offer you wine, unfortunately, as it is against my principles; one never fully recovers from alcoholism.'

'I'm fine, thank you.' I murmured.
She turned her back to me, and began busying herself with boiling the kettle and taking a cup down from the shelf, choosing a tea bag, a teaspoon; everything over-elaborate and unnecessary.

'Tea always brings out the best in people.' she said, almost to herself, her back still turned.

'I said I didn't want anything, but thank you.'
She turned back to me and handed me the cup of brewing tea:

'You are forgetting my profession, Ann,' she laughed, silkily. 'It is my job to interpret those feelings and desires that you are unable to communicate verbally to me. So, you say you don't want a cup.' She winked at me, and I felt like I was about to throw up over her marble counter top. 'But I believe that you do!' She added a dash of milk and turned back round.

I hadn't come here with a specific intent. In fact, I had no idea what I was going to do; but as if in answer to my sub-conscious longing, I suddenly noticed a small paring knife on the work surface, its blade glinting under the harsh beams of the kitchen spotlights. Doctor Blunt still had her back to me, and was now making an espresso for herself. In one smooth motion, I reached for the knife, and pushed it up into my sleeve. Jane turned back to face me. 'So, what was it that you wanted to talk to me about, again?'

'My son.' I whispered murderously.

'You seem very aggressive tonight, Ann. Have you been drinking?' Her head was cocked to one side.

'No.'

'I realise that sometimes it is hard for you to channel your hurt and upset, and expressing those feelings can sometimes lead to frustration, anger, even guilt; but you mustn't take it out on those around you; we've been over this: aggression is a hindrance to the healing process. Oh, I almost forgot: biscuits!' She clicked her fingers, as if filming some sort of kitchen advert on an invisible camera, and turned back round again to reach up to the top shelf.

Now was my opportunity. I was convinced now, more than ever, that she was responsible. I was going to make her pay for what she had done; I was going to cut through her body with the serrated knife and watch her bleed to death. I was going to wipe that lipsticked smile off her fucking face, and I was going to enjoy it. I lunged forward, the knife poised in my hand, when suddenly she turned to look at me, her grey eyes colder than ice.

'Now, now, Ann, what do you think you are going to do with that?' And before I could think, she grabbed me by the hair and slammed my face down onto the work surface. I was momentarily aware of the clattering sound made by the knife as it hit the tiled floor, before I lost consciousness completely.

*

When I came to, it took me a few seconds to realise where I was, and as the room gradually came into focus, I could see, from the duck-egg blue tiles, that I must be in Jane's bathroom. I could smell ammonia; it stung my eyes. I tried to itch my nose, but found that my hands were bound behind me with something. As I rubbed them together, I could hear a scratching sound, indicating that it was an industrial masking tape of some kind, such as you would use to protect the skirting board when painting a room. A sock had been stuffed into my open mouth, and as I tried to move my feet, I realised that it was one of my own.

'Wakey wakey!' Jane's sing-song voice floated through the air, and as everything finally became sharp and clear, I saw the doctor, sitting on a chair facing me, her notebook and pen in her hand. She leaned forward and removed the sock. 'Hello, again, Ann. Now, let's start the session, shall we?'

'How did you know that I knew?' I asked, quietly, but with my voice full of hate. She laughed, that high-pitched, tinkling sound, and crossed her legs.

'Ann, do you want to know why you are such an excellent patient?' I didn't reply. 'Because you are a terrible liar, and an open book. Even from our very first meeting together, I knew more about you than probably those closest to you.'

'I doubt that!' I spat.

'It's true. You might not want it to be, but it is. What you told me in our sessions wasn't really of any importance, well to you it might have been, it might even have helped you a little bit,' she paused, and smiled to herself, 'but for me, the goal was never really getting you to admit to anything. I could see everything that I needed to see just by looking at you, interpreting your words, and seeing your emotions. From our very first session together, you were so relaxed, your defences completely down with me; it made everything so easy, and of course it made you the perfect candidate for hypnosis.'

She caught me off guard.

'Hypnosis? What has that got to do with any of this? I don't understand.'

'Oh, you will,' she smiled. 'Very soon, you will understand everything.' She continued to stare at me, her eyes boring into mine, her expression unwavering. 'So, Ann, you wanted to find out tonight,' her voice switched back into her professional one, 'about Michael; is that correct?'

'Don't you dare say his name!'

'Tut, tut, defensive as always. You need to learn to be respectful, especially if you want to know what I think you want to know.'

I glared at her murderously.

'Now, this is how it's going to go: you are going to behave, you are going to be respectful, and you are going to answer my questions, honestly and truthfully, unlike in the past, when you always talked yourself around the subject, tried to make excuses for your behaviour, and lied constantly about your feelings. Today, you are going to be honest.'

'And why the hell would I tell you anything?'

'Because if you want to know what happened to Michael, I suggest you do exactly as I say.'

I didn't reply, but instead, looked around the room for an exit, a way out, for something I could use to cut through the binding on my hands.

'I will take your silence as a yes.' She uncrossed her legs, and flipped through her notebook, the same one she had always had with her during our sessions, during which I remembered always wondering what things she had written about me, what words she had used to describe me, how she had categorised me. 'So, question one: why did you have a baby?'

I looked at her in disbelief,

'Why did I....? What do you mean?'

She leaned forward, her face inches from mine,

'Answer the fucking question!'

'I... I...'

'Truthfully!' she hissed.

I closed my eyes, thinking back to all those years ago, to my relationship with Dave, to our wedding, to Karen's children being born, to my road trip with Alice.

'I always wanted to be a mother. It's what I wanted to be.'

She leaned back, glaring at me.

'Good. Now you can ask me something.' She smiled, and I felt sick.

'Same question.' I snarled, and she blinked; I had clearly not asked her what she had hoped I would.

'Don't try and outsmart me, Ann, it isn't a good idea, especially when I am the one with a knife and a bathtub full of water.' She paused. 'But I will humour you, this once. Having a baby for me was the key to survival; it was the one thing I wanted in this world more than anything else. I had succeeded in every possible aspect of life: I was married to a wonderful man, had a dream job, a successful career. It was my time. Time for me to have the child that I knew I deserved, and that I, unlike you, would welcome into a family that would love and always cherish it. But it was sadly not meant to be; we tried many times.'

'You said you had three miscarriages.'

'Do not interrupt me again! As I was saying, we tried many times; I had many early miscarriages, and three second trimester miscarriages.' Her eyes looked glassy:

'Do you know what it is like to lose a baby at six months, Ann?'

'I...'

'Thought not!' she snapped. 'It's classed as a stillbirth, these days, because you give birth to your dead baby. You lie in a hospital bed, waiting to hear your baby's heartbeat, only for the doctor to tell you that there isn't one, that even though you thought you were out of the danger zone, you weren't; that you will have to go through labour, but not take a baby home at the end of it, to the nursery that you have decorated and equipped, and with a stencilled name on the wall above the cot!' The words stuck in her throat. 'But then came Lucille, our IVF miracle. She helped me to fulfil my destiny. She was perfect in every single way. I had a baby because it was what I was meant to do, be a mother.' We both sat in silence for several moments. 'Now, question two. How did you feel about bringing a child into your relationship with your husband? And don't lie to me, because I will know.'

'I felt scared. I knew that it was... not the best choice.'

'Don't skirt around the question! I want facts; I want you to be honest!'

'Fine! I knew it was wrong. I should have had a baby with someone else. I should have fixed my problems, healed properly, before bringing a baby into the world.'

'Ah, thank you. But you didn't, why not?'

'I didn't want to wait; I wanted a baby so badly, I was prepared to... to...'

'Go on...'

'I was prepared to take the risk.' I said quietly, without looking up.

'Finally, some truth. You admit you were impatient and selfish, and in being so, you gave birth to a child, knowing that he was in potential danger, every single day of his life, in that house with you and his father! What kind of a mother does that?'

She got up and began to pace around in front of me; her mask was slowly beginning to slip, and I could see the anger and resentment that lay beneath. She noticed this too, and took several deep breaths, before sitting back down, calmly.

'Your turn.'

'Why did you take my son?'

'What a waste, Ann. Is that a rhetorical question? I took Michael to save him! How can you not see that? His life was in danger; you never really loved him the way a mother should love her own child, you only saw him as a thing, a possession. You needed your life with Dave; it was a vital part of you; you couldn't give it up, even for your own child. That's why, Ann, that's why. I'll let you have another question, as that one was far too easy!'

'What did the other parents do wrong? Why were they special?'

She looked at me strangely for a second or two:

'My, my, we have been busy, haven't we? So you know about them? About the others?'

'Laura, Tommy, Jennifer. Yes, I know.'

'Interesting. They were all replacements.'

'For Lucille?'

'Lucille, she was the sweetest little girl. I loved her, with a real mother's love. I would have given my life for her, made sacrifices that you couldn't even begin to understand, never mind make. When I lost her, I lost everything: my destiny, my purpose, my husband, even my job! I had to find something to do, something that would give me a new purpose, something useful. I wanted to save children who had never been given the chance that Lucille had.'

'But you killed them?'

I couldn't help myself, and before I knew it, Jane's face was level with mine again, her nose almost touching mine, a look of pure evil in her eyes.

'Watch your fucking mouth! I released them. I saved them. Don't you see it yet? Laura; her mother preferred a crack pipe to looking after her own daughter. Tommy's father used him as a punching bag, every day! And don't even get me started on Jennifer's sick father, do you have any idea what he did to her? Do you?' I nodded, withering in my chair. 'He raped her! He raped her, repeatedly, did things to her that you can't even begin to imagine. I had to save her, I had no choice!'

'Her mother was innocent, Jane! Her mother loved her; there were other ways to help her, to free her, you didn't have to hurt her!'

'What do you know about any of it? I offered love, warmth, freedom and a new home to all of those beautiful babies but...' she hesitated. 'No, my turn. Did you stop drinking, after Michael was born?'

I stared at her for a moment, before answering.

'No.' I whispered.

'And? No... no... no, what?'

'No, I continued to drink heavily, sometimes during the day.'

'When Michael was at home?'

'Sometimes.'

'When you drove Michael to school?' I nodded. 'I can't hear you! Speak up!'

'Yes, sometimes I would drink before taking him to school.'

'And you ask me why I took your son. What kind of a mother are you?' She smiled, triumphantly.

I sat there, my head down, thinking about what she was saying. Had I truly not deserved Michael? Had I been such a bad mother that I merited what came to me. I couldn't believe it to be true, yet what she said made sense. I had, against my own better judgement, stayed with Dave, in order to bring into the world a child that I couldn't possibly protect, with my vices and lifestyle choices. Was there some truth about what she was saying?

'Ann, your turn.'

I looked up at her finally, considering her for just a few moments. There was only one question that really needed to be answered, only one more question that I had to know the answer to, even if it meant losing my life afterwards. I knew she would never let me leave here alive, and I couldn't die not knowing.

'What happened to Michael?'

'Tut, tut, so unimaginative; I can read you like a book; but then again, that is what makes you such a good patient. Very well, I'll tell you what happened. I took Michael from your front garden, from right under your nose,' she sneered. 'You were busy pouring yourself another gin and tonic, vodka soda, wine spritzer, or whatever it is that you mix your poison with to disguise it, and pretend to the world it's just the cocktail hour. Michael came easily. He knew me, recognised me. It's amazing how naive and gullible children can be, even when they are taught not to be.'

I suppressed a sob, thinking back to the all the times that I had warned Michael about never getting into a car, or going off with a stranger, about always refusing snacks and sweets, if offered, and to only go with someone that he knew, or that mummy knew. Poor baby, he had done just that; after all, Jane was practically a family friend, my therapist, a woman who had entered my house and drunk my coffee, somebody safe.

'We came here, and I showed Michael his new bedroom. I had spent a long time decorating it; I had chosen the wallpaper covered in cars and trucks. I wanted him to feel safe in his new home. He asked if you were joining us and I told him that you would be coming soon. He believed me, and guess what, I think he almost forgot about you for the rest of the evening. He played on a Playstation that I had bought for him, he ate chicken nuggets for tea and I let him drink Pepsi.'

'All the things that I refused him...' I whispered.

'Of course! I wanted to indulge him, to show him that I would spoil him and give him exactly what he wanted, and he almost bought it.'

'Almost?'

'I had forgotten one very important thing; silly of me, really, knowing the kind of woman you are, I should have realised you would have been over-sentimental with the boy. Can you guess what I'm talking about?' she taunted, cruelly. I nodded:

'Bear Bear.'

'Bear Bear! Damn it, yes!', she said, slamming her hand on the window sill. 'Why did I not think to bring Bear Bear. I wasn't sure; I had planned so carefully but not carefully enough, so it proved.' My heart began to hammer in my chest. 'He was heartbroken, distraught. Sobbing into his pillow: "I want Bear Bear!" She mimicked Michael, in a high-pitched voice, and I wanted to slit her throat. 'Just like the others, never happy enough with a new home, a sanctuary where they could really be loved and protected.'

'Wait a second!' A thought suddenly occurred to me. 'Is that why you asked me to bring Bear Bear to one of our sessions? What did you think, that I would actually let you go home with him?'

'Perhaps. It was clear that there was no way that I could get you to part with it, but it made no difference anyway. I had already begun to realise that Michael was not the one. He had become unappreciative, disrespectful, and constantly whining for his mother!'

'He was five!' I pleaded with her. 'Five years old! Just a child! He wouldn't even have known what unappreciative meant! Please, Jane, you have to see, all this, all of it, is just crazy!'

'I told you not to interrupt me again. Be quiet, you're so close to the truth now, don't spoil it, or you'll be meeting your end before you know all of it!' she said menacingly. 'Now, where was I? Oh, yes, he was becoming tiresome. It was disappointing really, after all the meticulous planning and preparation. I had truly believed that choosing the child of a "friend", and waiting patiently in the wings, would be the answer I had been looking for. I really believed that Michael was the one. But after a few weeks, I knew that it could never work out.'

'What did you do to my son?' My face was wet with tears. 'Please, tell me.'

'I'm going to do more than that, Ann; I'm going to show you!' and she leaned in so close that I could smell her breath: 'Hell is empty, and all the devils are here.'

As she whispered these words, a memory flashed again before me: a memory that was becoming clearer each time: the memory of the moment that Michael was taken. The phone rang again; I answered it, and this time, I heard quite clearly, Jane Blunt's silky voice on the other end of the line:

'Hell is empty, and all the devils are here.'
And then I fell again to the floor, unable to move, my eyes open for a second to see the reflection of the car, hear the tap-tapping of high heels, Michael's voice, the tinkling laughter, the slamming of the car door, and then, as now, everything was plunged into darkness.

*

When I came to, the first thing that I was aware of was the cold, and then the rushing sounds of the swollen river. It was still raining, and I could feel the drops on my face. It was dark, but I could make out the dim glow of a flashlight.

'Hello again, Ann.' Jane's voice came from somewhere above me. 'Welcome back!'

And then I felt myself being pulled along the wet earth. She must have been hauling me along the river bank; my head knocked against small rocks; I felt twigs and small branches scratch the sides of my face, and I closed my eyes. She continued to drag me for another twenty yards or so. My head began to throb, and my feet hurt. She then propped me up against a tree, overlooking the river. I knew where we were. It was a place that I had visited so often over the past two years: a place where I came to talk to my son, to share confidences with him, to tell him how I missed him. My hands and feet were still bound, and my leg was bleeding. Jane Blunt was sitting opposite me. When she seemed satisfied that I had completely regained consciousness, she untied my feet.

'Let's make you a little more comfortable, shall we? Now, the thing that most people underestimate about intelligent killers, like myself, is that I do not require tools to inflict pain. I don't need knives or guns. I didn't even really need to knock you out back in my kitchen before, but it felt appropriate, and you had become tiresome. I have so longed to do that to you, for some time now.'

'The feeling is mutual,' I muttered, venomously.

'I can only imagine. Anyway the point is, with people like yourself: weak and open, the power of hypnosis goes much further than simply extracting memories and revealing secrets; it extends far further than the four walls of my office. And what you didn't realise, while you were with me, week after week, was that I was planting a suggestion in your brain: something that would have the effect I desired, with the utterance of a simple phrase.'

'Hell is empty, and all the devils...' I repeated slowly, stopping just in time.

'Yes!' She nodded appreciatively and continued. 'Yes, exactly! I planted the suggestion that on hearing those words, you would fall to the ground, and sleep. You remember how much I like Shakespeare, don't you? It's from *The Tempest*, and so apt, don't you think? Anyway, it worked wonderfully, in fact you are only the second person that I have successfully sent to sleep using this technique; the other was...'

'Laura's babysitter,' I finished. She actually looked impressed.

'I should have given your sister, Alice, more credit; she's clearly been hard at work on your behalf. So, do you have any more questions, any final words?'

'Why did you remove the shoes?'

'I'm sorry?'

'I never understood why Michael's and Jennifer's shoes were not found with their bodies?'

'Oh, I thought you would know the answer to that? I wanted to give them a chance; I wanted to give Michael a last chance to prove that he could be my son, and that I could be his mother. He kept saying he would do anything to go home, that he wouldn't tell, that he just wanted... you! So I gave him the opportunity, but I had to make it a little difficult, of course. I hadn't expected him to be so quick, even barefoot, at his age. I had to drive quite a way upstream to find him; he had got quite far, just not far enough.'

'You evil bitch! How could you? How could you do that to a little boy?'

'It is not wise to criticise me, Ann, especially given your current situation, and our location.' She indicated the swollen river below. 'Michael and Jennifer were both given the chance to go to home, but they failed to take it. I believe, subconsciously, that they wanted to stay with me. They wanted to be freed, safe, forever. I granted them their wishes,' she concluded. I felt numb all over.

'Just get on with it!' I said, finally. 'Do whatever it is you need to do.' I felt so tired, as if the adrenaline from all of it: losing Michael, the last two years, being rid of Dave, was finally wearing off; as if the sleeping pill had finally kicked in, and the insomnia was over. I knew the truth, and nothing else could change it now. I was at peace with all of it, and I had nothing left to live for. I was ready to join my son.

Jane led me down the embankment and gave me a push, which sent me sprawling head first into the shallows. I felt my head hit something, and then a warm trickling sensation on my forehead. The water felt cold and almost welcoming.

'I'm not sorry, Ann. I have no choice but to kill you. What alternative do I have? Perhaps you will have a second chance in another life, to be the mother you thought you wanted to be.'

And she pushed my head under the water. I didn't move, didn't try to stop the water entering my nose and mouth; I gulped it in, inhaled it. I wanted everything to be over. I closed my eyes, waiting for the release of death to come... but it didn't, and I was suddenly aware that Jane's grip was loosening. I began to feel light-headed, but my senses were heightened. I could hear voices, muffled above the water, but they were fading as quickly as they began. Suddenly, I felt hands on me, pulling me up, someone falling into the water beside me. I became aware of flashing lights and murmuring voices all around me.

'Ann, can you hear me? Ann, are you OK?'

Paul Stone's warm voice forced me to open my eyes. The woods were full of police, I could make out cars parked at the top of the embankment. Paul's arms were round me, and next to me lay Jane Blunt.

'Is she...'

'Dead? No, unconscious. I need assistance down here!' he shouted up to the paramedics.

'I'm fine,' I mumbled.

'Stubborn, as always, I see. But you are certainly not fine. They will take you to the hospital, OK?'

I nodded, unable to fight any more. I was out of witty replies and smart-arse comments. I just wanted to be warm and safe and as far from the river as possible.

*

'She's awake!'

'Oh, thank goodness!'

'Is she going to be OK?'

'She'll be absolutely fine, she's got quite a nasty cut above her right knee, and she took a pretty bad knock to her forehead, but once the swelling goes down she will look as good as new.'

'Thank you!'

I tried to open my eyes, and became quickly aware of how much effort it took. My eyelids felt extremely heavy, and the thought of giving in and going back to sleep was overpowering. I could smell hand-sanitiser and rubber, my mother's perfume and talcum powder. My entire body felt sore: my head throbbed continually, and my back and neck were incredibly stiff. So many thoughts and emotions flooded over me. I had to find Paul, to tell him that I had remembered exactly what had happened when Michael had been taken. I was torn between my urgent need to get up and do something, and to stay there in the comfortable haven, protected and safe and away from all the awful things I had experienced over the past twenty-four hours.

My mother and father were the first to come fully into focus: my mother, with a look of concern on her face; my father, holding his head in his hands. As I looked slowly around the small, white room, my sister and Karen became clearer too. Alice's laptop was open; my being in a hospital bed plainly had not outweighed her need to work. This made me smile. Karen was sitting cross-legged, not taking her eyes off me, biting her fingernails, a bad habit that she had never seemed able to kick, ever since our school days together. She smiled at me, when our eyes met:

'God, you had us worried!'

Alice snapped her laptop shut, and leaned over the bed,

'You just don't listen do you? What were my last words to you?' she scolded, but her expression was soft, and I knew that she was perhaps more angry at herself for not accompanying me, rather than at me for going it alone.

'Steady on, Alice, let her recover first, before you start having a go!' My father's voice of reason cut in between us, and Alice sat back down.

'Where's Paul?' I whispered, hoarsely. They all looked at each other.

'He's busy, love,' replied my father, eventually.

What were they not telling me?

'I need to find him; there's so much that I need to tell him: I know what happened - she told me everything - I even remember now what happened when Michael was taken.'

'What you need to do is rest, and you most certainly do not need any more excitement today!' my mother interrupted.

'But why isn't he here? I thought he would be waiting for me to wake up!' I felt disappointed and upset. I felt that I needed his presence, his reassurance. It was Karen who spoke next,

'He's very busy, Ann. They've arrested Elizabeth Bridge for all four murders; he's been working non-stop; I'm sure he'll come and see you as soon as he can.'

We all sat in silence for several minutes. These people were my world, my safety net. I could not have survived losing Michael, and the two years that had followed, without them. The silence actually felt nice, comforting in a way.

'Is it my fault?' I said, at last.

'Is what your fault?' my mother repeated, incredulously.

'All of this? Elizabeth, Jane, whatever her name is; she told me that she had planned it all, that she had chosen to take Michael before he was even born. Could I have prevented it?'

'God, Ann, if anyone's to blame, it's me. I recommended that monster to you in the first place!' Karen interjected. 'If I had known what she was capable of...' her voice trailed off.

'She said I was a bad mother, that I wasn't deserving of Michael. Do you think that's true?'

'How can you even think that?' said Alice. 'You were everything to Michael. You were the best mother he could have hoped to have! You loved that boy more than anything in the world. Don't let the words of a psychopath get inside your head and warp your perception. You are an excellent mother...'

'Was...'

'Are! And you will be again!'

'What are you talking about?'

'Listen, Ann, maybe you should get some rest. Paul will be here soon to see you, I'm sure.'

'I feel so tired!'

'I know, love, go back to sleep. I promise you that everything is going to be OK.'

My mother kissed my forehead; I felt her linger, her eyes closed, breathing my hair; I could feel the love emanating from her whole body. My wonderful mother! How glad I was to still be here, to still have my family. I closed my eyes and drifted effortlessly back to sleep.

I don't know how long I slept, but when I opened my eyes for the second time, it was dark outside. The blinds had been drawn, and a nightlight emitted a dull glow from the corner of the room.

'Hey.'

I turned my head quickly, hurting my neck. Paul was sitting on my left. I hadn't heard him come in, hadn't even felt his presence:

'How long have you been here?'

'A few hours. I've been watching you sleep.'

'Isn't that a bit creepy?'

'I'm glad to see that concussion and near-death has not dulled your sense of humour.'

'Paul, I remember; I remember everything!'

'Shh! Don't get too excited.'

'But it's important that you know. I wasn't drunk when Michael was kidnapped. I wasn't unconscious after downing vodka. It's so important that you know that.' He nodded. 'She had hypnotised me. Something about suggestive hypnosis: she had planted a phrase in my head, and when I heard it, I would just...'

'I know, Ann, I know everything,' he cut in.

'But... how ? Did she confess?'

'Unfortunately, Elizabeth Bridge is not speaking. She hasn't said a word since her arrest, and I doubt she will. I'm not exactly sure what will happen now, with a trial. Her lawyer will probably claim insanity.'

'Do you think she's insane?'

'It's hard to tell, I'm not a doctor. She doesn't seem to be an evil person. But she did evil things. It's for the prosecution and lawyers to decide what motivated that evil. My job's done!' He mimed washing his hands.

'But then, if she hasn't spoken, how do you know?'

'After we arrested her, we searched the house. We found a diary of sorts: random entries, over a period of years, describing her thoughts, and the things she had done; notes on patients, potential victims, children she was planning to kidnap. There was a long chapter on you, your therapy sessions, hypnosis. It was an interesting read, to say the least.'

He passed me the book that I had seen, almost every week, for the past seven years, the book that I had always wondered about, speculating on what things Doctor Blunt saw fit to write about me.

I opened it.

The Diary of Elizabeth Bridge.

June 7th 2011

Ann is proving to be an excellent patient. Not only does she believe that I can help her to overcome her problems, she seems so self-centred that she is blind to any deception on my part. A perfect subject for experimental suggestive hypnosis.

She is a masochist; I could tell, from the moment I met her. No sane, self-respecting woman would stay with that pig of a husband of hers for fun. I'll wait for her to make this admission, or maybe I will draw it out of her through hypnosis, make her feel like she had to tell me, she didn't have a choice. It's too easy; too easy to find unappreciative, lonely housewives, willing to pay thousands of pounds to hear what they already know, to be told that they are doing a great job, that their marriage will work if they try hard enough, and that the baby they think they want is the answer to all their problems.

But I have hope in Ann. She wants children, and I am going to convince her to make her desires a reality, something that she must give in to. Is she deserving of it? Probably not, but I will be the one to pass that judgement when the time comes and the opportunity presents itself.

I turned to another page, and continued to read:

September 18th 2012

My Lucille never stood a chance in this world, populated, as it is, by people like Ann. I tried so hard, and for so long to get her here, only for her to be taken from me, so needlessly, so harshly. I feel compelled by some greater power, or maybe just the power of my maternal instincts, to rectify the situation, to replace my loss and to find a suitable replacement for her. I see them everywhere: children; homeless, beaten, abused. Parents do not know how lucky they are to be given the gift of life, and unconditional love. I am convinced now, more than ever, that I know what must be done.

I continued to flick through:

December 10th 2013

Ann continues to disappoint and at the same time motivate me. She is the perfect subject. Her son is already one, and the thought of him living in that house, with those poor excuses for humans, continues to disgust me. What kind of people treat each other with such contempt, and lie to themselves that the love they feel for each other is genuine, is respectful and honest? Ann does nothing but talk in circles around her disdain for her own husband, yet she stays with him, despite my advice to the contrary. She believes two parents are better than one. She has hope, although for what, I am unsure. Her life is hopeless. I find it exhilarating to watch her move through the world with her son, talking about her plans for their future together, knowing full well what I must do when the time comes.

Turning the pages again, I came to a more recent entry:

May 23rd 2016

Ann reminds me a lot of Laura's mother, if you can call her that! She wasn't deserving of that title. The week before I tried to take Laura, her mother had locked her in the downstairs bedroom, all night. She had problems sleeping; I remember reading her sheet at Barts, when I was there, remember thinking what a perfect daughter she would make. Her mother couldn't cope; it wasn't enough having a beautiful baby, who, with the right nurture, would continue to develop, and grow into a toddler, a little girl, and finally, blossom into an adult. No! She wanted a child, who slept through the night, leaving her and her boyfriend alone, to smoke crack, or screw in silence. I couldn't let her stay with that family, it was against all my instincts, against everything that I believe in and have worked for until now. Laura needed my help; she needed to be rescued from her mother's negligent clutches, to be freed. I tried to give her that liberty, that chance! I wish in some ways she had been a better replacement, but she didn't have Lucille's loyalty. She wasn't appreciative of the freedom that I tried to provide; she refused to come with me, so I had to improvise, had to set her free a little earlier than planned.

And little Tommy. What a sweetie he was! Again, if he hadn't let me down, I would have cherished him: I would have made him the centre of my universe, if he had only let me. In some ways, I think it was a good idea to take a boy. It is difficult to have another girl in Lucille's bed, as all I seem to do is compare the two, and then I'm more or less doomed to failure, as no little girl could ever live up to my darling daughter, the most perfect daughter a woman could wish to have: my miracle, snatched from me so unfairly, swept away into the rushing river, leaving me alone again.

I handed the book back to him, not wanting to read any more; it seemed futile. Nothing I read would give me any more closure, and certainly would not make me feel any better about the inevitable ending.

'I know why she removed the shoes.' I said at last, and he looked at me, genuinely interested.

'Really? that bugged me for so long. Why?'

'Well you were kind of right. She promised Michael he could go home, if he could find his way. She removed the shoes and let him go. The same with Jennifer. I don't know whether or not she really planned to let them go if they succeeded. What chance did they have? I guess we will never know!'

He shook his head from side to side.

'I've seen so much ugliness over the years in this job; especially with what happened to my own sister, but nothing compared to this, to what happened to your son, to what happened to Michael!'

He leant over, kissing me. I reached up, grabbing at his hair, feeling his stubble outlining his jaw. I felt safe. Eventually, after what seemed an eternity, he let me go, and went over to his things in the corner of the room, returning with a box that looked familiar.

'There is just one thing that we don't have the answer to,' he said. 'Do you know what this is?'

'Yes.' I replied, 'It's Jane Blunt's sensory box.'

He blinked. 'Her what?'

'In one of our sessions together, we used the technique of the sensory box to identify objects that had good connotations and memories. She showed me hers first.'

'I see. Can you remember what was inside?'

'Yes, I think so, er, her wedding ring...' he pulled out a small silver ring and placed in on the table beside my bed. 'Let me see, a birthday card and a champagne cork, I think.' He removed both items and placed them next to the ring. 'God, I can't remember, I think there was some perfume, an ornament of some kind and a shell, like the ones that you can hear the sea in...' He retrieved the perfume bottle, a large sea shell, and the ornament, which was a frog. 'Oh yes, I remember that now, she said her grandmother had used it as an ashtray, I think.' He nodded.

'Good. Now are you sure there was nothing else in the box when she showed it to you?'

'No, nothing. Why is this important?'

He picked up his notes, and scanned the paper, stopping when he had reached the part that he was looking for:

'This is a list of missing items from three of the murders: Laura had just celebrated her fifth birthday, but her mother's birthday card to her, which had been on her window-sill, was missing.'

I sat up:

'And Thomas, what was he missing?'

'A pot frog; he loved animals, and had quite a collection of little ornaments.'

I felt cold all over.

'And Jennifer?'

By way of answering, Paul Stone carefully removed from the box an item that I was sure hadn't been there before: a tiny pink ballet slipper. I stuffed my knuckles into my mouth, and closed my eyes.

'I think these were all items that were accessible to Elizabeth Bridge at the time she abducted the children. I believe she kept them, as trophies, to remind her of what she had accomplished, the children she had "saved", as she liked to put it. Do you remember anything of Michael's being missing from the house, or more probably, from the garden, as he was out there playing?'

I nodded:

'His green spade. I've not been able to find it since, but I just thought it had got lost in all of his things. I didn't even really find it that odd.'

Paul paused for a moment, then opened the box again and turned it towards me. There was one item left: there, nestling in the corner, was Michael's bright green spade! My hands trembling, I reached out for it, held it to me, and wept.

Paul left me alone for a while, thinking, perhaps, that I needed a moment or two to hold it, to remember my darling little boy playing in the sand, and the mud. I had already said goodbye to him so many times before. I had visited the place where he died, I had buried him, and had almost come to terms with the fact that he was never coming back. It's strange: even now that I can accept that, now that I have found out all there is to know about what happened to Michael, I still don't feel ready to let him go. I had given life to him, had watched him grow, from a baby into a little person that I loved so much. It didn't feel right saying goodbye to him any more.

I would give my life for him to walk in through the door, his face covered in dirt from playing outside, his cheeks rosy from the cold, his little fingers slightly swollen because he refused to wear his gloves. I had done everything in my power to keep him safe, and having failed to do that, I had discovered a different aspect of motherhood: devoting every moment from then on to finding out who was responsible for what had happened, and the motivation behind it. I had succeeded, before the police, before the gentle, intelligent Inspector in charge of the case, with whom I realised I was in love. With Alice's help, I had managed to avenge my son, and bring his killer to justice. And as I sat there crying, I realised that these were tears of relief; relief that after so long, after so many unanswered questions and disappointments, it was finally all over.

'I brought you a cup of tea.' Paul appeared at the door, smiling. I gratefully accepted the small plastic cup from him and took a sip. The tea was weak, but warm and comforting nonetheless.

'I'm sorry I couldn't make that promise to you,' I began.

'Which one?'

'About feeling the same about you, when this was over.'

He waved a hand:

'I should never have asked you to make it. You were right about a lot of things, and I was wrong.'

I raised my eyebrows.

'Humility? That's a new side to you that I didn't know existed.'

He smiled:

'I hope there are many things that we will get the chance to discover about each other.'

'I meant to ask you: my family and friends were here before. They seemed very secretive, and a little off. Like they were holding something back, as if they knew something I didn't. You wouldn't happen to have any idea about that would you?'

He shifted uncomfortably in his seat.

'As a matter of fact I would.'

'Really? Do tell!'

'Well, normally, you would be the first to know, but under these circumstances...'

'Oh come on, Paul, spit it out.'

'The doctors took blood samples from you while you were unconscious; it's pretty standard procedure, and before administering any drugs, they have to know certain things about you.'

I sat up in bed, staring at him, completely confused.

'Certain things, like what?'

He held my hand in his and smiled:

'You're pregnant, Ann.'

Epilogue

I couldn't bring myself to cremate Michael. There is something so brutal, so very final about destroying a body in that way. The thought of his little coffin wheeling slowly into a blazing furnace seemed wrong somehow, too conclusive, too final. I suppose I have always been traditional in most aspects of my life: from marriage, to having children, and in death and burial it seemed I was no different. I couldn't bear the thought of Michael no longer existing, in a physical form at least. It had taken me so long to accept that spiritually, he was no longer there, but I had still sat holding his hand, even though the light and the life had left him forever. I suppose I am selfish, in that I wanted reassurance that my son was still whole, still a physical being, who would decay and leave in his own time. I had chosen the graveyard where my grandparents were buried, and their parents before them, a place that I knew I could visit, as often as I wanted, for as long as I could, until it was my turn to be buried there.

It has been nearly two years since I lost Michael, and every day without him is still painful, still difficult in many ways, as I continue with my life. It is impossible to forget all the wonderful memories that I have of my only son. I see him everywhere, in everything I do; but I can now accept that he is gone. One of his friends asked me if Michael was in heaven. I don't think he is there, but I can picture him in lots of other places. In a park, laughing with his friends, at my parents' house, cuddling up, eating his favourite food, swimming in the sea, building sandcastles and chasing the waves. And I told his friend that because he was in all those other magical, happy places, he couldn't be in heaven, or with us right now, but that one day we would all be together again. I can picture him waiting for me, holding out his arms for Bear Bear. I don't worry any more that he is lost or alone, because I know that he is safe, and that my grandparents and friends who have passed on will all be with him, looking after him until I get there.

I never bring flowers to the grave. Michael wasn't old enough to appreciate them, and as he will be five forever, I have to think of more appropriate gifts to bring him. This month it will be Christmas time, so I decided to bring a bauble like the ones we used to buy together. I placed it gently onto the small grey tombstone, my fingers trembling as I fixed it into place.

'Hey sweetie, I'm sorry I didn't come and see you yesterday, mummy was really busy. I'm teaching now, at your school! Miss Cliff finally managed to persuade the board of governors to include more artistic subjects, so I'm teaching two hours of drama a week. I have Tony in my class, and Lisa. They always ask about you, and tell me how much they miss you.

'And I miss you too, my love, so much. I miss your smile, I miss your bright face and your laugh. I miss your hands, your little legs and each of your toes. I miss watching you play, seeing you happy, and hearing you tell me that you love me too. I miss watching TV with you, and reading you bedtime stories, painting home-made cards for Grandma and singing our favourite songs during bath time. I miss your sense of humour, your hugs and your wet kisses. I even miss cleaning up after you, and changing your sheets after you've had an accident. I'd give the world to wash your bedsheets just one more time, to hold you just once more, walk you to school, watch you sleep, hear you breathing. I miss tucking you back into bed when you've thrown the covers off in the night, and separating the felt-tipped pens and the crayons that you mixed up on purpose, just to annoy me. I miss being annoyed by you. I miss all of it. I was so excited for the future that we were going to get to spend together, and now I just have a list of all the things that we will never do again, that live only in my memory.'

I fell to my knees, holding the stone with my hand:

'My sweet boy, my baby, I will miss you for ever.'

I closed my eyes, and knelt like that for a few precious moments, weeping into the cold stone, and feeling the love for him explode and burn away in my chest. I felt a hand on my shoulder, and wiped my eyes. Paul stood there, silently, and placed another bauble next to my own. It was the first time that he had ever come with me to see my son's grave, but it seemed appropriate now.

'I never knew you, Michael, but I came to know so much about you, through your incredibly strong and wonderful mother. She told me all about your tradition with the baubles, so we got one for you,' he paused and looked at me, 'and one for your baby sister. I promise I'll look after both of them for you.'

I got to my feet, one arm cradling my swollen belly, the other threading through his, and I kissed him on the cheek. He nodded, and we started to walk back to the car. I felt safe, safer and more positive than I had felt in years. I looked back, at Michael's name on the stone and blew a kiss:

'I promise, I'll make birthday cake with her, every day!'

ABOUT THE AUTHOR

N F Paupe was born in England, the daughter of two language teachers. After completing her BA honours degree in Theatre and Performance at the University of Leeds, she moved to France to pursue writing, where she still lives with her husband and two daughters.

QUESTIONS FOR DISCUSSION

- Most of the male characters in the book are flawed in some way: Dave is abusive and selfish, Paul is a recovering alcoholic, Lee Haddison is a paedophile etc. Do you think that Ann only sees the bad in people, especially men?

- "Karen was my best friend, my soulmate, my partner in crime." How do you feel about the character of Karen? Do you think she brings out the worst or the best side of Ann?

- "This was a house of only good memories, of unconditional love, and of hope. I would sit in this room and have so many dreams for the future: the person I would become, the career I would pursue, and the children I would raise." How is Ann's life different from the one she had hoped to have? What do you think she would change if she could do it all again?

- Throughout the book, Ann and Paul continue to disagree, butt heads, then make up again. Do you think their relationship is solid and realistically going to last, or did Ann turn to Paul for comfort during her grief?

- How has Ann's relationship with Dave changed her view on life? Is she a negative or a positive person?

- "I don't feel ready to sacrifice anything. I guess I'm incredibly disappointed with myself."

What do think Ann means here? Why do you think she is disappointed with her herself?

- Alcohol is an ongoing theme in the book. We see references to Ann drinking too much, Karen's social drinking, Paul's alcoholism. We rarely see alcohol depicted as something good. Why do you think this is and what do you think the author means by the continued negative references to alcohol?

- "It felt good to fade into anonymity." What do you think Ann means here and why does she feel this way?

- What is the significance of the weather throughout the book?

- "Doctor Blunt was wearing a red blouse. She always wore red." Having read the book, what is the significance, in your opinion, of Doctor Blunt always wearing the colour red?

- How do you think Ann feels about being pregnant again, after losing her first child? Do you think she sees it as a fresh start, a new beginning? Or is she perhaps conflicted between the fear of something bad happening and the joy of giving life again?

- Do you believe that Ann was always a masochist, and Dave just helped her to explore her deep-rooted feelings and desires, or was it something that he forced her into, that eventually she became accustomed to?

- (About Paul) "We had seen each other several times, since

Jennifer's funeral, and each time I knew that I would be with him, I applied lipstick. It filled me with a combination of both disgust and excitement." What do you think Ann means by this?

Printed in Great Britain
by Amazon